A MEMOIR OF THE LAST DAYS OF ATLANTIS

ISLANDS
out of
TIME

A MEMOIR OF THE LAST DAYS OF ATLANTIS

ISLANDS
out of
TIME

a novel by

WILLIAM IRWIN THOMPSON

BEAR & COMPANY
PUBLISHING
SANTA FE, NEW MEXICO

LIBRARY OF CONGRESS CATALOGING-IN-PUBLICATION DATA

Thompson, William Irwin
  Islands out of time: a memoir of the last days of Atlantis:
a novel by / William Irwin Thompson.
      p.   cm.
  Reprint. Originally published: Garden City, N.Y. :
Dial Press / Doubleday, 1985.
  ISBN 0-939680-83-1
  1. Atlantis—Fiction.   I. Title.
PS3570.H645I8   1990
813'.54—dc20   90-44377
                                                                CIP

Copyright © 1990 by William Irwin Thompson

Bear & Company, Inc.
Santa Fe, NM 87504-2860

Cover illustration: Kathleen Katz © 1990
Design: Kathleen Katz
Printed in the United States of America by R.R. Donnelley

9 8 7 6 5 4 3 2 1

FOR JOHN AND
DAVID SPANGLER

Foreword

Fiction appeals to us because the ego is a fiction. This conventionally maintained identity we call the self is a matter of perspective, and if we look too closely, as when we look at the dots in a newspaper photograph, the recognizable image dissolves.

If we take a good look at our minds, either through Western introspection or Eastern *zazen*, we discover that there are large gaps between each thought, and in the interval between we cannot be certain at all "where" we were, or where the "I" had gone. In *zazen* particularly there is a curious reversal of *figure* and *ground* that comes about as the gap between each thought widens. The gap becomes the *figure*, and thoughts become the background, or rather a kind of background noise that has no absolute and essential *ground*. In that groundlessness which we uncover, we no longer fill up the *structure* of consciousness with new *content*: either with sensory perceptions or psychic visions; we immerse that structure of *knowing* in *being*, like someone taking off his or her clothes to float in the sea. As we return to the condition of conventional mind, we see how it had been possible to stretch one thought to the next, to ignore the gaps and make the sequence of thoughts appear to be a continuous line with a solidly inked-in identity.

It is a simply plotted, linear fiction, this ego of ours, but one does not have to be a zen master to discover just how fictional personal identity is, for one only has to try to write an autobiography. It soon becomes obvious that our memories of childhood experiences are adult constructions that we never experienced in that way as children. The memories are not so much descriptions of the past as they are performances of the present; they are artifacts with an independent literary life of their own. And so we discover that the ego is a fiction in the act of creating a fictional narrative about the unfoldment of its "true" identity.

If autobiography, as a *recherche du temps perdu,* is a fiction, then a memoir of a past life on a lost continent in a mythical prehistory is even more of a fiction of identity. Or, perhaps, it would be better to call it a parody of identity, a parody of autobiography, a parody of prehistory, a parody of the genre of the science fiction novel.

People who believe in egos write novels with characters. And people who believe in the solidity of materialism write realistic novels. Not surprisingly, the rise of the novel is related to the historical period of the rise of the middle class and the expansion of industrial materialism. Every epoch has its dominant elite, and its dominant literary genre, and in these epochs the descriptions of these genres are so powerful that social reality soon begins to imitate art. The duke and the duchess take Don Quixote into their palace as an honored knight errant of old because they have read Part One of the book of his adventures. Even as far back as the time of Cervantes, the media could create reality. The instant feedback of Don Quixote's madness onto himself in play makes his obsession a shared fantasy, and the play of shared fantasies is what we know as *culture.* Whether the knight errant is Don Quixote or President Reagan, "the Great Communicator," the shared fantasy in which the media create reality is the paradoxical *nature* of *culture.*

In the age of aristocratic, land-owning warriors, from Homer to Ariosto, the cultures of Europe made the epic their dominant literary genre. In the age of industrial capitalism, books and money were printed, and gold and paintings became forms of accumulated wealth stored in banks and museums that, architecturally, tended to look alike. The middle classes believed in things and egos and liked novels that had characters and were "true to life." They were also brashly confident enough to think that they knew exactly what "true to life" meant.

Now we are in the period of transition from one age to another, and from one elite to another. With contemporary society being shaped by physics, microelectronics, and genetic engineering, it looks as if Thatcher, Kohl, and Reagan are the sunset-effect of industrial capitalism. Like Don Quixote on Rocinante, they ride forth in their Rolls, Mercedes, and Lincolns right at the time when the age of the automobile is in its climactic finale. The forests, orchards, and vineyards are dying in Europe, and even though the air pollution could be immediately reduced by 18 percent if the Germans would simply impose a speed limit, the middle class consumers refuse to do so, for the car, like the sword of old, is a symbol of manhood and power. For a German-speaking people, raised on the fairy tales of Grimm, the forest is the dark place where the evil witch lives; it is a place of female control; but the highway is a place of masculine assertiveness; consequently a speed limit is not simply a matter of rational environmental management. But there is also an archetypal power to wine in the European folk-soul and unconscious, and as Europe continues to lose its orchards and vineyards, the shock will be profound, and some new form of ecological management will be inevitable. It looks as if the scientists are going to become the new governing elite, but what the dadaistic and anarchic Greens of Germany do not seem to realize yet is that ecological management will require computerized, authoritarian forms of control. The law will have to dictate just what kind of fuel is tolerable, how big an engine can be, and how fast a vehicle is permitted to go. The feedback of pollution on culture will have to be electronically coded; therefore, some form of electronics is likely to become the Hammurabian Code of the future.

Artists and social critics have been aware for some time that we were living in an informational society, so they have been expressing themselves in new forms that are not the old genre of the bourgeois novel with its attendant English Department criticism, of Eng. Lit. Inc. Elsewhere I have called this new genre *Wissenskunst;*[1] other critics seem to prefer the Greek-Latin macaronic term of *metafiction,*[2] but from whatever point of view one adopts to look at our new society, it is becoming increasingly clear that realistic characters locally defined with a

sense of place may indeed map on to Faulkner's
Yoknapatawpha County, but they do not embody the new elec-
tronic-aerospace culture of the American Sunbelt. What is the
individual and where is the place for a person plugged into an
Apple and networked up to "The Source" in a conference that
is not occurring in real-time or real-space? *Per-sona* in Latin
means to sound through, and the term refers back to the masks
of the old medium of classical Graeco-Roman theater from
which the actor's voice sounded through. Who is the being
behind the mask? Who is the being behind the terminal? Literary man had a stable character he acted out through a lifetime,
through a *story* of rags to riches; but electronic humanity does
not have a stable identity, or even a stable sexuality. He-she flips
channels and sexes like a Boy George with a remote-control TV
switcher in its hand. Esoteric individuals in our cybernetic era
may watch their minds in *zazen*, but exoteric and electronically
conditioned individuals watch themselves experience identity
as the shared response of the medium to entry. Both the esoteric and the exoteric persons begin to experience identity as
something that the old Buddhists liked to call, not eternal essence, but "co-dependent origination."

Artists have always had a way of anticipating technological
innovations, and the multi-dimensionality and interpenetrating
spaces that are now so common in music video, thanks to video
synthesizers and computers, were first anticipated on canvas by
painters like Magritte and Escher. Similarly, James Joyce, in
Finnegans Wake, was one of the first novelists to replace characters with patterns. As "the pattern that connects" replaced the
character that holds identity, the barriers between fiction and
nonfiction broke down. Nonfiction, like Tom Wolfe's *Electric
Kool-Aid Acid Test*, or my own *At the Edge of History*, became
more narrative than expository. At the same time that the barriers between fiction and nonfiction were broken down, the barriers between political activity and journalistic reporting dis-
solved. And with the dissolution of these boundaries also came a
loss of orientation, as Left and Right lost their old meanings, for
the gonzo journalism of Hunter Thompson and the media performances of Ronald Reagan are *structurally* both emanations

of the same electronic culture. They are both pure Southern California.

We had been warned about all of this by McLuhan in Canada, Borges in Argentina, and Escher in the Netherlands, but Americans are quintessentially a practical, industrial, and middle class people; they are not inclined either to Buddhist Emptiness or European epistemological complexity. They always look at the *content* but rarely see the *structure*, so they go to Disneyland and see the Midwestern town. They look at Reagan, our first divorced President, who never goes to church, and they see him as a small town Midwesterner who is a pillar of Southern fundamentalism.

In my earlier books and public lectures I have said that "all scholarship is disguised autobiography," so it occurred to me that a disguised autobiography might provide an interesting approach to scholarship. An imaginary autobiography of a past life on a lost continent requires no historical research and gives the writer a degree of freedom that no historical novelist or seriously responsible autobiographer could ever hope to have, so the task was compelling.

Precisely because the ego is a fiction, identity is a guise. Conventionally, we like to think of heroes versus villains, but the *characters* are not the real descriptions of identity. The narrative itself is our character, for we as human beings are a story of beauty and beast, hero and villain. That is why Blake was right when he said that when Milton wrote about God in *Paradise Lost*, his spirit lay in chains, but when he wrote about Satan, his spirit soared. I find that in this archaeology of the unconscious I too became more interested in the voices of evil in the narrative, and so I must own up to the fact that the villains speak for me as much as the stupid genius who thinks the story is about him. In this chamber work for five voices, there are *personae*, but they are not so much characters as instruments of myth.

I apologize for having had to frame this narrative, to put it into a context, but I found that some readers wished to put it into the old historical context of the realistic novel, and this is a waste of time, even with a work about lost time. To put one historical context inside another historical context seems appropriate, especially since Atlantis is not admitted into the narratives of scientific prehistory, but that may be why it serves so well as a metaphoric description of scientific post-history.

May 10, 1985
Bern, Switzerland

Notes

1. See the author's Passages About Earth *(New York, Harper & Row, 1974), p. 3, for a definition of* Wissenskunst; *also his* Evil and World Order *(New York, Harper & Row, 1976), p. 77; and his* The Time Falling Bodies Take to Light *(New York, St. Martin's Press, 1981), pp. 4, 248.*

2. *William H. Gass coined the term "metafiction" in his essay "Philosophy and the Form of Fiction" in 1971. See Gass's* Fiction and the Figures of Life *(Boston, Nonpareil Books, 1978), p. 25. The term has been picked up and put into general circulation by Patricia Waugh in her recent study,* Metafiction *(New York, Methuen, 1984). Unfortunately, Dr. Waugh has added lead to the silver of Gass's brightly reflective prose. Professors of English Literature now seem so intent on protecting their employment and justifying their existence to educational management that they have retooled themselves to reappear in the marketplace as behavioral scientists. They now write as badly as educational administrators and sociologists. Consider, for example, Waugh's use of such words as "foregrounded" and "problematizes" in the following definition of metafiction:*

   In all of these what is foregrounded is the writing of the text as the most fundamentally problematic aspect of that text. Although metafiction is just one form of post-modernism, nearly all contemporary experimental writing displays some explicit metafictional strategies. Any text that draws the reader's attention to its process of construction by frustrating his or her conventional expectations of meaning and closure problematizes more or less explicitly the ways in which narrative codes—whether "literary" or "social"—artificially construct apparently "real" and imaginary worlds in terms of particular ideologies while presenting these as transparently "natural" and "eternal." (Waugh, p. 22.)

Both the philosophical playfulness of Gass's thinking and the artistic delight of his prose are lost in Waugh's academic approach. The kind of metafiction she seems to favor and promote is simply a professional and technical self-conscious discourse between the edges of genres and the margins of texts. Ultimately, the accumulating ironies of her favored self-indulgent authors end in a lattice of negations that permit the critic to have the last word by surrounding the artist with the containment of the dying cosmology, the careerist nihilism of the bureaucratic professor. Wissenskunst, *by contrast, plays with the narratives of science; it does not try to imitate science or chase after a scientistic professionalism. The* Wissenskünstler *lives at the edge of science the way the bard lived at the edge of kingly power. Always at an edge with socially accepted definitions of reality, the* Wissenskünstler *becomes a "Juggler of Our Lady" who found no room for his work in the corridors of the monks and so juggled alone at midnight in front of the statue. The juggler has to play the fool among experts to find a new place for the archaic in the contemporary. Metafiction need not, therefore, be merely an ironic commentary on its own composition; it can also become a shift of consciousness, a movement from* noia *to* metanoia, *from travel to homecoming, from domestic habituation to cosmic astonishment.*

A MEMOIR OF THE LAST DAYS OF ATLANTIS

ISLANDS
out of
TIME

Mostly the mind dwells on the Tower. Even in other incarnations millennia afterward, the mind is drawn back to that serenely wrought instrument of perfected terror, and only then brought back to those four who stand out against the backdrop of the brown volcanic rocks to remain more durable than temple stones or the rubble of broken desires. Enduring into other times, other cultures, they persist like some unknown architecture of the mind. In all the civilizations that were to follow there would be legends and esoteric murmurings, or sometimes even an obscure compulsion to re-create in form what had been stricken from history. And always, they would be there: unfree, untransformed, still seeking the ultimate deliverance, still unforgiving of the angelic violation that had raped their spirits and thrust their souls screaming into animal bodies.

It is too late to blame anyone. The four—no, call it five—are an entirety, even a single entity. Time has at least accomplished that much in writing. Still, the terror, the incomprehension of Evil, remains. Cresting a hill in San Francisco, you stop mechanically at a traffic light, and then become taken over by the horror of involuntary and impersonal memory at the sight of the Transamerica Pyramid. Of course, the builders cannot admit, nor can the members of the academy accept, the pull of racial memory; and so a dumb and brutal doom compells them to act it out again: to find great seismic faults in the earth and there of all places choose to thrust momentary towers into their acrid, rotting sky. More than a mere quotation, the Transamerica Pyramid is an evocation of the Tower: you have only to set the solar crystal into its crown to conjure it all up again.

The prehistoric bay, however, was not so large or irregular in shape. The remains of the collapsed cone of an ancient volcano, the bay was almost circular in form where the land with its crescent wings gave protection from the winds to favor its deep natural harbor. Upon these wings were the steep ledges into which had been set all the white buildings of the temple city of the High Priest. In the center of these mustard brown volcanic ledges stood the Great Tower itself, and immediately below it, the Palace of the High Priest and the great hypostyle hall. To the west of the southward facing Tower and Palace were the numerous buildings of the Temple Institute, which extended to the westernmost cliffs above the sea. And there at the extreme edge of the cliff stood the large double doors of copper that led into the Archon's Laboratory of Incarnation. Despite the spray of the salt seawinds, the doors were never allowed to cover with patina, but were polished every morning by the guards themselves. Sometimes at sunset they would glow a lurid red in the dying light, and on nights of the full moon they would glisten like the armor of soldiers hiding in the night.

On the opposite side of the Great Tower, to the east of the Palace, were the buildings and cloistered gardens of the Sacred College. The largest of these enclosed gardens separated the hypostyle hall from the residential quarters and the great room of the Convocation. To the extreme east was the small chapel with its seventy-two seats for the Members of the Sacred College.

Below the broad stone-paved street that connected the College Gate, the hypostyle hall, and the copper doors of the Institute, were the administrative buildings, and below these, the storehouses which extended to the quais at the water's edge. The storehouses, which had practically taken over the old capital, were here not allowed to extend to the center of the bay, which was reserved for the processional ramp that climbed from the moorings of the barges to the portals of the hypostyle hall itself. The boats would dock to east or west, depending on whether their affairs took them to the Institute or the College, but the center was always kept open for the processional barge that would take the High Priest to his garuda.

Lovely as the barges and sailing ships were, the greatest sight of all was to watch the great vessels of the air, the silver garudas, set down in the middle of the harbor and then glide swanlike to their appointed rest.

The peninsular City of the Tower was the creation of the High Priest himself. As the Empire had grown, commerce had grown with it, and the causeways and canals had become littered with the debris of merchants and farmers. With the extension of the Empire to the colonies in both the Eastern and Western continents, the Military too had pressed its demands for barracks, docks, and storehouses, until at last the imperial capital was more of a cluttered bazaar than the seat of the High Priest and the Mother City of the Theocracy. It was then that the High Priest conceived the vision of the City of Knowledge to be built on the isolated peninsula to the south. Here he imagined that the Theocracy could express itself in utmost purity. Here the traditional arts and the new sciences could be lifted to great heights in the very consummation of Atlantean civilization itself. To encourage the former, the High Priest created the Sacred College, and for the latter he established the Temple Institute. With these two strong institutions as his right and left arms he believed he could restrain the disordered growth of the military and the commercial classes to hold all within the form of the ancient and sublime Theocracy. And to that end the Temple Institute served the High Priest with loyalty and skill, for from its lore of herbs and medicines had come a new knowledge of drugs and poisons that made the ingeniously catapulted darts of the Atlanteans the most feared weapons in the world.

To abandon the old capital and to build anew the center of civilization was not only visionary, but costly as well. Provinces that had before participated in trade had become colonies providing tribute; but as great as this burden was, nothing caused as much hatred as the small, but steady stream of pregnant women and children that was led in small groups through the large double doors of copper into the Institute.

On one particular day of the final summer there was more than the usual flow of traffic in the bay. A Solemn Assembly had been called, for it had been decided by the High Priest that if the Provincial Governors knew how the City of Knowledge itself had become a vessel for the evolutionary transformation of the human race, then they could serve with renewed enthusiasm to direct the sullen peoples toward humanity's appointed destination. And so a call was sent out for all the Governors to meet with the Supreme Council of the High Priest, the Members of the Sacred College, and the faculty of the Temple Institute. The Solemn Assembly must have been a source of deep anxiety for Bran, the Captain of the largest garuda assigned to the Institute. As a provincial himself, an islander from Eiru in the Remnants of Hyperborea, Bran's sympathies were not always imperial, but he loved to fly, and there were no other flying vessels anywhere else in the world. It was only in the last year, when he had been set to transporting the pregnant women and children that his work had grown intolerable. Always before the conspiracy of the Society of the 144 had kept his spirits up with the thought that he had been called to flying to fulfill a great destiny: to escape the end of civilization that Abaris had prophesied and to carry the chosen ones into a new age. When he had only to wait and spend his time carrying officials from one colony to another, he could be patient; but now that he and his garuda had been assigned to the Institute, waiting on prophecies had become impossible.

The Society of the 144, however, did not seem to mind the wait. They would irritate Bran with their servile meticulousness as they went over, once again, their lists of secret storehouses, their roster of the chosen technicians and horticulturalists the colony would need to survive, and their maps of the chosen location by a large lake high in the mountains of the Southern Continent. But they had only to look at their plans, they did not, like Bran, have to look into the dark obsidian eyes of the Governor of Anahuac.

Bran would dwell on that scene often in the attempts he would make later to chronicle the last days. He would try to re-create the mood of that silent crowd of people standing in the clearing as the Provincial Governor of Anahuac himself came to protest the conscription of his subjects.

The day had been unbearably hot and clouds of steam hung

just above the red flowers on top the mimosa trees. Bran had wanted to rip off his silk uniform, but it had stuck to his skin like a plaster on a festering wound. The sweat had streamed down into his eyes, blinding him with salt, until finally he had tied his ceremonial scarf around his forehead as if it were a mere rag. Whatever authority he had once felt left him as he looked down at the small man with his amethyst medallion of office on his bare chest. Once the mythic quality of being the tall blond god descending from the skies and bringing the natives the mysteries of corn and tubers had appealed to him, but that was in a time when he was giving and not taking; now that little man seemed to tower over him.

The Governor stood there looking up with those alien black eyes under a severely straight edge of dark hair that covered his entire forehead. When he spoke there was no trace of rage or passion, only the stiff formality of words that were alien to his tongue. It was as if he had become a figure in some tragedy and his face were a mask:

"You are a disciple of Abaris. Under your robe you wear the emblem of the winged serpent. How can you do this?"

"It will come to an end *soon,*" Bran said with all the emotion missing from the Governor's voice. "Everything will come to an end soon, but we need this vessel if Abaris' prophecies are to be fulfilled. If I revolt or give myself away now, the whole plan will be lost!"

"What good will your plans do for those already inside your vessel, Captain? If Abaris is willing to sacrifice them for his plan, then he is no different from your High Priest. But I did not come here to argue. I came to go back with you. I will go with you now to your Solemn Assembly and there in front of all, I will kill your High Priest. In the civil war that is sure to follow, the Empire will not have time to bother about Anahuac. But when the army tries to return here, my people will be ready. This will serve more than waiting for the end of the world."

The Governor passed by Bran in a silent contempt that wounded him more deeply than any attack. He had taken the lead, and by turning to follow him into the vessel, Bran felt that at least he was doing something by ferrying this assassin into the beginning of civil war.

The Governor remained silent throughout the journey, nor did he speak as he left the ship to follow the pages up the processional ramp to the Palace of the Provincial Governors. As Bran watched him disappear, his words did not go away but continued to weigh upon Bran's conscience.

If civil war were to come, Bran wondered, would his garuda be taken from him? Was he about to lose the one thing that had kept him holding on to Abaris' plan? But if civil war were about to break out, that itself could mean that the final days were at hand. But why hadn't the leader appeared? Abaris had been so insistent on that point: in the final weeks immediately before the catastrophe another man who had been trained by Abaris would appear. Brigita would be the first to recognize him, but Bran was to know him from the passwords.

Then more than ever did Bran feel isolated and alone. With Abaris dead and Brigita on the other side of the sea in Eiru, there was no one who could tell him what to do. Should he report the Governor to stop the assassination and civil war that could result in the loss of his ship? Or should he move to escape with the 144 precisely at the moment of confusion?

Bran looked up at the City as if he could read his instructions from that citadel of knowledge, and then he dropped his eyes to his feet in disgust and began to walk toward the ramp that would take him up to the Institute. There was little in the City of Knowledge that he cared to look at anymore. The architectural power of the City had long since worn thin, and in the rigid symmetries of Institute and Sacred College, there was not enough diversity and life to hold him. All the ramps had been so constructed that only the top of the Tower could be seen as one climbed up from the harbor to the Broad Street, and this perspective made the Tower appear not to rise from the earth but to float above, weightless in the air. It was not until one came to the Broad Street itself that one could take in the whole expanse of the City, from the copper doors of the Institute to the west, to the Chapel of the Sacred College to the east. But Bran had seen it all before a thousand times; he knew every little vista at the turns of the ramps that celebrated the capital in prearranged instances of self-praise.

Bran had always preferred the old capital. Its architectural styles spanned the millennia, and its carefully planned symmetries were caught in a tussle with spontaneity, like a celibate caught in bed with a woman. Everywhere that order tried to transcend into perfection, just there disorder camped at its edges. All the races and occupations of the world flowed through the dirty streets and cluttered canals of the ancient city, and Bran knew how to find his way by smell alone: from fish market to flower stalls, from the sweet thick rot of the slaughterhouse to the hilltop temples where the tropical winds from the south were subtle and far more mysterious than the heavy and obvious incense the priests used to obscure the candlelight.

This City of Knowledge was a priest's dream of perfection, order, and control, and so Bran kept his eyes to the ground and pounded his decisions down into the stones with his feet: he would not report the Governor of Anahuac; he would not give the signal to move to the 144; he would simply wait to see what the Solemn Assembly would bring.

In disgust at his own powerlessness, Bran broke out into a run as he cleared the last three steps and turned to the left to come out of the ramp and onto the Broad Street. But the ramps were designed for a slow and meditative ascent and not an athletic race, and no sooner had he turned the corner than he smashed into a dignitary and sent the man sprawling to the ground. Bran recognized at once from the pale blue robes that he had collided with one of the chosen few, one of the seventy-two Members of the Sacred College.

"You clumsy ass! You wear the uniform of a Captain of a garuda, but you don't even look where you're going. Pity the poor wretches that have to fly with you!"

That hurt. And for that remark alone, Bran wanted to strike out at him, but the Members of the Sacred College were the aristocracy of aristocracies and outranked everyone except the Supreme Council of the High Priest.

"Please forgive me, Your Grace. I'm afraid that birds that can be graceful in the air are often clumsy on earth."

The dignitary reached up to take Bran's extended hand and smiled back at him:

"I like that! That's a good image, Captain. 'The bird that soars in air, waddles on the muddy earth.' For the sake of your poetic nature, I accept your apology. You just might have the beginnings of a good song there."

"Is Your Grace a poet?" Bran said as he bowed in deference.

"No, a composer. If you finish the words to your poem, Captain, come to me and I will set it to music. I am Viracocha. I am one of the precious hothouse flowers that decorate the morning end of the City."

The dignitary pointed in the direction of the College, smiled, and with a slight nod of the head, turned and moved off down the Broad Street toward the College Gate.

At least he doesn't take himself too seriously, Bran thought. What a life he must lead in his palace of arts.

As Bran watched the man walk rapidly down the street, he began to imagine himself as a Member of the Sacred College for poetry. He had no idea of what the living quarters would be, but he saw himself sitting at a desk by a window to the sea: he had been up writing all night and now he could see the sun coming up over the ocean. As clearly as if he had just written the words down, he could see the quatrain he had been working on:

> *Body burdened on the ground*
> *Startled heaven when it found*
> *Arms it had falsely used*
> *Were wings that force had bruised.*

But the image of wings only recalled to his mind the emblem of the winged serpent and the black accusing eyes of the Governor of Anahuac. The daydream of living the life of a poet ended in the pain that reminded him only too well of who he really was and what he had to do. As the dignitary disappeared through the College Gate, Bran turned around to face in the opposite direction of the Institute.

Bran moved toward the copper doors with a prayer that this would be one of the last times that he would have to report there. He couldn't see how it could go on much longer, for either the 144 would be discovered, or he would give the signal to go and not wait for the prophesied leader to appear.

The guards at the doors saluted him as he passed through, but the Officer of the Guard inside the entrance post surprised him with an unexpected message as Bran handed over his flight report:

"Good Morning, Captain. His Excellency the Archon has requested that you stop in to see him before you go to your quarters."

An immediate spiral of fear spun around in Bran's stomach. Had they learned about the 144? Had their spies found out about the Governor? Bran took a deep breath to slow his racing heart, saluted the Officer of the Guard, and continued down the long artificially lit corridor.

Bran thought it strange that for all the people he had brought into the Institute, he had himself never gone beyond the Office of the Guards. But he did not need to be told that the double doors at the very end of the corridor led into the Laboratory of Incarnation, and he knew at once that was where the women and children would be. He did not want to go in there, and he could see from the seal of the Archon on the door to his left, that he did not have to go further toward those double doors.

Bran knocked twice and waited for the silent page to open the door to admit him to the Archon's study. But it was not a page who admitted him, but another armed guard, and this made Bran feel more ill at ease. Was this normal, he wondered, or was the City already prepared for a civil war?

The guard knocked twice on the door to the inner study, and then opened it to let Bran pass. The Archon was standing at the other end of the room with his back to Bran. A row of Mercury Tablets neatly aligned on the table gleamed in front of the robed figure and gave an aura of pink light to his silhouette. The Archon turned slowly to look at Bran, and then with a welcoming smile, he moved with the help of his cane back to his desk.

"Good Morning, Captain. Please sit down. Don't wait for me

to be seated, for, as you can see, it will take me a little longer to settle myself into my own chair."

Bran tried not to be obvious as he considered the Archon's condition. The right leg seemed stiff and the right arm was not in its sleeve. It appeared to him as if the Archon had suffered some sort of a stroke since he had last seen him.

Slowly the stricken figure adjusted himself into the chair, took a breath of resigned acceptance, and smiled again at Bran in a very grandfatherly way:

"Ironic, isn't it? Here we are at the Institute studying the nature of the blood, and I become afflicted with a blood clot."

"I am very sorry, Your Excellency," Bran said. "I hope that your own staff here can find the remedy soon."

"There is much about the blood that even we don't know, but we are coming very close to a great climax in our work, you can practically feel the excitement in the air, so, perhaps soon we shall. For the present, I must concentrate on our primary work. Which brings me to the subject: we have had some reports concerning an emotional disturbance in the Governor of Ana-huac. I believe he traveled here for the Solemn Assembly aboard your vessel. Did you notice any unusual behavior?"

"He was strangely silent and withdrawn, Your Excellency. But I confess that I still don't understand what is 'usual' for these people. You look into their eyes, but it is like looking into one of their black obsidian mirrors. You can never tell what is going on inside. They never seem to signal their emotions before they express them. One minute they are peaceful, the next violent. All that I can report is that every time we prepare to ascend, the clearing is surrounded by hundreds of silent men. They do keep well beyond the range of our dart-catapults, but sooner or later, I think, they will revolt."

"I see," the Archon said as he began to toy with the handle of his cane. "And the Governor, do you see him leading such a revolt?"

"He or anyone of them could, Your Excellency. The Governor is an enigma to me. I must confess that I really don't like these people. Their moodiness disturbs me so that I always feel un-easy around them."

The old man nodded in silence as if to say that he knew exactly what Bran meant, and then in a manner that was so paternal that it bordered on the patronizing, he tried to explain the situation to Bran:

"You see, that is because their emotions are collective, not personal. But that is precisely why they are so good for our work here. The Atlantean race is too civilized, too highly individuated. We had need of a race that was more psychically malleable. You can have no idea of how important the work is that is going on here. But, soon, you shall. For now, let us say that the Institute has found a way to accelerate human evolution. These pregnant women that you have brought here are, in a way, truly the mothers of a new human race. I would like to thank you for the sensitive manner in which you have executed this mission. It is a delicate situation, but you have handled it with the appropriate delicacy. The people of Anahuac, of course, neither understand nor appreciate our work, but this Solemn Assembly should be helpful in bringing about a more sympathetic union among the peoples of the Empire. I believe that is all that I need to know for the moment, Captain. Thank you."

Bran stood up quickly to attention, bowed, backed up three paces with his head still held low, and then turned to go out the door. He passed quickly by the guards in the outer study and at the entrance and did not take a deep breath until he was beyond the copper doors by the low wall overlooking the sea.

As Bran took in a freer breath he tried to take in his whole situation. It felt to him as if the Archon had believed his report, but the remaining danger lay with the spies. Was there one of his own crew that was reporting to the Institute, and if so, who? It was clear now that the Governor of Anahuac would be arrested and that the assassination attempt would be aborted, but what about the 144? If the 144 were linked to a revolt in Anahuac, or were thought to be part of a coup by the military, then they could all be rounded up before the signal of escape was ever given. If only Abaris were still alive!

Bran turned away from the low wall, moved down the Broad Street, and then took the small alley to the left that led to the residential quarters of the Institute. He wished that there were some way that he could get into the Palace of the Provincial Governors to give the doomed Governor of Anahuac a warning, but he doubted whether the Governor would even try to escape. The person that he really needed to see was Brigita. If Brigita would only attend this Assembly, he thought that some solution to their dilemma could be worked out. But he knew that Brigita might avoid a Solemn Assembly whose only purpose was to worship the Empire.

Bran felt trapped: he couldn't warn the Governor, he couldn't get in touch with Brigita, he couldn't, like her, simply project out of the body to find the spirit of Abaris, and he couldn't give the signal to the 144. It was then that he began to feel the panic of an animal in a trap: had that seemingly kind and solicitous old man been toying with him? Did they already know everything? Was this Solemn Assembly simply a ruse to bring everyone into the City to eliminate the military coup and the 144 all at once?

Bran fought down the feelings of panic as he entered the officers' quarters and went into his room. The one thing he was not prepared to do was the one thing that he had to do, and that was nothing.

The light from the clerestory dropped onto the table as somewhere beyond a cloud moved out of the way of the sun. As the sunlight flashed on the engraved metal sheets, Viracocha took a step back from the table. He had already seen enough and the light of understanding had flashed for him within seconds of looking at these proposals for the increased elevation of the Tower: the whole project was a mistake, perhaps even a very dangerous mistake.

The old man, however, seemed happily occupied in his examination of the engravings. Viracocha studied the bent figure for a moment, observed the light bouncing off his bald head, watched the long bony finger moving slowly over the calculations, and listened to the little voice laboring the obvious as he hummed tiny exclamations of agreement to himself. When the old man thought he had found a particularly challenging point, his tongue would protrude from his mouth and remain exposed until the exclamation of agreement would allow it to return to its well-deserved obscurity. Viracocha found it difficult not to become annoyed.

Viracocha knew that the old man, as Member of the Sacred College for Architecture, thought he was being generous and companionable in inviting the youngest Member to join him in a look at the new and exciting project for the City of Knowledge. And he also could sense that the old man was trying to make him feel less isolated within the College, but, in fact, Viracocha preferred his isolation and had absolutely no desire to work in groups or be part of the circle of which the Member for Architecture was the most senior.

As Viracocha watched the long skeletal finger make its slow deliberate passage among the figures, he thought of a blue heron moving along an icy shore in winter in search of fish. Could he see himself as now this writing can from the perspective of the millennia, he might see himself as the wild horse. He was of medium height but for his broad shoulders and full chest had delicate hands. His thick shoulder-length brown hair contrasted with his red beard, but his eyes like the sea seemed to change colors with his moods: one minute they appeared to be blue, the next green. Even when he stood at rest, he raced on with an animal instinctiveness that did not think twice about its moves. Viracocha never needed to deliberate; words would rush out of him with such speed that it made thinking appear to be as natural as seeing or running. Conversation was only possible if one were to run along with him, but that rarely happened. Most people, like the old man, believed that sureness of thought and slowness of thought were the same thing.

While the Member for Architecture carried on with his official duty of examining the Institute's proposed changes in the Tower, Viracocha let his mind return to his own work. For the first time in Atlantean history, he planned to set two solo voices, a baritone and a soprano, against the chorus. He was excited and his imagination was pleased with the image of a man and a woman standing out against the massed power of the entire choir.

At last the old man came to the end of his examination. With a dramatic exhalation of self-importance and relief from his heavy responsibility, he sat down in the chair by the table and turned toward Viracocha with a priestly formality that seemed to say: "And now the Member for Architecture would like to ask a sometime architect and now Member for Theoretical Music and Composition to pronounce an opinion on the matter at hand."

"Well, Your Grace?"

As if he were thinking of more important matters, Viracocha remarked rather casually that the whole project was a mistake.

"I'm sorry, Your Grace, I'm afraid my hearing is going. Could you please repeat that?"

"Yes, of course," Viracocha replied as he closed his eyes to review his calculations. "No, it's very clear. If you change the alteration of the Tower, you will alter its resonance with the bay in the etheric range and the whole wave pattern will be disrupted. Rather than enhancing the etheric bodies of plants and animals placed in the foundation vault of the Tower, what will happen now is that the etheric body will be separated from its connection to the physical. I'm afraid it would be dangerous for anyone to be in the foundation vault when the solar crystal was activated. Surely, Your Grace, you can see that the Institute's calculations are so consistently wrong that they suggest a pattern of conscious misrepresentation."

"I must confess, Your Grace," the old man said in disbelief and discomfort, "that I do not see what you're talking about. It's true that the site for the Tower was chosen because of the etheric properties of the rocks and the depth of the bay, which provided a convenient collector, but surely with the sea all around us, the stabilizing quality of water will not be lost?"

"It is not simply the etheric quality of water," Viracocha answered with impatience, "but the geometry of the bay as well. The underwater configuration of the bay is nearly perfectly conical, and this organizes the etheric radiance of the seawater in a way that is adjusted by both the elevation of the Tower *and* the frequency-signature of the solar crystal. Change anything, and you change everything."

"But surely you can't think that the entire faculty of the Institute, not to mention the Supreme Council of the High Priest, has made a mistake?"

"I thought that was what I just said," Viracocha replied as he looked down at the seated old man in wonder that anyone so stupid could ever be appointed Member of the Sacred College. "Does Your Grace intend to approve the designs considering, at least, the questions I have raised?"

That was going too far for the Member for Architecture. He reached out to grasp the edge of the table to hold onto solidity as he stared up at Viracocha in state of shock and disgust:

"This proposal comes from both the High Priest himself and the Archon of the Temple Institute! You do seem to have a problem of reading perspective into these engravings. However, I will ask the Archon for a clarification. I'm certain he will be able to put your mind at ease."

The old man bowed to indicate that the consultation was at an end. Viracocha returned his bow and gladly left him to his afternoon rest.

I suppose he imagined that he was doing me a favor, Viracocha thought to himself as he left the apartment and walked out into the cloister, the oldest Member giving the youngest Member a sense of belonging by taking him into the project that all his cronies were buzzing about. Viracocha could understand why the old man had let him see the plans, but what he couldn't understand was why the Institute would want to alter the whole dynamics of the Tower.

Viracocha turned away from the colonnade that led to his quarters on the eastern side of the quadrangle and decided to walk out to the end of the southern peninsula. The puzzle of the Tower began to interest him precisely because of its obvious absurdity. He began to feel that intuitive pull of growth that had taken hold of him at critical times in his life to effect the most unsuspected transformations. It was in one of those earlier transformations that he had abandoned the formulaic conventions of temple architecture to take up music. And it was through musical composition that he had been appointed to the Sacred College, to become at thirty the youngest Member since its founding.

He could feel the pull, but this time it had an almost spatial quality to it. He looked around as if his environment could give him the answer he was seeking, but he knew the surroundings only too well. Viracocha had begun to feel a sense of confinement during his three years of residence in the great City of Knowledge. As he passed out of the quadrangle of the residential quarters of the College, he followed the colonnade through an enclosed garden with a fountain in the center. And in the center of the fountain was the required obelisk to the sun. He quickly passed through and came out on to the processional walkway that wound around the entire crescent directly above the bay. It all seemed so controlled, so boringly bisymmetrical, with the Institute on the extreme western side of the processional and the College Chapel on the extreme eastern side. Directly in the center was the Broad Street, the hypostyle hall, and above it, the Tower itself. Only the Tower rose above the level of the plateau behind it, but there was nothing on that plateau except sparse grass and scrub bushes. For the most part the isolation of the City of Knowledge was unrelieved by either village or town. It was more than forty miles of poor grazing lands dotted with a few goats before one came to the ancient capital, but there were no roads on the peninsula, and all traffic between the seat of the High Priest and the old capital was either by sea or air. Once one had taken the official promenades along the processional ramps, the Broad Street, or through the labyrinthine paths in the gardens and cloisters, there were very few places left simply to go for a walk. To the extreme east, on the fields and low cliffs in front of the Sacred College there was a goat trail that led down to a small cove with a tidal spouting cave, but to the western end by the Institute there was nothing but very high cliffs that dropped from the laboratories to the surf-beaten rocks below.

Viracocha turned to his left to follow the processional walkway to the entrance to the Chapel; as he walked along the edge he looked over the low wall down into the deep blue waters of the bay. He had never seen so many garudas at rest on the waters at one time. Although it had been explained to him on several occasions by the older Members of the College, it still did not make much sense to him. A Solemn Assembly was not a decision-making body, for that was the work of the Supreme Council. A Solemn Assembly was not a forum of discussion, for that was the work of the convocations of the College or the Institute. A Solemn Assembly was an invocation of the Spirit of the Empire, and although voices of questioning were invoked in the liturgy, they were not really intended to be anything more than occasions in which to appreciate the unanimity that filled the great hypostyle hall.

The whole thing seemed something of a farce to Viracocha. First, they sent over the plans for the proposed increase in the elevation of the Tower from the Institute to the College, but they didn't really want anybody to do anything but register a

ritual approval. Next, they called a Solemn Assembly to cele-
brate the approval that they hadn't really received. It was more
theater and politics than science or architecture, but perhaps,
Viracocha thought, theater was what the politics of Empire was
all about.

Viracocha liked to walk because he never had any need of
plans or writings. Whether he was doing the plans for a building
or the notation for a musical composition, the transcription with
emerald stylus onto the thin metal sheets was always for the
sake of others. He had only to look at a building to imagine its
original plans, or hear a piece of music to transcribe it into the
hieratic notation. So as he looked down into the deep waters of
the bay and then turned to look up at the Tower, he did not
need to go over the plates again to know for certain that he was
right.

The copper doors of the Institute gleamed in the sunlight in
response to his inquiring look across the bay, but no answers
came for the questions in his mind. Only an image came out of
nowhere, as if he were dreaming with his eyes open, and that
was the image of some maniacal idiot pulling on a head until it
was torn from the spine. In that instant he knew that he was
correct in his calculations, that the etheric body would be
pulled away from the physical.

Viracocha turned away from the Institute to stare at the stone
wall in front of him. He had no desire to move to the left and go
into the Chapel, so he reached up to the top of the wall, pulled
himself up and swung himself over onto the other side without
giving a thought to how ridiculous he looked scurrying over
walls in his priestly pale blue robes. At first glance nothing was
there but jagged brown rocks. The land did not drop away with
the high dramatic cliffs of the western side of the peninsula, but
simply leaned toward the sea with a collection of rubble that no
architect would care to landscape. Viracocha could see why the
architect had built a stone wall to mark the end of the city and
the entrance to the Chapel.

There were no goat trails to follow, but the slope of the land
seemed to pull him down farther to the eastern side away from
all sight of the harbor. He followed the inclination and moved

down out of sight of the Tower or any of the buildings until he came upon a collection of broken basaltic columns. One of the hexagonal columns was a foot or so lower than the other three surrounding it and so it seemed nicely formed to serve as a chair.

As Viracocha sat down in the natural throne, he felt free of the psychic confinement of the city and was simply happy to be able to look out over the sea and thankful that there was nothing human to look at. He stretched his legs out, placed his hands on his chest, and closed his eyes, as if to test whether or not the place could serve for composition. But he was startled to find that his mind did not return to his composition at once. Instead the elevated Tower stood out vividly in his imagination and he saw an inner shaft of light go from the solar crystal to the center of the earth. Light met light as the brilliant shaft was met by a stream of molten lava shooting up from the depths of the earth. And then he understood. The new space of the singularity would not be in the pathway from the crystal to the center of the foundation vault; it would go all the way down to the center of the earth: the distance from the solar crystal to the center of the earth over the distance to the sun. They were trying to alter the whole geometrical dynamics of the solar system!

In the very instant that Viracocha became aware of the project, he became opposed to it. He did not think about it. It was a completely instinctive response. Once he had decided against it, thought was needed only to determine the way in which to oppose the undertaking. It was at that point that the artist in him decided to take the most dramatic and unexpected form of all: he would speak out against the project during the Solemn Assembly. When the voice of the Oracle rang out in ancient liturgical Atlantean: "Who among you could even conceive of not being moved by so great a vision?" he would rise, sing out a newly created ancient response, and proceed up the aisle to the Speaker's Stone to challenge the entire project. If theater was the politics of Empire, then, Viracocha vowed to himself: Theater we will have!

Viracocha was enormously pleased with himself as he jumped up from his basaltic throne and resolved to rush back to the library to make certain that his responsorial chant would be composed in perfect liturgical Atlantean. The dramatic power of the challenge would be ruined if his strong tenor voice rang out in the great hypostyle hall in faulty grammar. It wouldn't matter if only the Member for Poetry recognized the error; the idea had to be perfect for Viracocha, or else the idea of perfection was lost.

Now Viracocha was truly excited in ways he had not felt before during his three years in the City. He jumped up onto his volcanic chair and leaped up into the air and began to run as fast as he could up the hill to the stone wall. The rocky ground was higher on the southern side of the wall, so Viracocha did not have to break his stride, but grasping the top of the wall with his left hand, he simply flung himself over with a great display of power, some grace, and much silliness.

He was the first to realize the silliness of it, for as he came hurtling over the wall he nearly collided with a dark blue hooded figure staring across the bay toward the copper doors of the Institute. As Viracocha landed scarcely a pace away from the figure, he put out his hand to the pavement to steady himself and looked up at the hooded face as it slowly turned to take notice of him. In the deep shadows of the hood all Viracocha saw at first were two green eyes staring at him without the slightest trace of surprise.

"Good Afternoon, Your Grace," the voice of a young woman said in a bow that by its slight inclination said that though she recognized the pale blue robes of the Sacred College, she herself was of no mean rank.

"Good Afternoon," Viracocha said as he stood up and brushed the dust from his hands. "I'm sorry to have startled you. No one is usually here at this hour, and, well, I was feeling celebrative for having made a decision."

"You didn't startle me, Viracocha. I was here to wait for you. So, you have decided to speak out against the Institute. I'm glad. It has to be stopped."

Viracocha stared at the woman first in disbelief, then in irritation:

"Whoever you are, young lady of the hooded dark, I wish you would come out into the open in *every* way."

She did not raise her arms immediately, but stood for an instant to study him, and then slowly two white hands lifted and folded the hood back over her shoulders. The skin of her face was as pale as her hands except for a faint bridge of freckles which passed over the nose and seemed to match the color of her long reddish-brown hair.

"As you can see, Your Grace, the hood is not for hiding but for protection from the sun in this southern climate."

"From the coarseness of your dark blue robe," Viracocha said as he began to examine her more closely, "I assume you come from somewhere near the ice sheets."

She was young, neither plain nor pretty, but a constantly changing relationship between the two that seemed to have as much to do with her own ambivalence as with any natural endowments. Her eyes were fiercely intense, almost threatening in a defensive way that said: "I'm not very good with people and I know it, so don't try to befriend me." She appeared to be slight and Viracocha thought she looked lost in the huge tent of her ankle-length robe. He imagined her as skinny, angular, and hard, with bony shoulders and hips that tolerated their fleshly covering the way she tolerated her ill-fitting cloak.

She looked at him with exasperation as much as annoyance and then blurted out with impatience:

"I am Brigita, the Abbess of the One Thousand of Eiru, and I don't understand how you can possibly be so ignorant of your own spiritual life not to remember me."

"Of course, I know *of* Brigita the Abbess of Eiru. Abaris told me about you, but unless I am getting feebleminded at thirty-three, I don't remember ever having had the pleasure . . ."

"Not in the body," Brigita interrupted, *"out* of the body *in* the spirit, in the *real* world."

"I'm afraid I don't work very well in your 'spiritual' world, and now I'm beginning to understand why you *seem* so good at reading minds. I'm not what you would want to call a good student of Abaris. I've never had an 'out-of-the-body' experience in my life, so although I'm flattered to have appeared as the man in your dreams, I must confess my innocence."

That annoyed Brigita just as Viracocha hoped it would. Her green eyes hissed in serpentine menace at the mere suggestion that he or any man was part of her dream life.

"Why are we wasting time with this silly banter? You are not the man of my dreams; if any man were to have that place, it would certainly be Abaris, and not you. You have had 'out-of-the-body' experiences every night for the last few years, and it is absolutely impossible for me to understand how you can forget that subtle life to focus your identity on this dumb, obvious, crude, masculine personality of yours!"

Viracocha looked over Brigita's shoulder to see two colonials coming up the processional walk to the Chapel. As he returned his glance to Brigita, she immediately turned around to consider the approach of the two men.

"I don't think we should go on talking like this here," Viracocha said. "I don't know yet what you want, but *I* want to talk to you again. We're not allowed to have women in the Sacred College, so we'll need to meet outside."

"Strange isn't it," Brigita commented with returning calmness. "You're allowed to take a concubine to your bed, even though you're all priests here, but you can't take a woman colleague into your study."

"That's because there is no such thing as a woman colleague here in this City of Knowledge," Viracocha replied. "The only women here are servants or concubines. Do you know where the spouting cave is on the eastern side of the peninsula? It's down out of sight from any of the buildings or gardens of the College. We could meet there tomorrow afternoon, after the Solemn Assembly."

"Yes, I can see the place you mean. I had hoped to be able to work some plan out with you, but, if they don't arrest you, I will meet you tomorrow."

"Why would they arrest me for a loyal observance of the most ancient ritual, me, a Member of the Sacred College? Even if you could read minds, I don't think you read the situation here in our City."

"You don't remember your spiritual life, and you can't see what's going on around you," Brigita said in disbelief. "And to think Abaris called you 'the new man,' the 'Man of the Future'! May the One help us, for I certainly can't see how I am going to be able to go through with it all with you."

Brigita did not wait for a reply, but pulling her hood over her face, she turned and went into the Chapel. Viracocha stood a moment in silent consideration of her face as it stood out so vividly in his imagination. Everything about her was at an edge. Her face was exactly at an edge and the slightest shift could make her homely or beautiful. There was not much body to her so she seemed to haunt the psychic edges of the physical like some wraith haunting a lover's bed: repelled and attracted to the physical copulation that would pull her soul into life.

In considering Brigita, Viracocha recognized that she brought him to an edge in himself, for part of him found her secretive plainness attractive, and he had erotic fantasies that if she were a concubine, he would find all sorts of unexpected and pleasant surprises in her nakedness. But another part of him found her to be an arrogant and condescending purist with a contempt for the world she could not understand, much less master. Except for the grandfatherly Abaris, she certainly did not seem to like men. The war of the sexes, Viracocha thought to himself with a smile. Well, you can't have that with a concubine, so unless they do arrest me, I will be there tomorrow at the spouting cave.

Viracocha returned the bow from the two colonial visitors to the Chapel, and then hurried down the walkway to return to his quarters in the College. He knew that he had taken up enough time with the Institute's business and that it was time to get back to his own. The High Priest had requested a performance of Viracocha's choral works for the evening's reception of the Provincial Governors. If he didn't attend the choirmaster's rehearsals, he knew he could always count on the master to work against him to make the work sound safe, conventional, and soporific.

When Viracocha returned to his rooms, he was surprised to find a large packet of drawings and a note from the Archon:

We at the Institute are pleased to learn that His Grace, the Member for Theoretical Music, has taken a keen interest in our work. We thought it fitting, therefore, that you have your own copy of the plates for study.

Nicely done, Viracocha thought to himself. He politely invites me in and tells me to be sure that I do my homework. The old man certainly did not waste any time in informing the Institute of my objections.

Viracocha did think that was curious, but he did not have time either to open the package or reflect on the Member for Architecture's motivations. He had the rehearsal, then the reception, the dinner, and then the performance. The package would have to wait.

When Viracocha returned to his rooms late that evening, he was too tired and too preoccupied with the problems of the performance to recall the packet of engravings on his desk. With his back to the table and his eyes set for infinity, he unbound the gold chain to his cape and let it drop to cover the images of the Tower like some velvet, enveloping wave. Within a few seconds, he was deeply asleep.

Only when he awoke the next morning did Viracocha remember the plates, but even then they did not seem to be central to his concerns, for he turned over the thin metal sheets in a quick and cursory examination that was only to make certain that they were simply copies of those he had seen before. Some other thought left over from sleep or dreams was trying to get at him, but he could not remember anything other than a feeling that it had to do with the Solemn Assembly. He picked up the emerald stylus and toyed with it absentmindedly for a moment, and then he moved to the side of the table where his Mercury Tablet sat.

The metallic gray liquid shimmered like the surface of a frosted mirror, but as he touched it with the stylus it transcribed his motions into gleaming figures of gold. With an elegantly artistic hand he inscribed the hieratic script for *Ome ulubi ra, se tata mak*, and then, with the head of the stylus, he activated the command for glyphic resolution. Within an instant the linear script of gold melted into six hieroglyphs with their tonal consorts.

Viracocha hummed the tones, but did not find them to be the melody that he thought he half-remembered from his dreams. He tried reversals and inversions, but it was not until he took the occult reciprocals for the tones that he discovered the chant he wanted. It was not simply a chant, but an astonishingly haunting call to the stars.

As he chanted the sequence over and over again, he began to remember what he was looking for. It was the Solemn Assembly itself that was the art form that held out the solution to the problems that had developed in the previous performance of his choral work. The Solemn Assembly could be transformed into an oratorio in which several soloists' voices competed with the chorus of the whole civilization. The Solemn Assembly was the most archaic, most collective ritual for celebrating the tradition of Atlantean chant, that ancient, droning monody that pulled the mind down into trance.

"What a perfect occasion for contrasting the soloist singing a melody even more ancient than the plainsong of the chant!" Viracocha exclaimed to himself and he returned the Mercury Tablet to its silent silver gray. As he rose with enthusiasm to dress for the part the day was to bring, it was hard for him to contain his own excitement.

What made it difficult to sustain such enthusiasm was the unanticipated long wait of the morning. The processions were unending. First came the line of green-robed Provincial Governors, then the long line of red-robed Military Commanders, then the even longer line of the indigo-robed faculty of the Temple Institute, and finally, the line of the seventy-two pale blue-robed Members of the Sacred College. When these had taken their places in the hall, then the Supreme Council of the High Priest entered, each attired in his robe of magenta. One by one, they came onto the raised dais at the end of the hypostyle hall: the Commander of the Military, the Governor of Trade, the Archon of the Temple Institute, the Master of the Sacred College, and, finally, the Oracle herself.

Ages before, the High Priest had been a woman, not so much

a priest as a matriarch. But as trade and warfare had grown, and with them the competition to control trade through superior weaponry, the clusters of villages had grown into cities, and a new priesthood had developed with the mystery of writing that could maintain control of life with facts. Conflict followed conflict, until at last there was an open civil war between tradition and innovation. The result of that conflict was the establishment of the Theocracy. The priests took on the ancient dress of the matriarchs, and the High Priest took over the role of the Great Mother herself, but to honor the gifts of the past, woman was given the role of Oracle. In trance, she would speak for the old gods in the new assemblies of men; but that was long before in the early days of the Theocracy. Now her role was restricted to being the conductor of the ceremony of the Solemn Assembly. She no longer sat on the Supreme Council of the High Priest, but stood alone in her tower-like pulpit, above all except the High Priest, yet more of a captive than an ancient voice entoning the monodies of a cherished tradition.

After all the dignitaries had taken their places, the minor colonial officials and provincial priests were allowed to fill the back of the hall. And then there was absolute silence for the space of half an hour.

Viracocha closed his eyes to meditate and to perform the kriya he had been taught by Abaris. Silently he intoned the solar syllable as he drew up a golden stream of energy from the base of his spine. He enjoyed the subtle physical sensation of feeling the energy spread out over the back of his brain and then pour into his inner eye. The cobra stood erect: the expanded hood was his brain and his spinal column was the long body of the snake. The image of Brigita came to his mind, and he saw again the bright green eyes peering out from under the shadows of her hood. Slowly, he pronounced the lunar syllable and felt the cool silver of the stream flow back down through the spinal channel to come to rest at the bottom, like moonlight on the surface of water in a deep well.

From somewhere, very far away, he heard the sound: two wooden clapping sounds, a metallic thud, and then a high tingling sound of a small bell. The sound was coming from behind.

He listened again, as now everyone did, and musician that he was, he was able to recognize the objects from their timbre. Someone was walking on wooden shoes, punctuating the rhythm of his slow gait with a heavy metallic staff that struck the floor and set the tiny bell on top of the staff to ringing. Viracocha was hearing the approach of the High Priest. Like a great drum roll the three beats and crystalline answer continued as the High Priest slowly came from outside the back doors of the hypostyle hall and moved down the central aisle. Over and over again the four sounds repeated themselves. The High Priest was chanting with his feet and staff even before a single voice had been lifted. An enormous physical power seemed to come out of those four sounds, as if the reverberations filling the entire hall had become the incarnate body of the High Priest himself. As the sounds grew louder Viracocha found that they penetrated his body and seemed to resonate in the centers along his spine. And then he opened his eyes and saw the High Priest.

It was his newly acquired height which first amazed Viracocha. The High Priest towered above the Assembly as he struck the stones with his *cothurni*. It was not walking, it was setting the earth under him into vibration until the earth itself became the shoes on which he walked before the stars. The golden staff with its silver bell on the top was the sun and the moon, which he had taken in hand to make his journey through space. The enormous headdress of peacock feathers was broader than his shoulders, and the golden spiral of twin ram's horns over his ears suggested that he was all-seeing, all-hearing. The brocaded robes were an epiphany of the colors of the robes of the other priests, for he was their summation. He had become "the Rainbow Body of the Higher Self," and in him humanity stood out and declared its rightful patrimony.

As the High Priest approached the ramp to the pyramid that held his throne, he stopped at the dais which supported his Supreme Council; then, very slowly, he turned to face the Assembly. Viracocha found himself wondering like a little boy how the High Priest was going to ascend that pyramid to his throne. As the High Priest faced the Assembly, he struck the platform with his staff and immediately a shaft of light came through the skylight and shone directly into the enormous emerald that was at the center of his peacock headdress. He began to turn slowly to face the ramp up to his throne, when suddenly a scream rang out through the hall: "Death to the Murderer of Anahuac!"

At first it was not fear that paralyzed everyone, but something more like awe at the inconceivable. No one in his state of religious peace had the power to jump to his feet to try to take command of a situation no one could yet understand. All saw one of the Provincial Governors break out of ranks, run into the aisle, and fire dart after dart from his catapult. But the High Priest did not fall; instead he raised his arms and his staff and commanded the guards and the Military Commanders in a voice that was much deeper than the high-pitched scream of the Governor: "Be still!"

No one moved. No one breathed. It was now a direct and elemental agon of the assassin and the High Priest. Raised upon the platform and his *cothurni,* the High Priest towered above the small man with straight black hair. They both stood motionless for an instant, and then the Governor threw down the catapult with disgust and drew out a long dagger from inside his robes. With another high-pitched scream, he started to run toward the High Priest.

A brilliant flash of flat, metallic white light burst from the staff of the High Priest, and Viracocha immediately closed his eyes in pain. It took several seconds for all the afterimages and colors to disappear so that he could see again. When he did open his eyes once more, the assassin was gone and the High Priest was seated on top of the pyramid in his throne. A single exhalation in awe of a miracle came out of the multitude, but even as they all began to draw breath, the Oracle sang out the opening words of the traditional chant and the whole Assembly answered in an enormous wave of emotion that seemed to express the very power of their entire civilization.

Over and over the hypnotic cycle of the chant turned, and as Viracocha stared at the green light of the great emerald on the High Priest's forehead it became the point where all sound and light gathered. Everywhere around him he could feel the pull of the entire Assembly moving into trance. Nothing could be other to the single mind of the Assembly in the purity of that consecrated time of miracle. Viracocha's breath softened, his heart slowed in its beat, and the interval between each pulse widened until his mind passed through. When his heartbeat would return, it reminded him who he was, and he began to wonder where or who he had been in that rich emptiness.

He could not discern just at what point the chanting receded into stillness, or for how long the Assembly rested in that silence that was not an absence of sound but a thick presence that filled the hall. Out of that presence a voice did come. The timbre was so perfect for that sense of presence that voice became for silence what soul was for body. There was no longer an inside versus an outside, for the voice of the High Priest filled the hall and yet seemed whispered inside everyone.

"*Children of the Sun, rejoice.*
You are the generation of the Great Return.
For thirty-five thousand years
Our temples have labored to perfect
This animal body into which our spirits
Were cast by an errant god.
For millennia we have striven to purge
Beast and monster from our troubled blood.
Abandoned by the gods,
We did not sink down
Into the wretchedness that was expected of us,
But instead we lifted our Towers up into the Sun,
Listened with our crystals
To the melodies that came and surrounded
All living things with robes of color,
Robes of Power.
We studied how sound and color touched
The hidden organs of the body,
And we placed our bodies in the color,
in the Sound.
Then like a snake sloughing off its skin,
We dropped the hairy mantle of bestial fur

To stand out naked, reborn in light.
This has been our labor,
And now it is finished.
Now begins the new work,
Not with the body of flesh,
But with the body of light
We receive from the sun.
As we have re-created a body of flesh,
So now shall we re-create a body of fire.

First, we shall begin humbly,
Taking small lumps of clay
To knead them together
To create a larger vessel.
With our new knowledge we shall take
A dozen bodies of light, make them one,
And into this form project
Our chosen spirits.
Mothers in the Tower shall conceive
A new race of gods.
And each generation will be greater
Than the last as we ourselves
Breed ourselves out of this oblivion.
We are the last Atlantean generation.
You are the first generation
of demi-gods about to become gods.
Then we will not need vessels
To carry us back to the stars!
We will be stars.
Now, in the condition of our exile and
Abandonment,
We are in space and time;
Ah, but then, my children,
Space and Time will be in us."

There was silence again: that pure, rich, and perfect silence in which the great bronze voice of the High Priest still resounded.

Then the high sibylline voice of the Oracle sang out the liturgical call, the summons to lift the spirits in response.

Viracocha opened his eyes as if to question space, to ask what could possibly follow the poetry of the High Priest's vision. Slowly, the Archon of the Temple Institute walked with the aid of his cane to the Speaker's Stone. His first word shattered Viracocha's mood. The voice was all wrong: it was flat, avuncular, without resonance, but with a practiced charm that seemed to be a mockery of human warmth. There was posturing, but no spiritual flow to the words for Viracocha. For him they seemed extruded from his mouth to drop still-born to the floor.

The aesthetic repulsiveness of the Archon's presentation annoyed Viracocha. This was not the time or place for lectures in biology and engineering. He could hardly bring himself to listen, until he noticed the pattern. The Archon was excessively technical concerning the obvious, but when he came to the difficulties inherent in the project, he quickly passed over them with facile glibness.

Viracocha looked around to see what response the Archon's speech was calling forth from the Assembly. He could scarcely believe it, but it seemed as if half the Assembly were asleep, the other half still in trance. Why was it such a foregone conclusion, Viracocha wondered. Why did no one else seem to feel the very wrongness in the timbre of the Archon's voice?

The Archon finished his presentation, and the Member of the Sacred College for Architecture voiced his affirmation without even bothering to walk to the Speaker's Stone. The whole thing was becoming sloppy and coming apart. They had destroyed the beautiful aesthetic space created by the High Priest, and Viracocha resented the fact that this was taking the *kairos* away from his own planned response. He could see so vividly that his own speech would have been perfect if it could have come immediately after the High Priest's. The dramatic opposition would be perfect. But now he wondered whether he should go ahead with his own presentation.

The Oracle sang out the call: "Who among you could even conceive of not being moved by so great a vision." As Viracocha listened to her soprano voice, he remembered the full baritone voice of the High Priest, and was grateful that the Oracle's voice was perfect for the moment. He could see it all so vividly: the single tenor standing alone in the central aisle of the great hypostyle hall and singing out the words that no civilization had ever heard:

"I am here. And here now do I stand against this act that would destroy the very ground on which we all stand."

Viracocha could feel the shock waves move all around him, but he could also feel how dramatically perfect the moment had become, and how right he had been to take that step out into the central aisle. He had shattered the collective trance, and now everyone's attention was on him.

Slowly, gracefully, with his arms crossed and hidden in his sleeves, he began to walk and sing the ancient-sounding chant, *Ome ulubi ra, se tata mak.* Few were there who could know its meaning of "How shall we be, if this is done?" but no one was there who could not feel the haunting cry of a melody that called to the stars to question the sad origin of the human race.

As Viracocha reached the Speaker's Stone before the dais, he bowed to the Supreme Council, to the Oracle high in her stone pulpit, and then he faced toward the High Priest and bowed very low, with his palms covering his knees. When he raised his head, he looked again into the eyes of the High Priest. There was no anger or hostility, but simply a curious fascination.

"Your Holiness, were not your spirit inspiring me, I could not stand here before you. And though it would seem that I am here to stand against this action, that is only an appearance. The moon seems to oppose the light of the sun as it fills the night, but a higher knowledge can show us how the moon takes its light from the sun. And so do I from you. But as the moon gives a different light and a different mood to the beauty of the night, it can only be true to the sun by being completely different.

"Your Holiness, alter the geometry of the Tower and you will lose the geometry of the bay. A great rift will appear in the nature of things: between the land and the sea, between humanity and the earth, between the physical body and the etheric. A person asleep or in trance in the Tower would have his etheric body completely severed from his physical form.

And the space from the solar crystal at the top to the foundation vault in the bottom would no longer be the space of the singularity. The opening would extend from the center of the solar crystal to the very center of the earth. The ground under the Tower would crack open and all the volcanic fury of the underworld would become a new darkness brought to light.

"Your Holinesss, it is loyalty to you and to our whole civilization that moves me to stand here. This proposed change touches death as it reaches out for life. Perhaps because the Temple Institute has been so taken up with war, its genius is found in destruction, and it falls to the more ancient role of music to question this misuse of vibration. But now I fear it is not the enemies of civilization that we will destroy, but civilization itself. And so it is that I must say to the call of the Oracle, *'Ome ulubi ra, se tata mak' "*

The strong clear tenor voice of Viracocha filled the hall with the beauty of ancient liturgical Atlantean, and it did not matter that the meaning had been forgotten; all recognized the language and knew the power of tradition it summoned. No one could suspect that this archaic-sounding chant had been composed by Viracocha. No one, except perhaps for the High Priest, could appreciate that Viracocha was making his inconceivably individualistic action seem to be part of a tradition of which they all were ignorant.

As Viracocha ended his chant, he bowed low before the High Priest, and then turned to bow to the Oracle, to the Supreme Council. With his head still held low, he stepped down from the Speaker's Stone, took three paces back, and then turned round to walk up the central aisle. He could see and feel the confusion all around him. No one had any way to judge what had just happened. No one knew if one should be outraged or honored; it was so completely outside of any frame of reference, that none knew what to think or feel, and so all began to drop their eyes to their feet to avoid looking at Viracocha in the hope that someone would do or say something so they would know how to react.

Viracocha returned to his place and sat down. Once again the Oracle sang out the liturgical call, but this time the Archon and the other members of the Supreme Council sang out the opening words of the final hymn, and relieved to know finally what to do, the entire Assembly sprang to its feet and began the cycle of the closing chant. Over and over the droning chant spun on its circularly linked syllables, and as Viracocha entered into the collective monotony, he began to think of the ways he could turn the Solemn Assembly into a new form of oratorio. He would need a stronger ending than this mumbled chant.

The trouble with the work, Viracocha thought to himself, is that there are not enough female voices; there is only the Oracle. Viracocha looked up to the pulpit and noticed that they had all left: High Priest, Oracle, and Council. The emptiness of the dais brought no ideas on how to end his work, and so Viracocha decided he would finish the choral work at hand before he took on this more ambitious project.

As the chanting continued, the Members of the Sacred College began to file out, followed by the faculty members of the Institute. As Viracocha's turn came to join the recessional, he noticed that everyone was trying to keep a good distance from him. By the time he reached the end of the hall he was completely isolated, and so it was all the more noticeable to those who came behind him when the page of the High Priest approached him and signaled that he was to follow at once.

Viracocha had expected the page to lead him outside the hall and then around to the twin staircases that led up to the balcony just before the Palace, but the page turned in the opposite direction down a narrow corridor that went along the entire length of the hypostyle hall. Since they seemed to be heading in the direction of the heart of the rocky ledge on which all the buildings stood, Viracocha began to wonder if he was being led into the foundation vault of the Tower itself.

After a few moments they passed beyond the length of the hypostyle hall, left the corridor of polished stone behind, and approached a wall of enormous megalithic masonry composed of the darker, native rock. Viracocha could see very clearly in his imagination of the path they had taken that the open spinal passageway inside the Tower had to be not very far on the other side of that wall. The page, however, was not interested in the wall itself, but the corner where the white polished stone facade came to touch the megalithic wall. He felt with his fingers for a moment, and then when he was satisfied, he held his ring to the point until the panel of veneered stone slid to the side and revealed a stairway moving up to the left.

Viracocha followed the page, then waited while he set the panel shut with his ring, and waited for the panel to close and the dark steps to brighten like an activated Mercury Tablet. As they began to climb up the stairwell, Viracocha knew that they were now moving up to the level of the Palace, immediately above the hypostyle hall. When the page touched the wall with his ring, another panel opened, and they stepped into a hall lit with sunlight from the skylights above the broad corridor of polished white marble.

The page walked down the corridor toward the light coming from the great balcony above the harbor. Guards were stationed everywhere at intervals of a dozen paces. As they came into the great reception hall near the balcony, Viracocha began to wonder why the page had taken the long way around, and then he saw the two squads guarding the stairs at the end of the balcony, and knew the answer. A state of emergency had been declared after the assassination attempt, and now all strategic positions would have a doubled complement of guards with their catapults at hand.

As Viracocha considered the squadron of soldiers blocking the twin stairway that led up from the sides of the entrance to the hypostyle hall, he felt again the strong sense of confinement he had always felt in the City of Knowledge. A slight change of emphasis and the whole place became a true prison.

"Your Grace?" the page called to lead Viracocha out of his musings and to prepare him to enter the presence of the High Priest. They stood in the center of the hall and looked toward the double doors in front. Like the entrance to the hypostyle hall, they too were framed by stairs to left and right that led up to the High Priest's study. Viracocha knew it well, for it was in this study that the High Priest had first informed him that he was to be appointed to the Sacred College.

The Captain of the guard marched out from the squad guarding the double doors, and after having satisfied himself that Viracocha's robes did not conceal catapult or dagger, he pointed to the stairs to the left, and the page proceeded to lead the way once again. Once at the top of the stairs, the page motioned for Viracocha to wait between the two guards as he moved to knock twice on the door, then open it, and with a bow and gesture of the hand, give the signal for him to pass through. Viracocha stared for a moment at the enormous mosaic on the wall in front of him. For the uninitiated, it was simply an abstract mandala, but for the few it was an open explanation of the celestial dynamics by which the Tower affected the flow of energy from the sun into the earth.

After he had waited for the length of time required by protocol, Viracocha turned to his right to see the High Priest seated at his table and staring at him with his eyes out of specific focus. The table was a thick slab of white marble that looked more like an altar than a working desk. Absolutely nothing was on the table, not gold stylus or Mercury Tablet, nothing except for the clear quartz crystal skull. Viracocha had often wondered what purpose the crystal could have—humorous, decorative, or gnostic, but he had never seen it touched or even recognized in its presence by the High Priest.

It seemed to Viracocha that the High Priest was letting him stand there in silence for an inordinately long time. Viracocha began to look more closely to determine his situation. The High Priest had removed all his ceremonial outer robes and headdress and was wearing a simple white sleeveless robe, a gold chain about the neck, and a large pectoral emerald crest. Everything about him was as before except the eyes. The eyes kept their blank and lunatic stare, and Viracocha began to feel uncomfortable. Then suddenly the eyes snapped back into focus, the High Priest smiled warmly, and motioned to the chair of pink quartz and inlaid lapis lazuli. As he moved closer to the table, Viracocha saw the hem of magenta curling round the side of the second throne-like seat in front of the High Priest's altar-like table. He did not need to see the tip of the cane to know that the other person hidden in the chair had to be the Archon of the Institute.

"Please be seated, Your Grace. His Excellency and I were just remarking on what an extraordinary display of courage that was this morning."

As Viracocha approached the twin thrones of pink and blue that faced toward the center of the white marble table, a flash of sunlight came from the noonday sun through the tall slender portals that overlooked the bay, gleamed on the polished surface of the table, and forced him to avert his eyes to look to the floor. The light passed beyond him as he moved more closely, bowed, first to the High Priest, then to the Archon, and took his place in the chair to the left.

"Before we discuss your dramatic presentation this morning," the High Priest said with a gleam of amusement in his eyes, "let me congratulate you on last night's concert. You have come a long way since you first introduced polyphony into our court. I still remember quite vividly how amazed I was when I heard your 'Canticle to the Sun' for the first time. By the way, Your Excellency, do you love music?"

"Love?" The Archon responded with a slight tilt of the head. "That would be going too far. I do enjoy it as much as time permits, but given my age and illness, there is nothing now for me but to see the work completed. I think, Your Holiness, that music has a much larger place in your life than mine."

"That is a pity, Your Excellency, for, as I think you learned this morning, music and General Vibration Theory are not all that far apart, and an initiate in theoretical music can offer a technician a few surprises."

"I will certainly have to concede that point, Your Holiness," the Archon said as he shifted his cane and placed both hands on its top. "But, then, that is the reason you founded both Institute and College, isn't it? I must say, however, that I do think His Grace is wasted in the College. We certainly could use him in the Institute."

The Archon turned toward Viracocha and regarded him with what Viracocha imagined the Archon considered to be companionable warmth:

"After all, Your Grace does seem to be more interested in

innovation and not the conservation of tradition. What is the Institute but the very embodiment of the spirit of innovation?"

Why is it, Viracocha mused to himself, that I always get the feeling that he is playing at being human. There is something strangely abnormal about this studied normalcy. But what he said, turning from the Archon to the High Priest was less troublesome:

"I am grateful to His Holiness for the appointment to the College precisely because I am more interested in composition than technical research. At the moment I am working on a new form, not a simple chorus, as we heard last night, but a dramatic oratorio. There will be two or three soloists who will stand out against the chorus, and it is precisely *that* tension between tradition and innovation that interests me."

"I see," said the High Priest. "Then what we witnessed this morning was a dress rehearsal of sorts. Be careful, Your Grace. If you begin to confuse life with art and start to live your life as if you were *in* a work of art, you just might turn yourself into a tragic hero. It is one thing to command the elements of sound into a harmonic whole, and quite another to command living human beings into a civilization."

"If I needed to be convinced of it," Viracocha said in earnest, "this morning's miracle is certainly overwhelming proof of that. I still don't quite understand what I was seeing, or not seeing."

"And you may never know. The only one who will know is my successor, and I have not selected him yet—though the problem is beginning to interest me. But now, let's turn to the matter at hand."

"How may I serve Your Holiness?" Viracocha asked.

With a wave of his hand, the High Priest gestured to the Archon to answer Viracocha's question.

"First of all, Your Grace, you might begin by not opposing our project in public with such rapid sketches and caricatures," the Archon said, not bothering to mask his annoyance with politeness. "If you do have questions, your position certainly entitles you to be granted some answers. We regret that we could not send you copies of the plates much sooner, but we only learned of your interest on the day before the Solemn Assembly. And, as you should have been able to envision, you with your exceptional powers of visualization, Solemn Assemblies do not take place every year, so we were rather pressed to be prepared for the arrival of all the Provincial Governors."

"All of that says nothing about the conceptual flaws in the project," Viracocha said with an immovable resolution that indicated that although he was willing to respect the High Priest's authority, the Archon had yet to prove himself. "It seems clear to me that you were purposely hiding things this morning. You were elaborate, almost tedious, on the obvious and deceptively facile on the difficulties. For example, your calculation of the singularity is dead wrong. There is absolutely no geometrical restraint to limit the field of the singularity to the foundation vault. It will extend to the center of the earth."

"That is one opinion, and is the opinion of a musician and not a scientist. Over a hundred trained specialists in the Institute would choose to differ from Your Grace's recently discovered expertise. What Your Grace does not know—and, of course, how could you?—is that the sun is coming into a new galactic alignment with a geometrical pattern that is appropriate to our needs. You have not seen the sheets for these calculations, and, considering your irresponsible and arrogant approach, we doubt that you will."

"I am being responsible to the lives of those living on this island. It is Your Excellency who is irresponsibly toying with the geometry of the solar system for some still unidentified, but I suspect, personal ambition," Viracocha said, and stared defiantly into the Archon's eyes.

The Archon turned his glance away from Viracocha and looked to the High Priest. He was quite surprised to observe that the High Priest did not seem to be so much disturbed as fascinated by Viracocha's assertiveness.

"What you seem to be overlooking, my dear Viracocha," the High Priest said with enjoyment of the scene before him, "is that neither you nor the Institute is working in a vacuum. We knew that the Governor of Anahuac was opposed to the project, but we did not know whether we were being confronted with a single act of revolt or the stirrings of a revolution in which the military class would join with the Provinces to overthrow the Theocracy. In such a context, it was important to bring everyone into the City of Knowledge, use the intended assassination to our advantage, but not give out all the details of the project to our enemies. If I thought for a moment that your narcissistic display was part of the designs of the revolution, you would find yourself to be the permanent guest of His Excellency in the Institute."

"You mean that Your Holiness walked into that hall knowing full well that there was going to be an assassination attempt?" Viracocha said in a realization that he truly did not know what was going on around him. "But why not simply arrest him beforehand?"

"And why did you not simply go to His Excellency the Archon of the Temple Institute beforehand? Why did you choose to use the vehicle of the Solemn Assembly as a medium for personal artistic expression?"

"I really am confused," Viracocha exclaimed. "Was this morning miracle or theater?"

The High Priest smiled and leaned back in his chair as he regarded Viracocha with affection:

"I must say it is a pleasure to see you confused and not so sure of yourself. It won't do you any harm. So you will understand why I choose not to satisfy your curiosity."

Viracocha bowed his head in submission and then turned to the Archon:

"Well, whether this morning was the theater of miracle or the miracle of theater, I am not likely to know. And supposing that you are correct that the new galactic alignment restrains the singularity, I still cannot see why you want to sever the etheric body from the physical. It seems to me that the project could take us back to the Dark Ages when the soul did not penetrate into the body, but hovered above the dumb animal form."

"What you interpret as a vice," the Archon said, "is in fact a virtue. What this transformation will bring about is a condition in which the spirit will be able to inhabit a body completely."

"But that transformation is reckoned to be millennia away from us in the future!" Viracocha exclaimed in a growing sense that his original intuition was right and that something was deeply wrong about the Archon.

"Millennia, as expressed in the oracles," the High Priest interjected, "is simply a poetic figure for a goodly length of time. Evolution moves by sudden transformative innovations and long consolidating pauses. No one can be certain as to when an opening will appear. Not even the ancient sages would have thought we could be ready in this cycle, and so they prophesied that it would be the next one. But we have moved faster than anyone would have imagined. It is going to be in this cycle, which interestingly enough, just happens to be during the period of my ascendancy. So, I have not hesitated to move with speed, a quality, I am told, Your Grace can appreciate."

"I confess that Your Holiness moves too fast for me," Viracocha said with a slight tilt of the head, and then turning again to the Archon, he went on the attack: "But just what galactic geometry are we discussing, Your Excellency? Surely, you can't mean the Lemeurian Path? That would hardly provide an excuse for ripping off the etheric body, nor would it likely produce cosmic results."

"Will you please restrain this penchant for irresponsible caricature!" the Archon said as he lifted his cane and stamped the tip on the floor. "We are not 'ripping' etheric bodies away. We are surgically removing them with sound in an act of the utmost medical precision."

The High Priest rose, but in extending the palms of his hands, he indicated that both the Archon and Viracocha were to remain seated. He walked slowly to the corner of the room and looked out of the portals at the harbor far below:

"The view is much different up here, Your Grace. Human beings are fragments to begin with. They are not yet a unity that can become integral with the universe. The universe is open, full of novelty and surprises, like your music. But human beings are only fragments of machinery, moving about in complete unconsciousness. You seem to wish to treasure and protect this individual as if it were a unity. But the individual is only a metaphor for a unity that may evolve tens, perhaps even hundreds of thousands of years from now. We are not going to wait."

The High Priest turned round from the portal, leaned against the wall, and folding his arms over his chest, looked at Viracocha as if he were considering the amount of knowledge he could impart to him.

"What you think of as the solar system is merely the seed inside a fruit. But two different suns in complex rotation nourish the growth of this fruit, and one of these suns is more stimulating for the new genetic information in the inner seed. So first we must remove the fruit, then subject the seed to the influence of the primary sun, and then the new tree will be the true unity, the unity that you mistakenly now apply to a mere human being. If you understood your own 'Canticle to the Sun' as well as I do, Your Grace, you would be more fully aware. I appointed you to the Sacred College because that piece of music, in its inner structure, is isomorphic to the new galactic geometry."

Viracocha concentrated as he had never done before in his life. The silence in the room became infinite. In his imagination he transposed his score into geometrical correlates, but not knowing enough astronomy he did not have any memory images of star charts to lay over the patterns of geometry. In frustration, he discarded the imagery and became very quiet again. Not till he was secure in that silence, did he dare to speak again:

"The subtle bodies are a recapitulation of the larger pattern of fruit and seed. They form the most natural singularity of all."

"Not quite, Your Grace," the High Priest said as he walked back to the center of the white marble slab. "The human race, yes; the individual, no. When you die, my dear Viracocha, what happens? First, your physical body begins to decay and return to its constituent elements. Then the etheric body disintegrates and returns to the universal stream of life-force that flows down from the sun. Your consciousness drifts away in its vaporous psychic body and then unites with the emotional afterimages of other lives and other beings. Then this steamy gas swirls around in the chaos of the dreaming collective mind of the human race, and there other images begin to cling to it. Bits and pieces of other times, other personalities, begin to mix with the residuum once called Viracocha. Clusters of images mass and form more patterned, but still conglomerate images of desire. Unfulfilled longings, unsatisfied desires, and dominant appetites begin to collect, like garbage floating in a canal at the end of market day. And whatever image of desire is strongest begins to pull it down where living human beings excrete their thoughts into the collective psychic sea. The soldier thought-form comes down to haunt battlefields. The dream of sexuality is drawn to linger over copulation after copulation until finally its fascination causes it to congeal in the liquids dripping into a womb. And where, please tell me, is *Viracocha* in all of that?"

The High Priest regarded Viracocha with an affectionate but mocking smile as he slowly pulled out his chair and returned to his throne before the white altar of his desk. Viracocha did not answer but he found himself thinking that the High Priest's words would make a perfect aria for his oratorio. If he could make the denunciation of the individual strong, then the yearning of the individual to free itself from the pull of the collective could become all the stronger and much more hauntingly beautiful in its passionate longing.

"Precisely," the Archon said as he broke in on Viracocha's artistic reverie with his flat avuncular voice. "We simply take a dumb, mechanical process of *karma* and turn it into a conscious process of initiatic transformation. We surgically remove the etheric bodies from a dozen 'individuals' and then we forge them together through controlled emotions. This controlling of the emotions stops the random driftings which create these mindless clusters. The new etheric vessel is placed inside the singularity in the foundation vault of the Tower where it forms the incarnational vehicle for a more highly evolved entity. Through this more immaculate form of conception, generation by generation, the dark ocean of floating garbage will become thinner and thinner. Finally, it will disappear altogether and there will be no more sea separating Spirit and Matter, and when these two realms come together, our exile will be over. His Holiness said it better than I ever could when he said this morning that space and time will then be inside us."

"Although there is not much time," the High Priest said with a change of tone that indicated that he had made a decision and the philosophic discussion was at an end, "there is still some time. It should not take more than a month to add a mere seventy-two feet to the Tower. You are known, Your Grace, to disappear for periods of solitude and composition. I have been informed that you have a small cabin on one of the tiny islands near the great western continent, not far from the province where you were born. So, you will 'disappear' for a month. Some will think that you are being banished for impudence, and that perception will serve me nicely. Perhaps you do need discipline, if not disciplining. Genius without wisdom or self-restraint can become a very self-destructive force, and you might give that some thought when you think about a proper aria for the hero of your oratorio.

"I confess, Your Grace, that you fascinate me, and if I were inclined to write oratorios or epics, I would make you my tragic hero. Part of your being is restless and growing unsatisfied with its sheltered environment. It has a longing to see the whole. It is that restless part of you that pushed you out of the ranks of your colleagues and set you down, alone, in front of me this morning.

"Very well, we shall begin to let you see the whole, to understand what it means to create, not simply a work of art, but an entire civilization—not a militaristic state, but an expressive civilization of genius in which works of art such as your own are valued *parts* of a greater whole. And yet, and this is the fascinating aspect to your character, I can also see that another part of your being is afraid and suspicious of the world of power. It is the infantile part of you, the part that loves its own creations and sees the whole world as simply material for its own artistic manipulations. That part of you likes to protect itself through innocence, naïveté, even ignorance. It will be interesting to watch how you will deal with this little civil war between the need not to know and the restlessness to know.

"So, I banish you, Viracocha, but only for a month. Return from your hermitage, and I shall see how it stands with you. If I approve of what I see, then I shall personally supervise the next stage of your education. But now, although I am giving you some time, I cannot take any for myself. There are a few matters concerning Anahuac to clear up. Please excuse us, Your Grace."

Viracocha stood up immediately, bowed, and took the three customary steps back before he turned to leave. This time the page escorted him down the stairs, through the reception hall, and out onto the balcony. When the page bowed and left him at the stairs leading down to the Broad Street, he stopped a moment to steady himself.

It felt as if the High Priest had reached down into the flowing stream of his soul and stirred up the bottom. All the debris and images were swirling around inside with such force that he no longer had that clear perception of himself.

Viracocha walked to the edge of the balcony above the entrance to the hypostyle hall. As he gazed out over the bay below he struggled to find a new orientation. He noticed that the point on the low wall before him marked the center of the bay, and as he lifted and extended his hands, the right hand covered the copper doors of the Institute and the left covered the wooden doors of the Chapel. Where do these points come into balance? he thought to himself as he felt the pain in his chest.

With no clear resolution in his mind, he dropped his arms and walked slowly past the guards down the stairs to the Broad Street. His thoughts sank down to his feet and as he watched one foot after another take its step, he did not pay any attention to the path. There was no path, he was not walking on firm ground but was creating a path by walking.

He passed mindlessly through the College Gate on the Broad Street, but rather than going directly back to his quarters, he turned and wandered out to the eastern slopes in front of the walls of the College. Once his feet were on the narrow goat trail that went through the low-lying scrub, he remembered. He was startled to find that both the pace of his heart and his feet were quickening, and even his imagination began to race on ahead to wonder whether or not she would still be there.

She was. He could see her as soon as he came to the cliff's edge and looked below. She was sitting on the rocky ledge that he had always used when he fled his colleagues to come down to watch the waterspout and listen to the wind and surf thrust the darkness deeper into the cave. But it was low tide at that moment and no jet was being hurled up into the air.

Viracocha waved, but he was too high and directly above her, and to shout might call too much attention to them both; so he ran down the path as it continued along the edge of the cove to come to the fork where the second trail turned toward the sea.

There was an outcropping of rock at one point of the path that jutted overhead and blocked all sight of the ledge from the plateau above. Viracocha felt almost conspiratorial as he crouched down and made his way under the overhanging rock. When he stood up again he could see her sitting and staring into the darkness of the cave. Her hood was folded back this time and her long braided hair curved round her neck and fell from her right shoulder into her hands. She toyed with the knot at the end of the long braid, then, as she noticed him, she stood up quickly, almost in embarrassment, to face his approach.

Her hair seemed redder in the afternoon light, and the contrast of its color against the dark blue cloak with its silver clasp made her seem to belong to no land he knew: from another world and not simply from an eastern province. As Viracocha walked toward her he decided it was her large eyes that made her seem so strange. If they had been dark, and her hair black, she would have been considered beautiful. But her large green eyes were disturbing. He knew that if he came upon her in a crowded market, he would stare at her, just as he was, in an effort to decide whether her face expressed an unearthly attraction or an unsettling distortion.

"I'm glad you've come," Brigita said as he came nearer. "I was afraid that after this morning's assassination attempt that they might not be so tolerant of your views."

"So, you were there this morning," Viracocha said. "I didn't see you."

"I was in the rear of the hall, next to one of the columns, but I could hear you very clearly. You have a beautiful voice. But how did they take such a song of rejection?"

"The Archon is angry, and I would imagine that I have made a real enemy there. But I think that the High Priest was fascinated. He banished me for a month but promised to supervise my reindoctrination personally on my return. Look, why don't we sit down. You'll be more out of the sun if you sit here on the end of the ledge."

As Brigita sat down on the rocky slab, she put her arms around her ankles and pulled her legs in tight against her chest. She seemed to huddle in her cloak as if it were a protective tent.

"You know," Viracocha said, "I still find it hard to understand how you can stand to wear that great cloak in summer."

"It's my shield. I don't really feel comfortable in this world here on the Great Island, and I won't be relaxed until I am in my vessel on my way home. I don't see how you can live and work in this place. The Institute has poisoned the whole atmosphere." Brigita looked at Viracocha questioningly, but also accusingly.

"You seem angry at *me*. What would you have me do? Storm the Institute, free the peoples of the Empire, and fly off into the dawn of a new era?"

"Now who's defensive?" Brigita responded. "No, I'm not accusing you. Obviously, I wouldn't sit here waiting for you if I thought that you were part of all this. Let's just say that I am constantly amazed by your powers of concentration and self-absorption. You can focus so intently on your work that you just shut everything out, not only the Institute, but your own psychic life as well."

"You mean these 'out-of-the-body' experiences I am supposed to have had with you?"

"Yes, I do. You see, for me what goes on in my psychic life is so much more real, more vast, more important, that it is always a shock to wake up in the morning and find myself encased in the fleshly body again. It's as if every morning I die *from* the spirit *into* the body."

"Well, then, there's your answer. Every morning for me is another birth, another call to work and creation. Though it's true that some mornings I do wake up feeling that I have just come from some place where I was listening to the most beautiful music in the universe. Then I rush to my desk to write out the melodies before they fade out, and it's always a race between my hand and my memory. But I have to write, to work with it. If I simply listened to the music, I would become entranced and float in it forever, making a kind of hell out of heaven."

"I'm not saying that I'm right and you're wrong," Brigita said as she began to relax her defenses slightly. "I'm just saying how hard it is for me to understand you and to accept Abaris' remark that we were to work together. He said that you were 'the man of the future,' that you represented what I needed to understand, I in my ancient ways. I suppose I'm being resentful. I wish merely to study with Abaris, but he keeps lecturing to me about you."

"I'm flattered. But you keep talking about Abaris as if he were alive. I thought that he died over a year ago."

"Death is irrelevant for someone like Abaris," Brigita said with a smile of love and respect that indicated just what depths of admiration she had for her teacher. "I will probably see him again tonight. . . . You know, you don't look very Atlantean. Your skin is too olive."

"My mother was a native woman from the Western Continent. Only my father was Atlantean. I wasn't born on any of the Great Islands. Brigita, excuse me, but what are we doing here? I mean, you said that you wanted to talk to me?"

Brigita looked at Viracocha as if she were thinking over her reasons once again. She hugged her knees with her arms and looked down to the ground as she spoke to him:

"You said that you've been banished for a month. I would like to talk to you, but not here. I want to get out of here. Could you come with me to Eiru? I mean *right now*, without going back or letting anyone see where or with whom you were going?"

Viracocha looked at her in surprise as she turned her face toward him. What surprised him even more was that he liked the idea of leaving immediately.

"I haven't exactly come here prepared to leave, but then again I guess I have been wanting to leave for some time."

"Oh, don't worry," Brigita laughed at him, "we have plenty of heavy woolen cloaks for you to wear on Eiru. My house is small, it's Abaris' old house, but it's large enough for both of us."

Brigita's laugh and her flirtatious references to her house made Viracocha take a deeper look at her. She in no way was as beautiful as the concubines chosen for the College: her alien eyes, her sickly white face with its bridge of freckles across the nose, and her hair that was neither red nor brown but something in-between made her seem plain and strangely a-human at the same time. There was no way of telling what kind of woman's body lay hidden in the vast recesses of her great cloak, but he guessed from her delicate wrists that she would be bony and flat-chested. And yet, there was something very compelling about her, as if some hidden treasure were within her, something more subtle. He knew that he did want to go away with her.

"All right. For a moment I thought you were simply asking me to come to Eiru, but I'd much rather stay with you. You know, I've never lived with a woman for a whole month. It's never been more than two days . . ."

"Wait a moment," Brigita interrupted. "I think there is something I had better tell you about myself. We have no concubines, male or female, on Eiru. Celibacy is a serious vow in our religion, and I took my vows when I was sixteen, and I have *never* broken them."

"Good God! Then why on earth ask me to come to live with you? Perhaps I had better tell you a few things about myself.

Yes, I am a priest, but that is only because you cannot be a musician, not to mention a Member of the Sacred College, without being a priest. And, yes, that does mean that technically I have taken the official vows, but, Thank God, no one takes those archaisms seriously anymore. In fact, it was our High Priest himself who created the institution of the temple concubines to make certain that no one threatened the priesthood by doing something silly, like falling in love. I don't know too much about the other priests here, for I'm not exactly the kind of man who goes off with the fellows, but I do love the female body. I have been known to get lost in it and disappear for hours, sometimes even days."

"You mean that you couldn't live with me for a month," Brigita said in genuine astonishment, "having meals, going for walks, and talking late into the night, without making love?"

"For a day, perhaps, even two. For a month, I doubt it. Besides, the best heart-to-heart talking late at night is in bed."

"I don't know why you have to translate everything into sexuality. Why can't we just *be* together, simply. I mean, if you like to talk in bed, why can't we just sleep together, simply, like children?"

"Because we are not children anymore. Besides, *life*, you know *living* things, is the translation of everything into sexuality. That's how they got to *be* in the first place. You can't just *be*. Being means thinking, walking, composing, eating, sleeping, making love. I mean, why on earth would you want to sleep with someone and not make love? It sounds perverse."

"It may be *re*versed, but it's not perverse. I had a vision once . . . there is a way to make sexuality into a sacrament, a way of reversing the fall into the body, to create a sacred ritual."

"But sexuality is already sacred. It doesn't need to be *made* sacred. And I didn't fall into the body, I jumped in. And you might too if you didn't try to deny in your religion half of what the body is all about. Look, you have spent, I almost said 'wasted' all these years in virginity. Then you have a dream or vision in which you see the other side of life, how sexuality is not profane and chastity sacred, and the vision threatens your whole life as a priestess. You can't accept that, so as you try to reach out to a man, you tell yourself that you're not. That it is 'pure' and that you're just going for a walk, or taking an innocent nap. I accept your extending yourself to me, but not on the basis of some 'out-of-the-body' fantasies, but on the basis of a real in-the-body friendship. I've never had a woman as a friend before."

Brigita's eyes grew distortedly larger in anger: "Friend! You don't want a friend, you want a concubine. Do you really think you can exert some kind of control over me to give me an ultimatum that if I don't become your concubine, you will not come to Eiru."

"Control!" Viracocha laughed in amazement. "Who's trying to control whom? Who sets herself into my path, claims to be my old out-of-the-body companion, tells me what position to take in College matters, and then wants me to escape to Eiru to spend a month in some 'Let's live together, but not love together' arrangement. Can't you see the contradictions? Can't you see that you've set this whole thing up?"

"And what you can't see in your patronizing psychology and your demeaning of my visions is that they are not the product of some sex-starved virgin. I am as familiar with the psychic world as you are with the world of music. I know the difference between dream and fantasy, projection and experience. What I saw did come out of the mind of the future. You love counterpoint so much, then why can't you see that two notes held in unresolved proximity can produce another sound?"

"The overtones of sexuality?" Viracocha became silent for a moment as he let the metaphor play about in his imagination. "I'm sorry if I seemed to be demeaning your own religious experiences. I guess I'm really trying to protect myself. I don't know whether I could take the intimacy of living with you for a month."

"Is that an insult or a compliment?" Brigita said beginning to speak with increasing speed and intensity. "But then you're not sure whether I satisfy your 'love of the female body' or not, are you? Of course you're protecting yourself. You're always protecting yourself, whether through concentration on your work in complete oblivion to what's going on around you, or through some hedonism that you like to think of as a 'contemplative meditation on the cosmic mysteries of the female genitalia.' But while you were losing your abstract mind in all those women's bodies, I'm sure that the concubines probably gained a better understanding of you than you ever did of them!"

"We're even," Viracocha said softly. "I flippantly demeaned your visions. Now you have demeaned both my art and my sexuality. That doesn't leave much of me, does it?"

"Oh God!" Brigita exclaimed in frustration and anger at herself. "How did we get into all of this? I'm sorry. I really am. Anyway, there is a lot more to you than your art or your sexuality. I know one and don't know the other, but it wasn't on the basis of either that I asked you to come to Eiru."

Viracocha looked at Brigita in surprise. Brigita did not avert her eyes but looked all the more strongly into his, as if she were trying to make him see what she saw in him.

"Then on the basis of that," Viracocha said, "I accept your invitation. Brigita, I don't know you or what I am getting into. All I do know now is that there is nothing in me that wants to turn and go back into that closet of a Sacred College."

"Then that makes two of us who want to get out of here. My vessel is down here in the little cove around these rocks."

Viracocha followed Brigita down the path around the rocky walls of the inlet. He was just beginning to wonder how long it would take to sail from the Great Island to Eiru when he came out of the narrow canyon and saw the small silver garuda floating in the rising tide of the cove.

"But how did you ever get one of these?" Viracocha asked in surprise. "All garudas are restricted to the Empire."

"This is imperial," Brigita answered. "And the pilot is Atlantean. I am the hereditary custodian of the Treaty of Atlantis with Hyperborea. The vessel enables me to stay in official communication with the Empire, so effectively it is there whenever I need it."

"I've never seen one this small. They are actually more beautiful on this scale," Viracocha said, as he admired the grace with which the vessel responded to Brigita's signal and began to glide toward them.

When the garuda reached the edge of the rocks where they stood, it lifted silently into the air and the hull opened to extend a footbridge to them. Brigita gathered up the hem of her cloak and her white smock and stepped up. She did not turn around until she was inside, where she stood at the door and waved to Viracocha to follow.

There was almost a dream-like quality to the floating vessel and the foreign woman beckoning, and as Viracocha stepped up off the island he felt a great sense of excitement and anticipation.

As the hull closed behind them, one of the two crew members turned back to face the controls. Viracocha looked around to orient himself.

"The best view is from the observation room all the way to the back," Brigita said. "The sleeping cabin is here, the storage room here, and the toilet there. I'll join you in the observation room in a few moments after I have met with the crew. We won't arrive in Eiru until night, but the summer sun will still be up."

Viracocha began to explore the trim little ship, from the small closet of the toilet, to the storage room, and to the small sleeping cabin with its two bench-like beds on either side of the narrow aisle.

The observation room was the largest of all and had a curving oval portal that enabled one to see up as well as to the side. Two swivel chairs were mounted to the floor, but there was a low curved, padded bench all along the stern of the vessel under the window. Viracocha moved to the portal and watched the ship pass out of the cove. As he looked up at the cliffs above him, he noticed a figure standing at the edge and looking down on his departure. Even at that distance he recognized the colors of the uniform of a page of the Palace, and Viracocha knew that his own pale blue robes and Brigita's small garuda would make no mystery of where he was going and with whom. Even at the moment of his flight, his world was still maintaining its hold on him.

Viracocha stood by the window, watching his observer grow smaller as the vessel moved away from the shore. It sped along just a few feet above the surface of the water and it was not until they were several miles from the coastline that the garuda began to rise in the air to pass through the clouds. Yet even from that distance, Viracocha could still make out the Tower as the afternoon sun struck it and displayed its great corona of light. He stared for a long time at the tip of the Tower, for he knew that the next time he saw it, the slender pinnacle that housed the solar crystal would be unstably higher in an unbalanced sky.

As Viracocha turned away from the window to step up into one of the observation chairs, he saw Brigita leaning against the entrance and studying him silently with that same diffused gaze that he had first noticed with the High Priest. She had removed her cloak and was wearing a white sleeveless linen smock that was bound at the waist with a simple hempen cord. Her hands clasped her elbows so that the upper arms framed her breasts. His attention was immediately drawn to her breasts, for he had wondered what kind of feminine body lay hidden in the folds of her great cloak.

Her breasts were small, which did not surprise him, but what he noticed with a growing sense of fascination was the outline of her nipples, which showed very clearly through the white material. The areolas were quite large, but there was no suggestion of a nipple thrusting through the smock. She appeared to have those delicate, full, virginal areolas that were not tough and leathery with a stubby teat protuberance sticking out. He had only known one concubine who had had areolas like that, and he had been amazed to discover how different the satin texture of the skin was where the breast gathered itself into the concentration of the circle. He had become so fascinated with the young concubine's girlish breasts that her areolas had become a fetish, an icon that allowed him to become lost in astonishment. Viracocha found his breath quickening in surprise and anticipation. Now he wanted to know everything about Brigita's body: would she have those long and full thighs, the very soft and straight pubic hair. Almost as if in answer to his question, Brigita's knee moved forward, and the smock fell around the form of her thighs. Viracocha could not sense through the linen smock just what the texture of her maiden hair would be, but he raised his glance to examine her eyebrows, for he knew from experience that you can tell the texture of a woman's pubic hair from her eyebrows. But as he raised his glance from her thighs to her face, he found himself staring into the fierce, wide eyes of an angry Brigita:

"You're beyond belief!" Brigita exclaimed in exasperation. "I've seen men look at women before with lust in their minds, but you've turned lust into a religion. I mean admiring a pretty face is one thing, but you've got a shopping list of thighs, pubic hair, and nipples, as if they were all separate items you could pick up in market stalls."

"Oh God!" Viracocha exhaled. "So you really do read minds, and it wasn't a joke. Well, if I've just undressed your body, you've just undressed my mind, which just might be the greater invasion of one's privacy and personal integrity."

"Believe me," Brigita said as she reached down to grasp the hem of her smock, "it's not a talent I worked to develop, for it's *my* privacy that is lost." The last word was mumbled into the folds of her smock as she pulled it over her head and threw it to the floor in defiance and disgust. "There! Satisfy your wretched curiosity, so we can get beyond this completely absurd level."

Viracocha stared in amazement at the naked Brigita and watched her areolas shrink, shiver, and harden into defensive points. But he accepted her defiance with his own defiance and did stop to notice that, though she was slight, she was not bony, and her thighs and hips were well proportioned for her light frame. As his glance descended along the inner line of her legs, his eyes came to rest on the crumpled linen smock on the floor. With a bow that seemed as much to express honor to her body as much as a request for forgiveness, he stepped toward the white cloth, reached down to return it, and said nothing as she lifted her arms to dress. And yet, for all his surprise at the display of her naked anger, Viracocha could not stop from noticing just how her small breasts stood out as she lifted her arms above her head.

Brigita smoothed the smock over her hips, threw the cord to the side on the bench and walked over to the second observation chair. She remained silent and looked away from Viracocha toward the vanishing land.

"It's my privacy that is lost," she said without turning to face him. "I can't go for a walk without people's thoughts coming to me, like the scent of manure on the wind. I can only have peace in absolute and total privacy. But you," she said as she turned round to consider him, "your mind is a booming chorus. No wonder you're a composer. I don't know how I'm going to get through this month."

"Then why did you ask me?" Viracocha said as he moved to sit in the other observation chair.

"Because of the prophecies of Abaris, of course, and because of my own visions," Brigita said, and sat down in the chair next to him. "But I had no idea that it was going to be so, so difficult, and so irritating. I mean, why can't you accept a woman for what she *is?* Why all this fussiness over disconnected bits of anatomy?"

"I don't know. I guess I'm trying to find out what woman *is.* It's an aesthetic response, much like a response to certain sounds or colors. Who knows? Maybe I am precognitive, the way you are telepathic, and I have had this vision of you from the beginning and have been searching about among the bodies of other women for the breasts of Brigita, the thighs of Brigita, the . . ."

"Stop! Please stop this, this courting of me! Thank God, I have not had to put up with all this courtship nonsense over the years. *Please* don't court me. I loathe it. It's like watching a little boy trying to show off in front of a little girl, and all the time he makes such an ass of himself and can't see what it is the girl really likes in him."

"So, you see," Viracocha said smilingly, "you do have your own aesthetic response to what is pleasingly masculine and what is not. There are certain masculine *actions* you like, just as there are certain feminine physical *forms* that I like."

"But that's just the point," Brigita said, "these forms are objects to you. The woman isn't a person to you. She's either a collection of objects, or an idea, *Woman.*"

Viracocha laughed in enjoyment as he noticed just how much

this young woman liked being courted with the mind. Small wonder that the only man in her life had been a teacher, he remarked to himself, but said: "In other words, women are right and men are wrong. Now, please tell me what is a mere object? If one truly *sees* a flower, a mountain, a woman's breast, it is full of power and Being even at rest. It declares *presence*. It celebrates the Creation . . ."

"But—" Brigita exclaimed.

Viracocha held up his hand. "Wait! Don't interrupt me yet, my solitary hermit. We're in the Great Male-Female Debate, the cosmic dance of opposites, and you have to move according to the rules."

"And if I don't play according to the rules?" Brigita asked.

"Then you lose by default and I win."

"And if I do play according to the rules?" Brigita asked in mock flirtation.

"Then I will win and you will lose. That's what rules are for; just ask any civilization and it will tell you that."

"I thought it was something like that," Brigita said. "But go ahead, finish your point."

"I was going to say," Viracocha said with a grand flourish, "that if you look at an *action*, a bird flying, a horse running, a woman making love, the action too declares *presence*. It too is a celebration of the Creation. So, if you truly see an object saturated with Being, or if you see an act that is truly expressive, they both come from the same center, or the Center. So, I don't see, for example, those large, marvelous, virginal areolas of yours as mere objects, or disconnected bits. You know, the difference that seems to keep coming up between us is that you keep talking about 'Being' as if it were limited, almost contaminated, by bodies or physical forms . . ."

"You do promise to finish, don't you?" Brigita interjected.

"I'm nearing the dramatic end, don't go away. As I was saying," Viracocha continued, gesturing with his finger in a magisterial fashion, "I see the physical form as projected by the being, much in the way an organism will extrude a lovely and delicate shell. Yet if one looks at the geometry of the shell, the 'pure' mathematics of the *thing,* then one sees into the Mind of God, and the *object* declares the *presence* of Creation. Finished."

"In other words, my dear Brigita," she said mockingly, "thus we can conclude that Men are right, and women are wrong."

"Precisely." Viracocha nodded in approval. "I couldn't have put it better myself. By the way, if you can read minds, why am I talking? Am I supposed to just think at you?"

"You're talking because you obviously enjoy it, so far be it from me to deny you *that* pleasure. But as for thinking at me: no, words are better. They sharpen the images and give clarity and sparkle to what would otherwise be a muddy stream of confused emotions."

"Good," Viracocha said as he began to swivel in the chair and noticed that his feet could just touch hers. "I would rather talk to you than think at you. I would also like to let our great cosmic debate drop to understand a few more simple things, basic things, like information."

"As for example?" Brigita said as she turned her chair so that her feet touched his. Then she closed her eyes, as if she were listening to a faint sound. Without opening her eyes, she pushed off her sandals and placed the tips of her toes, tentatively, against his feet. Viracocha quickly kicked his sandals off and placed the soles of his feet against hers. Two neat parallel lines appeared on her forehead as Brigita seemed to concentrate. She move slightly in her chair to adjust the position of the soles of her feet against his, and then slowly opened her eyes.

"What are you doing, Brigita?"

"I don't know, listening I suppose. Close your eyes, and listen with your feet for a change. There are more vibrations than sound, you know."

Viracocha closed his eyes and then became aware of a very high hum. He sensed that if he could only move his mind up to its level, the hum would begin to differentiate into a more melodic pulse.

"What's going on?" Viracocha asked in serious puzzlement. "Is this part of your 'Mind of the Future'?"

"I don't know," Brigita said very quietly, as if every sense in her being was alerted. "I think we should let it be for the moment. You said you wanted to have some basic information?"

Viracocha closed his eyes again to try to hear the melodic line at the edge of his perception, but it was too far away, so he decided to relax. Perhaps, he thought, if he didn't strain to reach toward it, it might descend naturally. He opened his eyes and looked at Brigita and was amazed to notice how different she seemed. All her features were the same, but now everything that had once seemed plain or distorted became arrestingly, dynamically beautiful. Yet at the same time, she was frightening, and the energy that poured out of the soles of her feet made bands of color appear to pulse around her whole body.

"Try to relax," Brigita said with a calmness that expressed both knowledge and authority. "It's too soon to jump into analysis and interpretation. What did you want to ask me?"

"Well, for one thing," Viracocha said as he gave up trying to understand or control what was happening, "what do you mean when you say that you are the hereditary custodian of the Treaty with Hyperborea? You can't be Hyperborean, can you? I mean, they left for the Pleiades ages ago."

"The colony returned, yes. But a presence was maintained until just a few centuries ago. On my father's side, my lineage goes all the way back. On my mother's side, I am Eireanne, though I wasn't born on Eiru, but on a small island to the northeast called Iohnah."

"That accounts for the large eyes then," Viracocha said as he moved the soles of his feet away and then discovered that he could no longer hear the ethereal humming sound. Quickly, he placed his feet against hers, and almost in gratitude, Brigita pressed her feet against his. "And my second question is: How did you first meet Abaris?"

"To answer that question," Brigita said, leaning back and placing her hands behind her head and closing her eyes, "I would have to tell you something about Eiru."

Once again Brigita's forehead became creased with two tiny lines as she seemed to be listening to the sounds: "Yes, I think this is the beginning of what I saw in my vision."

Viracocha closed his eyes again. The sound was still high and undifferentiated, and yet one part of him knew that at another level it was a melodic pulsation. It seemed stronger now; he could feel it move up from the soles of his feet into the base of his spine. "What does it mean?" he asked, unable to contain his need to know just what was happening to him.

"I think it means," Brigita said as she opened her eyes to look into his, "that the subtle bodies are becoming harmonized, or perhaps even becoming connected."

"A mind is a strange thing, isn't it?" Viracocha commented as he returned her gaze. "I don't know what your explanation really means, and yet I feel better already. Perhaps, because you make it sound so, well, sexual."

"It is sexual," Brigita said as her eyes went out of focus and took on the diffuse stare he had first seen in the eyes of the High Priest. "Don't be alarmed, I'm just looking at your aura, at the edges where ours pass into one another."

"The High Priest looked at me that way," Viracocha said. "Does that mean he can see auras and read minds?"

Brigita's eyes snapped back into sharp focus. "I'm sorry to hear that. That will make him more dangerous. If he can see auras, he can pick up your feelings. It doesn't mean that he can read minds. God! I'm glad to be off that wretched island."

The mood snapped with Brigita's change of feeling, and Viracocha felt completely and suddenly disconnected as Brigita removed her feet, wrapped her arms around her knees, and huddled into a tight defensive position.

"No!" Viracocha found himself almost shouting. "I feel ripped apart. That was too sudden a move. Please, let's go back where we were."

"I'm sorry," Brigita said quietly, then placed the soles of her feet against his. "Close your eyes, then, and listen. It will take me a little while to answer all your questions about me, about Abaris, about Eiru."

Viracocha leaned back into his chair and was relieved once again to feel her naked feet, and to enter again that atmosphere of color and sound that was erotic, and yet completely alien to any sexual touch he had ever experienced before.

"Let's begin with God," Brigita almost whispered. "You Atlanteans see God in the image of the sun: powerful, life-giving, transcendent but remote. We see God in the image of earth: powerful, life-giving, close, and intimate. You see God as masculine, but for us God is the Mother, the womb from which everything comes."

The sound of the high vibration that surrounded them seemed to descend and begin to penetrate the vibrations of Brigita's voice. Her voice became physical, as if Brigita's tongue were not simply speaking but passing all over his body like the kisses of a skilled concubine. Just as Viracocha loved to stretch out, close his eyes, and drift into trance as the concubine would kiss, lightly trail her free-falling hair, or softly move her breasts over his thighs, so now did he stretch out and float into an erotic reverie as Brigita's entrancing voice moved through and over his entire body.

"Because you Atlanteans see God as a star, a concentration of light, you see society in terms of cities, star-like concentrations of power. We have no cities on Eiru. Oh, we have great fairs in the summer when thousands of many-colored tents are set up. And then we have plays, dance and song, and the recitals of the poets. But these cities of summer melt away, and people go home to prepare for the harvest and the coming winter. Because we see God in the earth, we have no temples. It is difficult to build a temple more beautiful than the earth itself. Ours is a religion of listening, but yours a religion of chanting. Your temples are always full of a hypnotic droning. You'll notice the difference between Eiru and the Great Island right away in the landscape itself. Your island is raw, rocky, elemental. Human civilization has been imposed on those volcanic rocks by an act of will, and you can feel that the spirits in the rocks are indifferent to you, almost anti-human. Since you're not listening to them, they're not listening to you, and the concerns of your civilization are irrelevant to them. We've built up a whole culture from listening to streams and rocks and trees, and the spirits like it. They reach out to us, and when they appear, they put on a half-human form to please us. So we're part of the landscape, and they're part of us."

Almost as if he too could read minds, Viracocha followed Brigita's narration, seeing the images exactly as she must have seen them. The tone of her voice, the rhythm of her speech, and the strong sense of physical connection through the soles of their feet worked upon his whole being. The stream of her words entered and moved deeply inside him. It was not what she said, but the way in which she said it that seemed to exercise such complete authority, as if she were the absent owner of his own mind who had returned at last, not to claim it, but simply to move in to make it her home. The boundary between them had shifted, and as Viracocha opened his eyes to question the edges of his own body, he looked at Brigita and it seemed as if he were standing on a mirror in which the images had become reversed: male had become female, Atlantean had become Eireanne.

In some part of his being, Viracocha knew that Brigita had put him into trance, but he did not care, anymore than he had cared when the voice of the High Priest had put him into trance. The voice of the High Priest had expressed dominion, not dominance. The voice of Brigita expressed entrance, not intrusion. It felt as if he had become a woman and now her voice was the masculine power impregnating him with visions of a life to come.

"Please don't stop," Viracocha said softly, in an effort not to break his own receptive mood. "Go on, tell me more about Eiru. I can see it as you speak."

"Because we know that the rocks are alive," Brigita said in her foreign accent that Viracocha was beginning to find not alien at all, but the right way, the most musical way to pronounce the words, "we do more than talk to them, we compose poems to them. There isn't a great rock, stream, or mountain that doesn't have five poets competing for her favors. The poet who wins the prize in the summer festival spends the year traveling around the countryside and being taken in as a guest everywhere. It's considered an honor and a blessing to have a prize-winning poet stay in your home. The competition among the poets during the summer fairs is very keen. And if there is a tie, the rock or stream is consulted, and a person like myself is called in to ask the opinion of the spirit."

Viracocha opened his eyes to look at Brigita. The passive trance began to recede as his mind returned to try to interpret just what sort of woman it was who held the naked soles of her feet against his. "And have you always been able to see these spirits in nature?" Viracocha asked.

"From childhood, yes," Brigita said in a changed tone of voice, as if she accepted his coming up from the depths to resume normal talk. "If a child is strongly favored by the spirits, the parents will bring him or her to us, and we begin the slow training. It's all fairly simple. Since we have no temples or cities, there are no taxes to levy. The people donate the little that we need, and in return we will officiate at the festivals, or at a birth, a marriage, a funeral. I lived with my parents until I was twelve, then I went to live in the forest with a priestess."

Viracocha was now fully alert and his mind began teeming with questions. He wanted to know everything about her:
"But you are 'Brigita, Abbess of the One Thousand of Eiru.' That sounds like a fairly large temple to me."

"The one thousand huts are spread all over the island. We prefer the solitude of prayer or communion with the spirits. The men and women who live apart only come together for the celebrations of the four quarters of the year. When I left my parents . . ."

"What were they like?" Viracocha interjected.

"My father was a craftsman, a goldsmith, but one who knew a great deal about the healing qualities of various gemstones. My mother was a singer and a weaver. When I left my parents I went to live with a foster-mother, a hermit who had her hut in the forest nearby. It was a good life in the forest. I had a hut to myself, next to the old woman's, and my only chores were the small domestic ones for the two of us. Then, when I turned sixteen, I started to have intense visions, nightmares, and I was beginning to spend more time out of my body than in it. That was when the old priestess realized that I had a special calling. So she sent me to Abaris. He was living in a rock house on top of a mountain by the sea, the house where we will be staying."

"But Abaris didn't come from Eiru, or did he?" Viracocha asked.

"No one knows for certain," Brigita answered. "I always assumed he came from Sham'vahlaha, the etheric city above the great lake within the Vast Continent. Abaris was always traveling, and yet he always seemed to be there when I needed him. He taught me several meditational practices and insisted that I dance with intense physical exertion every day. That helped. The nightmares went away; my lunar period came, and then as the meditational practices began to work on my body, my lunar cycle went away entirely. It was then that this sensitivity to people's thoughts and feelings developed, though I have always been able to see auras."

"You make me feel positively leaden and crude," Viracocha said. "I've never seen an aura in my life."

"Yes, I can see that. But the strange thing about you is your ability to see archangels. I can only see the angels in nature or the ones that come down closest to the human level."

"I hate to disappoint you, but I don't know what you're talking about."

"Then what do you call those ice-blue crystalline forms that dance in your imagination?" Brigita asked as she lifted her hands to hold them behind her head. She stared through him in such a peculiar way that he felt awkward and embarrassed at the thought of just how completely naked he was to her sight. Almost in a compensatory defense, his glance was again drawn to her breasts, which were lifted by the raising of her arms. He looked again in wonder at the very large circles of her areolas, but he found his mind drawn back to the original experience of wonder when he first saw those ice-blue crystals:

"I wouldn't call those archangels. I think of them more as ideas of pure form that seem to underlie the performance of nature. I only see them when I am really deep in the best kind of concentration for composing. And I wouldn't say they dance, but that their movements seem to go in and out of more than three dimensions as they rotate. I think of them as the perfect notation. I'd like to re-form musical notation to make it like them, for then musical notation would be to a concert what they are to external nature."

Viracocha closed his eyes, for he felt from the energy that

seemed to pass between them now that perhaps an old problem would find a new solution.

"That is exactly how Abaris explained archangels to me," Brigita said, lowering her hands to her lap. "He said that I was the ancient mind of humanity and could see and feel into the spirits of trees and streams. But he said that you were the new mind that stepped back and away from nature to see beneath into the architecture of being, the archangels, the ideas in the mind of God. I can see now that that explains your peculiar sexual intensity."

"What!" Viracocha exclaimed in complete astonishment. He felt as if he were a musical instrument in Brigita's hands, and that she was testing it by going from one end of its range to the other very quickly to see the chromatics of the extremes.

"Can't you see?" Brigita asked as if it were patently obvious. "You don't *express* lust; you lust after lust. You're fascinated by the female body, but you're no more in the physical body than I am. We just seem to move in different directions when we leave it. I can begin to understand now why Abaris thought we would be drawn together. It's not just the crisis brought on by the work in the Institute. It's something else."

Viracocha remained silent as he tried to understand the emotions swirling around inside him. Strangely, he felt surprised that his confusion was making him angry. This baffling woman was constantly alluding to knowledge she never explained, constantly plucking at his emotions, and constantly leading him around like a cow that was too stupid to go into the shelter before the storm. As he stopped to consider just exactly how little he knew of where they were going and what they were going to do during this magical month alone together, he began to become really annoyed. But Brigita made matters only worse by beginning to laugh at him.

"I like you!" Brigita exclaimed in delight. "When you're confused, you get angry and would slap the world that dared to toss you around. When I become confused, I close up like a sea-anemone and huddle deep inside myself. All right, I'll stop being so cryptic. I may be a virgin, but I have seen men's thoughts in all their physical vividness. You are different. You didn't 'jump into the body,' as you claim. You were pulled in and you awoke with astonishment to find yourself within it. You're drawn to women's bodies because you're searching for the exact shore of incarnation where the ocean of Spirit touches the continent of the flesh. You stare up into a woman's vagina as if you were looking for the secret of the universe. And yet you can't, or I should say that you haven't yet been able to join that fascination with women's bodies with the vision of the archangels that takes you over. The picture I see of you as I press my feet against yours like this is of a solitary man walking along high cliffs and rocks. He knows that somewhere the immensity of the cosmic sea touches the earth in a gentler way, but he has not yet found the sandy beach where he can lie down and be *in* the sea and *on* the land at once."

Viracocha's anger disappeared as he felt just how much Brigita was alluding to the thought that everything he had been looking for in woman, he was now going to find in her. The sheer flirtation of it was tremendously exciting as he began to appreciate just how much more of everything marvelously feminine there was when a woman was not a concubine but a companion on every level. As he looked at her he felt a deep hunger for everything that she was. The energy pouring out of her body into his awakened every cell in him and as an intense erection began to rise up, he felt the erection go inward as well as out, as if his whole spinal column were part of it.

Brigita looked down at Viracocha's erection lifting up beneath his robes like some volcano coming up to alter the ground between them, and then she looked to his forehead, as if she were looking for something in his aura. With a quick movement she released the touch of the soles of her feet, swung her legs over to the side, and stood up and stretched.

"Before we deal with that kind of hunger," Brigita said as she twisted and released her body in some dancer's exercise, "I think we should start with a more basic hunger. I'm starved. I waited for you for hours, and I don't think you were exactly having lunch with the High Priest, so let me serve you, Your Grace."

Brigita bowed with the gesture of a concubine, and Viracocha thought to himself, as he felt the intense pressure of his erection, "I really wish you would."

Brigita looked into his eyes, smiled, and then looked down at his robe:

"You're like the Great Island: a volcano hidden and waiting for release. But here, there's another way to treat this situation, something I'm sure your concubines haven't shown you."

Brigita moved closer and placed her hands on Viracocha's head. The touch was gentle, almost compassionate, and the energy was even stronger than what he felt when their naked feet had touched. Then slowly she dropped her left hand to the base of his skull and with the tip of her finger she began to move in little circles right at the point where the spine entered the base of the skull. The sense of pleasure at her touch was exquisite. Then slowly she moved her right hand down, and with thumb and forefinger she began to pinch and shake the bridge of his nose. Whereas the touch of her left hand had been gentle and entrancingly relaxing, the touch of her right hand was strong and almost harsh. Instantly, he felt a snap, then a crack of lightning inside his spine, and his eyes rolled up, almost it seemed, to the top of his head. He could feel his eyelids begin to flutter like the wings of hummingbirds, and then he went up in some brutally fast ascension into a state of complete and thoughtless energy.

"Stay up *here,*" Brigita said as she pushed hard on the point between his eyes. Then she released her hold on him. He heard the panel slide as she moved into the galley, but he remained stunned, suspended in some state of etheric shock.

Very slowly, Viracocha came down, opened his eyes, and exhaled in mental and physical exhaustion, He stood up and moved to the bench to stare out at the sky. His erection had not dropped, but it had let go of its intense claims on him, and he knew that as soon as he ate some food, it would go away.

Is this what it is going to be like for an entire month? he thought to himself, and then realized just how completely ignorant, powerless, and confused he really was. Part of him wanted to follow her lead into whatever secret states of mind she had knowledge of; the other part of him wanted nothing to do with it, but wanted to end this frustrating flirtation and make love to her immediately, then and there in the garuda flowing through the clouds. With the energies she had aroused in him, he knew that he could make love to her again and again and again and again.

"I'm sure you could," Brigita said behind him as she returned with a tray of food. "But you must let *me* lead in this. We will become lovers all right, but not in the simple and prosaic way you imagine from your experiences with the concubines."

"You know, for a self-proclaimed virgin, you certainly seem to know a lot about sex," Viracocha said as he turned to watch her carry the tray and set it down on the cushioned bench under the rear portal. Brigita sat down on her side of the tray and then motioned for him to sit on the other.

"That's because you make the mistake of thinking of virginity as the absence of sexuality. It isn't, anymore than silence is the absence of prayer or thought. In fact, virginity, at least as I know it and practice it, is an intensification, a concentration on the mystery underneath sexuality."

Once again Brigita spoke of sexuality in a way that seemed to hold the promise of numerous undiscovered delights.

"I wish you wouldn't flirt like that," Viracocha answered. "If you can't stand to be courted, I am beginning to think that I can't stand to be flirted with, at least, by you. You get me so damned excited that I begin to feel like a mastodon in raging must."

"Yes, I can see that is going to be a problem for us," Brigita said with a lovely smile that made Viracocha realize that defenses were too late and that he was already hopelessly, stupidly infatuated with her. The grand scheme of the High Priest, to protect his geniuses from emotional stupidity, had failed. Brigita had him eating out of the palm of her hand.

With a laugh at his thoughts, Brigita reached down for a grape and placed it at Viracocha's mouth:

"Here. For heaven's sake, stop feeling sorry for yourself. If you'd only bothered to remember our out-of-the-body nonsense, as you call it, you'd know why I am here with you. Whatever vision I had of the future was a vision of us. I may be leading in some of this, but I'm not manipulating you. You're not clay, and I'm not the potter. *We* are being called. But let's drop it for the moment and enjoy the food. Here, try this; it is a dry mead that we make on Eiru."

As she held out the clay cup to him, Viracocha looked at the strange inscription that encircled the lip:

"What does this mean? Is it Eireanne?"

"Yes." Brigita said. "It's the prayer of the maker of mead. It says: Men are flowers, gods are bees, and honey what we shall become."

"Then I will take that as the grace and drink it in gratitude," Viracocha said as he held the cup aloft. "But this is good! It doesn't taste like wine or brandy. I confess I thought it would be rough and sweet, sort of like you."

"And instead, how do you find it?" Brigita asked with a smile filling out her lower lip in a way Viracocha found to be very attractive.

"Unpredictable, an interesting combination of sharp, precise, but unidentifiable herbs, and very smooth in a sensuous way that is kind to the lips and tongue. Is it strong?" As he spoke, Viracocha returned Brigita's smile, took the cup to his lips, and looked into her eyes as he took another exploratory sip.

"Very," Brigita said in acceptance of his little game. "You had better be careful."

"Good," Viracocha said, and took a very large drink and then turned his attention to the bread and cheese.

They ate silently for a moment, but Brigita never took her eyes off Viracocha and seemed to be studying him intently as he ate and drank the entire beaker of mead. After a few moments, she looked at him more quizzically and asked:

"What is the name of that island in the middle of that blue lake? It seems to keep returning to your thoughts."

"You mean Tiahuanaco?" Viracocha answered. "Yes, for some reason the smell of the herbs and the taste of the mead started me thinking of it again. I haven't for some time. It's a small island high in the mountains of the Southern Continent. When I was very young I worked there on an agricultural mission establishing varieties of tubers that would grow well in the high altitude. We were studying the effect of cosmic rays at high altitudes and their ability to enhance certain enzymes within these foods."

Viracocha turned to the side and stretched his feet out and became silent once again as he ate and thought back on Tiahuanaco. After a moment, he began to speak again:

"The top soil by the lake was very good. We could sink one of our metal rods into the earth until it completely disappeared. There was a little village there by the shore of this incredibly blue lake. But though the soil was good, the natives did no farming, for the marshes by the edge of the lake provided them with plenty of fish and game. I keep remembering the place because that is where I decided to go into music. One morning as I was working in the fields I kept hearing this strange music that seemed to be coming from the small island in the middle of the lake. The natives were afraid to go to the island, and only the shaman would go there once or twice a year, but I knew he was still in the village. I tried to ignore it, but it only called me the more strongly. So, finally, I threw down my tools, took one of the small reed boats, and paddled out to the island. When I came to the shore I found a stream flowing down the hill, so I followed the stream up to its source in a rocky crevice on top of a hill overlooking the bay where I had left my reed boat. I could hear the music very strongly there, as if it came out of the spring, so I sat down to listen. I seemed to drift off into some reverie as a stream of images began to flow into my mind.

"I saw a priest playing a flute—but I seemed to be behind him. We were on the top of some huge man-made mountain or temple. The priest felt me standing behind him and turned around. I asked him where I was, and he said: 'This is the land of the serpent that has learned how to fly.' Then I woke up, but it was already dark. I drank some of the water from the spring, and then curled up to sleep there until morning. I don't remember dreaming, but I heard the music again and simply floated in it. There was no sense of time passing, but when I woke up again, it was morning.

"Anyway, I forgot about it all, returned to the Great Island to study architecture, and then one day, about ten years later, I saw a tall, gray-bearded figure alight from one of the barges in the harbor. He did not look at me, but walked past, but as he did I saw the medallion on his chest, the winged serpent. I ran after him, insisted he tell me the meaning of the medallion. And that was it. I spent the day with him; he gave me various meditation practices like kriya, and then I never saw him again."

"You mean, you never saw him again in the physical body. Actually you saw him every night. It's quite unusual that he gave you so many advanced practices so quickly. But clearly Abaris knew what he was doing, for all your centers are intensely bright."

"Well, as you know, I don't know about those sorts of things. I have absolutely no memories of any 'out-of-the-body' experiences at all, with you or Abaris. I kept up the practices because, . . . I don't really know. It was simply that there was something about Abaris, his eyes mainly, that had taken hold of me. They seemed to express a love that had been forged in hell. I had fantasies that he had confronted an Evil that was beyond me. As if he had been tortured once and found even in the torturer the desperate act of man screaming for God, a man twisting and negating, but all the time screaming out to God: 'How can you let this be? What do I have to do to make you destroy me?' As I talked with him on that single day, I had the image of a torturer wringing infants' necks with his bare hands and crying out: 'How can you let this be?' "

"That was no fantasy," Brigita said quietly. "What you saw was one of his past lives, only it was Abaris who was the torturer. We, all of us who are now his students, were once his victims. Even you, or else you would not have so quickly recalled those images."

Viracocha's eyes darted away from Brigita's glance. He looked down to his feet, then realizing that he did not want to look at anything, he closed his eyes tightly. He could feel it coming, and he worked to get control of himself: "I don't want to hear that! I don't want to hear that!" He started to pound the cushion of the bench as if he could beat back the wave of emotion that was rising up and beginning to knock aside all his controls and definitions. He did not want that wave to touch him. He did not want to sit there with Brigita looking at him. But more than anything he did not want that wave of emotion. He jumped up, as if he could run away from it, ran toward the door, flung it aside, and saw nowhere to go but into the small sleeping room to the left. He was just able to reach the narrow cot and throw himself face down onto it before the wave struck him.

He had cried before in his life, but always from his eyes. But these tears did not fall gently from his eyes, they were torn out of his guts in great, wrenching sobs. He struggled to gain control of himself, to get up on top of that totally irrational wave of emotion that had engulfed him, but there was no longer the person there that he knew as himself. He had been violently knocked to the side by this other being of a thousand lives, a being that dwarfed and mocked the feeble definitions of self that he liked to think of as "Viracocha." There was no way that that tiny little aggregation of habits and opinions was going to control this other being. The emotions that had nothing to do with being Viracocha tore him to pieces and he sobbed into the corner of the wall as if that other being were wringing the tears out of him, twisting him and smashing him on a rock like a piece of washing in a stream. He could not stop. One spasm of tears was followed by another. There was no object to his crying, no feelings of guilt or innocence. He was both torturer and victim at once and he cried out in memory of the agony of both. Pathetically, in moments when he struggled to catch his breath, he would try to gain control of himself, but it did no good. He could not stop it; it had stopped him.

He sobbed violently for more than half an hour, and then finally the attack ceased, and he lay ravaged like a landscape through which an earthquake had passed.

When Brigita sensed that the seizure had passed, she came from the observation room into the sleeping cabin and slid the panel door closed behind her. She did not try to reach out to console him; she simply let him be and came in to be with him.

Brigita sat down on the opposite cot against the other wall and stretched her legs out on the narrow bed. Viracocha turned his face from the corner to look at her, and then slowly he sat up.

"I'm sorry," Viracocha said.

"For what?" Brigita replied in a very subdued voice.

"I guess I'm sorry for everything, everything there is. My God! Where did that come from?"

"You're very raw and open now. You'll have to be careful. Kriya can work like that. You go on for years, thinking that nothing is happening, almost becoming bored with meditation, and then all of a sudden, everything changes. All kinds of seizures of consciousness can take you over."

"I don't think it's simply kriya. Everything seems to speed up when I'm with you. Sight, touch, smell, they all seem more intensely heightened. It's like the cactus they chew in Anahuac. Or is this all coming from the effect of the mead? Just what kind of herbs do they put in it?"

"It's not the mead," Brigita said. "Maybe it is us, for I can also feel something that is working on the two of us. I don't know what it is yet. I suppose I will have to be careful as well. It looks as if there are going to be risks in our coming together like this. Do you want to turn back? We still can you know."

"No." Viracocha said with conviction. "From the moment you placed the naked soles of your feet against mine, for me that was the point of no return. But I do think it is time for you to tell me just what you saw in this 'mind of the future.' "

"I don't know if I can," Brigita said, closing her eyes to see the vision more clearly. "It's like learning how to dance. The teacher has to move your body into place. Even if I could express it, what would the words mean? What if I said: 'Come on, let's take our sandals off, touch the soles of our feet together, and then you can go off and have a good cry.' Those words wouldn't begin to touch what you've just gone through."

"No, they certainly would not," Viracocha exclaimed as he looked down at the floor. "Wherever this vessel we're in, and I don't just mean this garuda, is taking us, I know I don't want to turn back. I couldn't. When I'm with you, my emotions begin spinning around like a compass needle gone mad. I feel myself constantly switching from one emotion to the other."

Viracocha moved from his cot to Brigita's. He lay down with his head in her lap, and then encircled her waist with his arms. The odor of her body began to excite and overwhelm him, and as if to find its source, he began to slide down to place his face between her thighs. He rested there for a moment, then he reached down to try to slide the hem of her smock up, but Brigita stopped the motion of his hands: "Don't. Don't leap into action. Go inside yourself, not inside me." She spoke softly, compassionately, and began again to massage the point at the back of his neck where the spine entered the skull.

Viracocha released the hem of her smock and brought his hands back to encircle her hips. Her touch was so gentle and yet so precise that he shivered in pleasure as the motion of her finger expressed the power to lead him softly into trance. As he began to relax and let go of his efforts to take possession of her, Brigita shifted her body slightly and eased his face more comfortably between her thighs. He could feel his mind slowly falling like the feather of a bird in still air, and he could feel his head moving easily with his mind until it came to rest on the cushion of her hair underneath her smock. And all the time she continued the slow circling massage with the tip of her finger at the base of his head.

Her touch was more tranquilizing than exciting and he found himself slipping into a state of mind removed from the familiar actions of making love. The odor of her vulva was like a drug. He could smell an amethyst scent that he imagined was her "aura," but it blended with the less ethereal and more exciting odor that came from inside her. He inhaled deeply and felt the odor become a colored stream that passed into his lungs; his own breath seemed to be affected by it, by her presence inside him, and then he saw his breath flow out and pass into her vagina. It was as if his breath had become the penis that would enter her, and then it would reverse as his lungs became the vagina and her odor the full sexual presence that filled his chest and penetrated into his heart.

The slow sexual rhythm of breathing in and out, in and out, continued, and all the while Brigita slowly turned the tip of her finger that pulled his eyes upward and made his eyelids flutter with flashes of light. The light grew more intense as a window seemed to open right at the point on the bridge of his nose that she had squeezed so tightly before. And at the same time he felt this high vibrating sound humming in his genitals and giving him an intense erection. He wanted to move inside her, and yet another part of him, a part that felt to be she talking inside his mind, seemed to say: "You are already inside me. What makes you *think* that touch is more real a sense than smell?"

As if he were following Brigita's suggestion, Viracocha let go of his habitually sight-interpreted world and passed back into a time before the mind had been thought of, back into a world, not of objects separated in visual space, but of mingling odors and interpenetrating presences. The light touch of her fingertip seemed to draw up the pressure and lessen the demands of the independent animal of his erection, and she made his entire spine feel phallic and alive and offered her whole body to enclose it. How wrong he had been to think of the dark as the absence of light. Space was not void. Space too had her thighs around the sun. Everything was here. Everything came from here in joy, returned here in joy. There was no need to strive toward ecstasy or seek some other sexual consummation. It was here. Words dropped away, and then images: like someone slipping off his clothes to go to bed, he slipped out of his mind and fell into dreamless, unfathomable sleep.

He was free. He had run too far and too fast for her ever to be able to catch up with him. He could slow down now, but he didn't want to; instead, as he came down from the mountain path on to the level plain, he picked up speed. Now it was no longer simply a matter of escaping from her, but of finding the true physical mate for the energy throbbing in his gut. The exhilaration of speed had taken hold of him and he knew he could run himself to death and never feel the need to stop. The sheer wild perfection of breath and heart, mind and muscle, put him together into a unity of terror he had never known before.

The full moon, like a conspirator in his escape from her, lit up his path and the pieces of flashing quartz in the gravel seemed to signal the way of his release. He knew he should be feeling the pain of running in his bare feet, but the fury of running stark naked in the night, with the silk robe still clutched in his hand and streaming behind him like a banner, was so elemental that he was beyond the reach of pain. Now he knew how warriors could run screaming naked into battle, picking up arrow after arrow in their pierced flesh, but continuing to run until they had come to the enemy and with one slash cut off the head to fling it high over the armored lines of astonished eyes, and then and only then to collapse in death on top the bleeding trunk. He could do that, for he saw now those parts of himself that had come from afar to be with him that night.

But what he did not know, could not understand, was why he still had an erection. Why would it not drop? Why did it feel as if it were straining to reach up and touch the throbbing point below his navel? Had she drugged him again, or was it the witch's scum that still covered it? He would not be completely free until he had washed every trace of her body off his own.

He would wash in the sea. The stream was here, but he would not wash there, for that stream had to have its source in the spring by the side of her house. No, he would wash only in the open sea.

He was out of the meadow now and past the stream. He could see the village up ahead, see the silver gleam of the garuda at the end of the quai. But first he had to be clean, to be completely free of the gelatinous coating of witch's slime.

With one last effort of driven speed he ran to the edge of the wharf, flung down his streaming pennant, and screamed, slicing the air apart, before he struck the sea. The shock of the cold salt water broke the demands of his raging body. The irritating buzzing in his lower stomach mumbled and receded as his erection dropped, releasing its hold on him. When his head broke through the surface of the water, he hovered with his arms extended and gasped for several minutes. When he had finally regained his breath, he washed himself thoroughly on the groin to cleanse himself completely, and then he began to set his mind back to strategies of escape.

Viracocha swam over to the stone steps that descended into the water and then climbed up to the street. He saw the clump of his robe lying at the edge of the dock, slipped it over his shoulders, and swept his wet hair back and away from his face. As he turned he saw them all: every villager, man, woman, and child, leaning out of their windows and staring at this strange man from Atlantis. They knew who he was. But when they had heard his high-pitched scream they must have thought that the Angel of Death had come to announce the flood that was to end the world. They were ready.

But they were not ready for this man, this man who was out of his place, and perhaps now, they must have thought, even out of his mind. One by one the shutters closed as he passed by. But that was all right with Viracocha. He didn't want them, he wanted the crew of the garuda, and he knew which house on the quai was theirs. His only strategy of escape was to commandeer that garuda, to intimidate them into returning before she could awaken from her trance to find him gone.

The pilot was there, standing in the light of his doorway.

Puzzlement blended with uneasiness as he looked into
Viracocha's eyes.

"It is a matter of the highest imperial urgency that I return to
the Great Island immediately," Viracocha said.

"Immediately, Your Grace?" the Captain asked. "We are prepared to take off in the morning. The vessel is ready, for we
received the Supreme Council's summons to its presence this
evening . . ."

"Then that's all the more reason to stop this quibbling about
delays and leave *immediately*. If I am not standing in front of
His Holiness by tomorrow morning, you are going to regret it in
ways you can't begin to imagine."

"Very well, Your Grace." The Captain bowed and turned into
the room to address his partner, who was seated at the table:
"Get your things. We leave now."

"And one other thing," Viracocha commanded, "is there another sleeping cabin besides the one she uses?"

"No, Your Grace. There's only the closet behind the control
room. It has a small cot that one of us uses for long flights . . ."

"That will do fine," Viracocha interrupted. "You can use her
cabin. Now, let's go quickly."

Viracocha moved to the vessel and stood there glowering in
his impatience, an impatience intensified to cover his anxiety
that she might appear before they could leave. But he had made
his point and the crew servilely rushed about to prepare the
vessel for the overnight journey. As soon as the door was open,
Viracocha rushed in, found the narrow closet behind the control room, and closed himself in. He stood there waiting in
nervousness and dread for the moment when the vessel would
begin to move. When the garuda finally began to glide away
from the stone quai, he relaxed only slightly, pulled off his soggy
robe, and wrapped himself in the blanket on the cot.

As he sat back on the narrow bed with his back against the
wall, he could see the full moon come into the window and
disappear as the ship turned to face into the southwest. Still
shivering with horror and repulsion, he remembered the moment the moon came into the little window in her meditation
chamber to reveal her completely. The horrible faces that

flashed across her head came back to him, each one more hideous than the last. But one face seemed to sum up them all and hold them in her true identity: those white bulbous eyes over which the eyelids fluttered like the leather wings of bats, the evil ecstatic grin, and that line of drool falling from the corner of her mouth.

How could he have not seen it before? It was all so clear now, from the drug in the mead she had given him on the flight, to the hypnotic suggestions she murmured as he fell asleep in her fetid embrace, to the day by day meditations of the last month. It was so clear now that Abaris himself must have set him up for her. All the teachings of kriya had been nothing but a hypnotic lock to which she had held the key. The so-called secret and mystical teachings were nothing but a preparation for her takeover of his mind. It was all a plot. Abaris wasn't dead. He was waiting to use him to get at the High Priest. It was all his own fault. He had no business with any of it.

As the garuda began to lift off into the air and pick up speed, Viracocha felt his fear begin to dissolve and flow away in streams of self-disgust, and he resolved to stick to his music.

But how many other young men, Viracocha began to wonder, had that witch lured into her trap, maintaining the illusion of her beauty while consuming them? He should have known from the start. She was too flawlessly embodied in all those erotic details of a woman's body that were his own private fascinations. Nothing was there to break the spell: the long and full thighs, the soft and puffy large areolas, the lightly spun and fine pubic hair. If she had had only tough leathery nipples that stuck out like pig's teats, or short squat legs, or a thick black bush of pubic hair that hung down in snarls, he would have been delivered, and the spell would have been broken long ago. But there was nothing, not even mole or momentary pimple, to break the bewitchment. She had drugged him and then simply reflected back to him everything he wanted to see.

For a month he had never left her house. For a month he had been closed in like a shaman in his cave. He would touch her, kiss her, sleep with her, but never was he permitted to enter her. It was as if she were making some witch's brew and his body was the cauldron. Each day she would look at his aura to see how he was doing, the way a cook would check a pot. And after a few weeks of cooking over the stove of her body, he began to feel as if he were reaching the boiling point. They would kiss endlessly for hours, but always she would murmur in his ear about the need to control, to retain the semen. As she sucked on his tongue and tried to drink in his saliva, she kept mumbling about the mysteries of the seed and seemed obsessed with it, as if it were the heady brew she was boiling up inside him.

And boiling he was. In the last week he began to feel his lust turn into rage and he filled up with visions of raping her and flooding her with the semen she had dammed up inside him. But then she would smile, look at his aura, and say: "Soon. Not yet." And so she would stir the pot, smack her lips, and promise endless delights to come.

He had decided that he could not go on, that the next time she began one of those long kissing sessions, he would overpower her and put an end to the whole ordeal. Then she stood in front of him and said: "It is to be tonight, the night of the full moon."

She prepared the meditation chamber, but would not let him enter it, and, of course, now he knew why, knew why she didn't want to let him see what was hidden there in the dark. Then she came out into the bedroom, stood before him, smiled, and pulled the silk shift over her head. Always before, she had slept with him in that thin light shift; always before, except for that brief moment of anger on their journey in the garuda, she had kept that almost transparent covering on her body. Always before, he had waited eagerly for those moments when, with her back to the light, the form of her body would show through like reality through appearances. The power of illusion and suggestion that thin white shift had created had been unlimited, and now it was at her feet like a cloud on which she stood to come down tranquilly to the earth of his raging desires.

The witch's powers of deception were enormous, for she stood there like an apparition: with her long hair brushed out and falling to her waist, but not covering those little breasts that did not weigh downward but lifted up with all the emphasis of those large areolas that then in the warm summer's swampy night did not shrivel but relaxed, waiting for his touch, and with those long thighs that framed the triangle of bright hair, copper hair, not hair at all, but, like her eyes, traces of innumerable illusions of reflected, intimately held, candled light.

She walked toward him slowly, savoring her powers and the state of his astonishment, then, kneeling down before him, she took hold of the hem of his robe and slowly began to lift it. And when the erection leaped into her face, she simply smiled, kissed it, and continued to pull the robe over his shoulders and arms. But how many men must she have known and consumed to get that precise knowledge of a man's body? She knelt down in front of him again and taking his penis between her prayerfully folded hands, she began to lecture to him, in that soft murmuring voice, about the esoteric nature of the phallus:

"Don't let the seed flow until I tell you. There are really two penises here, the outer and rather obvious one," she said with a flirtatious smile, "and the other, inner and secret one. One is the penis, but the other is the phallus. With one you give birth to the race, with the other you give birth to the Higher Self. The inner ones goes as far inside you as this one goes outside of you. But there is a point inside where this inner penis is rooted, and that is where you must place and hold your mind. I will show you precisely where this point is."

And then, putting her mouth over the head, she hummed a deep "Ommm" and he shivered as the reverberations went down the rigid shaft. As he felt the vibrations inside, she reached up behind the scrotum and with one finger placed the tip precisely where the vibrations ended:

"There is where you are, and there is where you must remain until you have transformed the seed inside you."

She cupped the testicles with her hands, as if she were blessing them, bowed with her forehead resting on his erection, said a prayer in a language that was neither hieratic Atlantean or Eireanne, and then stood up to lead him by the hand into the meditation chamber.

"I will not be able to take all of you inside me," the lying witch had said, "since I am still a virgin. But we need only touch there for the energy to pass back and forth between us."

It was completely dark in the chamber. This time there were no candles lit on the low altar, but she knew the arrangement and position of every object in the room. She sat him down on the cushion, and then, placing her hands on his shoulders, she eased herself down and wrapped her thighs around his waist. With her left hand still on his shoulder, she reached down and placed his penis so that it gently touched but did not enter her vagina.

Instantly he felt a humming vibration and heard again that sound he had listened to when first their feet had touched. His eyes were pulled upward, and again with precise knowledge she touched the point between his eyes and spoke quietly:

"Keep your mind poised there, and at the place I touched below. Those two points of light are now far apart, but soon the point of light below will rise to meet the other. When they touch inside you, it is I coming up inside you, then, and only then, release all your semen into me."

The witch shifted her hips a little back and forth to settle into position. He should have known then, for immediately the head of his penis passed without obstruction into her vagina. But his mind was too drawn up into his eyes, seeing with astonishment a third eye open like a window in his brain, and hearing now more clearly the vibration begin to differentiate and become, not a buzzing hum, but a melody. She clasped her hands together behind his neck, exhaled deeply, warmly on his chest, and then became very still.

His breath quickly joined with hers until it had become a single lifting and falling tide. Then their breathing grew softer and softer until it stopped. Now there was no sound other than that high ethereal melody that seemed to pass into the crown of his head. But as it grew more ethereal, higher, and more rarefied, the point below began to vibrate in a denser, more physical way. The vibration in his testicles was thick and buzzing like a swarm of bees, and his penis became so distended that it felt as if it were twice as large as it had ever been before. It kept expanding and moving deeper inside her, and then when it was fully and completely inside, he began to feel this vortex roar around it. Inch by inch the great black vortex began to pull him up inside her until it seemed as if the head of his penis had to be up inside her womb, but still the vortex did not stop but began to pull that inner, hidden penis from its roots. How could she be a virgin, he wondered, when she was so enormous that it felt as if his whole body was being sucked up inside her?

It was then that the moon came into the narrow window and caused him to open his eyes to question this dark vortex that was dragging his whole body up into her womb. He opened his eyes and in that flat, deathly white light, he saw it shine in reflection. On the low altar by her right hand, they were there, the chalice and the dagger. He pulled back to look at her face and then he watched in horror as her faces changed in rapid succession until the demonic in her lay fully revealed and he realized just for what abominable rite the witch had prepared him. He was her witch's brew, her elixir of eternal youth. She was waiting for the moment when he could no longer contain himself, then she would strike, slash, and squeeze every last drop of blood and semen into her chalice, her demented fountain of youth. Already he could see a line of drool falling from the corner of her mouth, see the white of her teeth where her lips curled up in a wild, maniacal grin.

He tried to pull himself out of her, but it was as if she were a parasite moistly fastened to his groin. Her womb had a lock on him, but by using all his strength he was able to lift her up by the elbows to pull her off. She did not awaken, but seemed intently concentrating in her ecstasy, waiting only for that moment of phallic explosion before she sprang into life with death.

He prayed to God she would not awaken as he unlocked her legs and eased her down onto the floor. In the shadows of the room there was still moonlight enough to see her sagging breasts, distended nipples, wrinkled skin, and withered thighs. As he let go of her, she stayed with her eyes all white and her lips pulled up into a leer, but her bony knees fell to either side of her gaping, devouring maw.

He backed out of the chamber, always afraid that it would awaken. He could imagine it stiffen, arch its back as the shape-changer became a spider and that open maw a consuming mouth. Every object around the room was filled with menace as he turned to find his way out, seized his robe from the floor, and fled thoughtless in terror into the still, warm, stagnant summer night.

He did not go over it merely once in his mind, but again and again, trembling in shock and self-disgust. With his knees held tight against his chest he tried to pull himself together and clear his mind of the effects of the drugs she must have been feeding him ever since he went away with her. He was still huddled in that position, asleep, when the vessel set down in the gray light of a foggy morning and floated toward its mooring at the western quai in the City of Knowledge.

Viracocha was grateful for the fog of that cloudy morning, for more than anything he did not want to be seen as he returned, depressed, embarrassed, and an unpriestly mess of damp, wrinkled robes and stringy hair. But when he came to the gate of the quai and saw the guard he realized in anger that the pilot had docked in error at the quai of the Institute. Of all the places he did not want to be, it was certainly at the western side of the City. But even more, the guard at the gate did not want him to be standing there:

"I'm sorry, sir, but you cannot pass. May I see your permit for entry into the Temple Institute?"

"I'm not going to the Institute," Viracocha said. "The pilot of my garuda did not know the proper procedures and set me down here on the western quai. I am a Member of the Sacred College and I was expecting to be taken to the quai on the other side of the harbor."

"I'm sorry, sir, but you cannot pass," the guard said, now beginning to look at Viracocha with even more suspicion. "A guard will have to escort you to the Institute to have your identity confirmed."

"This is getting a little ridiculous," Viracocha said as he thought to himself just how much he did not want to end up in the Institute in his present condition. "If you simply send up a page to the porter of the College and say that His Grace

Viracocha requests an escort upon his return from Eiru, that will be sufficient."

"It is no longer sufficient, sir," the guard said flatly. "Since the Solemn Assembly, no one is allowed in the City of Knowledge without a permit, and the permits are administered by the Temple Institute."

The guard saluted as an officer approached with his aide.

"Good morning, Captain. How many are in your party today?" The guard spoke with a familiar warmth that contrasted sharply with his officious tone, a tone that only annoyed Viracocha all the more.

"Twelve," the tall Captain said as he looked down at the strange figure beside him.

Viracocha pretended to be deep in concentration, but managed to sneak a sideward glance at the Captain, who returned his glance and rather impolitely continued his examination of the absurdly dressed Viracocha. As the guard placed a seal on the Captain's documents and returned them to him, the Captain suddenly snapped to attention:

"I'm sorry, Your Grace, I did not recognize you immediately."

The guard looked back and forth between Viracocha and the Captain.

"Do you know this man?" the guard asked.

"Yes, of course," the Captain replied. "We are in the presence of His Grace, Viracocha, Member of the Sacred College for Music."

"Now I remember," Viracocha said, "you are the Captain of the Institute's garuda, the officer who also writes poetry."

"I will need you to sign this confirmation of identity, Captain, before His Grace can enter without the new permit."

"Certainly," the Captain said as he stepped forward to write down Viracocha's name and sign his own. "I must say, Your Grace, that I find it surprising to see you down here so early in the morning."

"It was an error made by my pilot," Viracocha said. "I have been away in Eiru for a month and they have changed the procedures in my absence."

"From Eiru?" the Captain said with quickening interest. "But

I am from Eiru. May I accompany Your Grace to the Central Stairway?"

"Yes, of course," Viracocha said. "I appreciate your assistance."

The Captain turned back and stepped over to his aide, who stood standing with catapult in hand by a small group of children:

"Go up ahead of me. I'll walk with His Grace to the Central Stairway and then join you to make our report."

The aide saluted in silence, took the sealed documents from the guard, and ordered the small group to march on ahead. Viracocha's ears picked up as he heard him speak in Anahuacan. The group moved out of the fog and passed them in silence. As they went by, Viracocha noticed that they were all about twelve years of age. He thought it strange that children would be led to the Institute under armed guard and he turned to the Captain, but as Viracocha noticed the lines of strain around his eyes, he thought better than to ask in the presence of so many.

Viracocha watched each of them as they passed into view and then disappeared into the fog ahead. The sadness seemed to be as thick a medium as the fog, but not one of the children was crying or showing any emotion at all. The girls were wearing the traditional embroidered costume of puberty that would be changed after menarche, and the boys wore the blue sash that would be exchanged for a red one at the time of their initiation.

After the children had filed passed them in silence, the Captain turned to Viracocha and with a gesture of the hand indicated that Viracocha should precede him through the gate. When they were outside and on the street alone, the Captain moved up to walk by Viracocha's side.

"My name is Bran, Your Grace. I confess that I have been working on the poem, as you suggested a month ago. What does Your Grace think of this quatrain:

> *Body burdened on the ground*
> *Startled heaven when it found*
> *Arms it had falsely used*
> *Were wings that force had bruised.*

"The meter of the last line is a little stiff, I think," Viracocha answered. "What about something more like:

It had no arms to fight
But only wings for flight.

Bran stopped in his steps and turned to Viracocha with strong interest. "May I hear that again, Your Grace?"

"Of course," Viracocha answered. "I would suggest 'It had no arms to fight/But only wings for flight.' "

Bran smiled, bowed to Viracocha, and looked up with a strong expression of approval:

"That is indeed better, Your Grace. The meter of mine was too mechanical, too martial. Yours is lighter, freer, more appropriate to the subject at hand. Your Grace, I wonder if I might be permitted to make an unusual request?"

"To make the request? Certainly," Viracocha answered. "I at least owe you that much for rescuing me from this morning's embarrassing situation. Whether I have the ability to grant it is another matter. But what would you wish?"

"I would like to request permission to visit Your Grace this evening. I have never been on the Sacred College's side of the City, and I am told that the gardens are extraordinarily beautiful. But more than that, I would simply appreciate the opportunity to speak with you. Life in the Military, I am afraid, can become narrow and, well, culturally boring."

"That seems an easy enough request to grant, Captain. The porter at the entrance to the College's residences can show you to my door. If you don't mind missing the evening prayers, why don't you come before dinner?"

"Excellent," Bran exclaimed as if his life had just taken a happy turn. "That would work out well for me. Thank you, Your Grace. Until this evening."

Viracocha returned his bow and watched Bran turn at the Central Stairway to the left and begin his climb up the series of ramps and staircases that led to the Broad Street. Viracocha watched him move away and wondered about their coming conversation. It was clear that the Captain had a fanciful image of the life in the College and more than anything wanted to be a poet, and it was also clear from his manner and the tone to his whole being that he was not likely to become one.

Oh well, Viracocha thought to himself as he turned to the right to take the opposite stairway, an evening of polite artistic chatter would be welcome relief after the intensity of the last month.

As he climbed up the series of ramps and stairs, Viracocha felt as if he were an invading party of one, for the fog was so thick that he passed by all the posts of the pages and guards unseen and unheard. It was not until he passed into the quadrangle in the center of the residential quarter of the College that the porter saw him and greeted him:

"Good Morning, Your Grace," the old man said without registering any notice of Viracocha's unusual appearance. "It certainly is a thick morning, isn't it? Reminds me of the times I was back in the sheds at shearing with the fleece flying around in the air. There's a message here for Your Grace. I'm to send over a page to inform His Holiness of your return and you're to wait for word of when your audience is to be."

"Thank you. Instruct the page to say that I have returned and wait upon His Holiness's further instructions."

Viracocha continued under the portico of columns that surrounded the quadrangle and came to his room. He was tired and wanted little more than to go to bed and sleep for the whole day, but he suspected that his audience with the High Priest would be sooner than he wished.

As he opened the door to enter his own rooms, Viracocha stopped for a moment, and then slowly kicked the door shut without turning round. All was clean and in order, for the servants had not let the dust of a month settle on anything except the thin metal sheets that covered his desk, but it was precisely in its order that the place felt so foreign, as if he were coming to stay in an inn or guest house. The College was not home, but where then was home?

Viracocha walked through the room, trailed a finger through the dust on the metal sheets on his desk, and walked into the bathroom. He stood there for a moment before he pulled his robe over his head and then reached down to pull out the stops to fill the pool with the water that was fed by the volcanic hot springs on the island. There was no place that was home, he realized, as he stood there completely naked; his work, like his official robes, defined him. But even his work did not belong to any place or tradition; it was so purely mathematical, more a celebration of the architecture underneath things, the sacred geometry beneath appearances, a bony skeleton of celestial anatomy.

Viracocha stepped down into the pool and screamed out as the hot sulphured water touched all the cuts and blisters on his feet, but he did not jump back out of the bath; instead he clenched his fists, closed his eyes, and forced himself to remain there standing as the water slowly moved up higher in the pool.

What has this pain to do with that skeleton under the flesh? he asked himself, and then slowly eased down into the bath. It seemed so perfectly clear to him, in the pain of that moment, how ridiculous it would be for him to try to write some oratorio that was a musical parody of the Solemn Assembly. A Solemn Assembly was a celebration of an entire civilization, and he hadn't any idea of what this or any civilization was about. It was one thing to write a "Canticle to the Sun" that cleverly played on the geometrical relationships of the inner architecture of the solar system, but a Solemn Assembly had to have real voices, real people. The opposition between himself and the High Priest was not one of innovation versus tradition, it was a competition of two vain concubines competing for favors.

As the pain in his feet began to subside, Viracocha stretched out to let the tightness in his body float away in the water. Now that the pain was gone, he began to be more aware of the strange buzzing sensation in his lower abdomen and the uncomfortable feeling of engorgement inside his testicles. He thought of releasing what would have to be a flood of semen right then and there, but the metaphor of two vain concubines set him to thinking. After a month of unrelieved excitation, he needed much more than relaxation. He had never been with two concubines at the same time, and as he stretched his arms out to float in the pool, he began to let his mind drift in imagination of what it would be like to have the lips of two women moving all over his body, trailing their long hair lightly over his skin as they moved from place to place.

The erotic fantasy began to take him over, began to take control of his imagination, but one of the concubines became the young Brigita, while the other turned into Brigita, the aged witch. Viracocha bolted upward in the bath and grabbed his head with his hands as if he could force it to envision what he wanted. A feeling of weakness overcame him, weakness filled with doubts, frustrations, anxieties. Was Brigita a witch? Or just simply a stupid woman playing with drugs? Was Abaris part of some conspiracy, or just a silly old man who thought he knew the secrets of the ancients?

The truth was that he didn't know anything: not about Brigita, Abaris, Eiru, or Atlantis. He was some sort of idiot-savant that had absolute pitch and could work in music or architecture without plans or transcriptions, but he couldn't see, know, or understand anything that was going on all around him. It was ridiculous for him to send for a concubine, he was the biggest concubine in the place. In fact, the whole Sacred College was nothing but a collection of artistic concubines kept for the pleasure of the High Priest.

Viracocha stood up in disgust, grabbed a towel with an angry jerk of his wrist, and stepped out of the bath. He had always taken some pride in his reputation as a fast thinker, but now the absurdity of that description shamed him. He realized for the first time that he knew absolutely nothing about what was going on around him. The Archon of the Institute could be joining with the Military to overthrow the High Priest for all he knew.

As Viracocha dried himself vigorously, he continued his line of attack against himself until another voice seemed to enter the tribunal. "Now you're indulging yourself in an orgy of self-abasement," it seemed to say. "Don't be silly. You know you had to position yourself in this civilization through music, and it has served you well. Now you are in position. Today is the beginning of the new pattern." And then the voice disappeared, as if any further word on the matter would only cater to Viracocha's tendency toward self-indulgence of one kind or another.

The voice inside him had a peculiar effect on Viracocha, for he felt as if he had just stepped out of some sort of psychic bath that had washed away his confusions. Although he did not *know* anything yet, he did know that his orientation to knowing had shifted. He looked back in amazement at himself to consider with what complete ignorance he had walked up the aisle to challenge the Solemn Assembly. He had acted in an arrogance so pure and unselfconscious that it amounted to a peculiar kind of innocence. But whatever innocence or stupidity had moved him that morning, he knew that it was gone now. Now he was no longer interested in acting in complete self-absorption. The High Priest had been right: he had been protecting himself with a need not to know. But now he wanted to know. He wanted to know whether Brigita was a witch, or whether she and Abaris were part of some plot against the Empire. He wanted to know why the High Priest was moving so quickly to change the elevation of the Tower. And he wanted to know just exactly what was going on inside the Institute.

Viracocha had just time enough to dry himself and put on his pale blue robes of office, when the knock came on the door. He knew at once that if the page was ignoring the sign on the door that warned visitors he was not to be disturbed at his work, then it could only mean that the page had come to summon him to an audience with the High Priest. Clearly, the little voice in his head had been right. Things were not going to wait for tomorrow. Today was the beginning of the new pattern.

And somehow Viracocha felt ready for it. He did not want to wait in his ignorance any longer. He moved quickly across his rooms at the sound of the second knock, opened the door, accepted the page's bow and silent gesture of summons, and followed him out into the courtyard. The morning fog had lifted and although the sun was shining brightly there was a change of season in the quality of light and the odor of the wind. The oranges on the trees were ripe and as they walked through the quadrangle, Viracocha reached up and pulled one off a tree to take his breakfast casually on the run. The taste of the orange was sweet, and as he deposited the heap of peelings into the hands of the startled but still silent page, he appreciated through his own sense of well-being that it really was a beautiful morning. Soon the great rainstorms and raging winds would sweep up from the south, but now was one of the lovely moments of change when the summer was going, but the hurricanes had not yet come.

They had better be finished with the Tower by then, Viracocha thought, or else the winds will blow everyone off the scaffolding. But as he came out of the College Gate onto the Broad Street, Viracocha could see that there was little reason to be concerned about the weather, for they had already finished the increase of elevation and were now at work on the new housing for the solar crystal.

Viracocha knew that the real challenge of the project was not in the architectural engineering of the increased elevation, but in the geometrical accoustics of the foundation vault. The normal approach would be to build an icosahedron-shaped room out of iron, but if the Great Year of 25,920 years was coming to an end, and the geometry of the earth's position in the galaxy was going to be altered, then the old foundation vault would not be strong enough.

As they walked down the Broad Street to the stairs by the entrance to the hypostyle hall, Viracocha tried to imagine what configuration would be powerful enough to effect what the High Priest had described. There were only three possible frequency-signatures that could be induced into the crystal, and only the strongest would most likely be effective. If they were seeking . . . and then it burst into his imagination in completely finished detail . . . they were not simply seeking to enhance plant and animal growth by placing seeds in energizing fields aligned to the sun; they were realigning the earth to this second sun to make the earth the center of the old solar system. As if he were dreaming while he walked, Viracocha could see the new geometry needed for the foundation vault: the five Hyperborean Solids constructed out of their corresponding metals and set inside one another according to the planetary intervals. The distance from the center of the solar crystal to the center of the five Hyperborean Solids over the distance from the center of the sun to the center of the earth.

The foundation vault would recapitulate the geometry of the solar system so that the earth would receive the galactic emanation directly! They were actually going to try to take the energy from the sun to reach out into the galaxy.

But why? Viracocha almost yelled inside himself. If they were going to try to invoke that much energy, he knew that there was no way that they could contain the singularity simply inside the Tower; it would pass through to the center of the earth itself, and then anything could happen. The crust of the earth could crack open, if they were lucky, or, if they were unlucky, the sun could be pulled closer to the earth.

Now Viracocha began to get some sense of what they were doing in the Institute. They were working in haste because they were planning on skipping more than one Great Year's cycle of human evolution. They were trying to rush on ahead to the very end and consummation of human evolution to escape the earth. This kind of daring could not come from the Archon. Only the kind of man who had single-handedly rebuilt his civilization would be willing to press on with the reconstruction of human evolution itself.

As they reached the middle of the Broad Street, in front of the twin stairways that framed the entrance to the hypostyle hall, Viracocha stopped momentarily and looked down the street toward the copper doors of the Institute. The doors shown brightly in the morning light, and Viracocha thought of the children he had seen that morning in the fog. What were they doing in the Institute? How could removing the etheric body through sound affect this attempt to change the geometry of the solar system? As he turned away to follow the page up the stairs, Viracocha decided that he would ask the High Priest's permission to visit the Institute.

They moved up the stairs and across the balcony to the entrance of the Palace. The guards were everywhere, at every door and stairway, and their dart-catapults were not suspended in their leather slings but were ready at hand. Had there been another attempt on the High Priest's life? Viracocha wondered as they passed through into the entrance hall of the Palace and encountered yet another squadron of guards. He listened to his own footsteps in the echoing hall and could feel the impact of the watchful eyes of the guards as he came to the final set of stairs.

The guard knocked twice on the door. Viracocha waited and tried to prepare himself for that diffuse glance that would tell him that the High Priest was looking at his aura. But as the door opened, it was no page who stood there, but the High Priest himself who grabbed Viracocha by the arm and commanded him to follow as he practically ran down the internal corridor of the Palace:

"Good Morning, Your Grace. Welcome back. Come on, don't stand there, come with me." The High Priest laughed at Viracocha's amazement and stopped momentarily in the hall. In his white sleeveless robe his muscular arms stood out and he seemed far more physically powerful than one would expect for a man of fifty.

"Come on, will you. I told you that I would take you personally in hand when you returned. They've finished with the elevation of the Tower this morning. Let's go up."

And without a further word the High Priest turned and continued down the corridor at such a pace that Viracocha had to run to keep up with him. They passed through the double doors that separated the study, the reception hall, and the private dining rooms from the residential quarters, and kept moving deeper into the heart of the Palace. As Viracocha considered the layout of the rooms, he realized that the High Priest had either his bedroom or a meditation chamber directly against the spinal axis of the Tower.

As they passed through the last set of double doors, Viracocha could see that there was nothing ahead except the naked megalithic stonework of the Tower itself. The High Priest reached the wall first and then turned to Viracocha:

"Hurry up, now. For 'the fast Viracocha' you can be amazingly slow. I've told the engineers to clear the Tower, so we will have it to ourselves."

"Are we going up to the solar crystal, Your Holiness?" Viracocha asked as he caught up with the High Priest.

"To the housing, yes," the High Priest said. "But the crystal itself has not been remounted. They're restudying the facets again to determine what the new frequency-signature should be."

The High Priest turned and touched his ring to a hidden point in the stone and waited as the large trapezoidal megalith began to shift to the side.

"There are only three possible frequency-signatures, Your Holiness, and only the highest, and I might add, the most dangerous will work."

"Ah, so you still are the fast Viracocha, even if you seem to have become the timid Viracocha. Here, follow me."

The High Priest passed through the opening onto a small platform, motioned to Viracocha that he was to join him, and then pressed his ring to a second point that began to close the opening just as their platform began to lift upward. High above them Viracocha could see the light from the pyramidal apex of the Tower, but as he looked below he could see only the darkness of the empty vault. He could not take his eyes off the vault, and he saw in his imagination the thin metal models of the Five Hyperborean Solids all inside one another, and all vibrating with their appropriate frequency-signatures in resonance with the solar crystal. Finally, he turned back to the High Priest:

"No, Your Holiness, there is only one signature that will work with the Five Hyperborean Solids in the vault."

The platform reached the apex of the Tower and came to a stop. The High Priest stepped out onto the ledge that went around the four sides of the open square directly under the pyramid.

"*Five* Hyperborean Solids, you say?" the High Priest said with quickened interest. "You know, I think it's time that I sent you over to the Institute. You may just have come back in time to save them from making a mistake. Look at it, Your Grace!" the High Priest said as he gestured to the entire city and bay spread below.

And it was beautiful. On one side of the Tower to the north, all was green and natural, and no human settlement was permitted for miles; on the other all was cultural and man-made with the priestly city cut into the steep ledges of the living rock.

The whiteness of the Tower and the Palace contrasted with the darkness of the megalithic rocks and the deep blueness of the curved bay in which a dozen metallic garudas gleamed in the sun like the stones in a necklace. The air was bright and the wind carried those tropical odors that indicated that the season of storms would soon come. And yet at that moment all was peaceful, and it was hard to hold on to the sense of anxiety, unless, of course, one turned with Viracocha to look directly down into the darkness of the central channel into the foundation vault that was level with the sea.

"You look down, Your Grace, when you should look up," the High Priest said. "But I can see that you've had quite a shock. And yet, our dear Abbess seems to have awakened all your spinal centers. You're in for quite a change, Your Grace. But your sense of timing is perfect! We may be able to take this great voyage together."

Viracocha turned away from inspecting the darkness in the Tower to see the High Priest looking at him with that diffuse stare that he now understood.

"Voyage?" Viracocha questioned. "I'm afraid Your Holiness is too fast, no matter what my reputation may appear to be."

The High Priest did not take his eyes off Viracocha but continued to stare in complete concentration. And then, almost with a snap, his eyes came back into direct focus and he smiled warmly:

"Yes, perfect timing. When I sent you off into solitude I had no idea you would use your time so well. It seems you have chosen the fast and dangerous way yourself. You were not in this condition a month ago. The center in your solar plexis is much more active. Despite the shock you seem to have sustained, I think that a good dose of fear and an awakening of the perception of power are two qualities you needed to develop. You were too self-indulgent, too self-centered and impulsive before. Just what were you and our esteemed Abbess of Eiru up to in your absence?"

"I'm not certain I know, Your Holiness. I believe it's called witchcraft. Whatever it was, it certainly has an amazing power to make appearance seem reality."

"Witchcraft?" the High Priest said. "Witchcraft *can* make appearance seem reality, but it can't effect those changes inside you. I think I'll need to find out more about our esteemed Abbess of the One Thousand of Eiru, but I didn't bring you up here to discuss Eiru. Look at the Tower, Your Grace. It's finished. Tomorrow we remount the solar crystal. Just look at it! No moving parts, no noise, no sweaty slaves grunting in labor. Simply a silently vibrating crystal: pure geometry, all unheard music. There's no instrument that you can compose on, Viracocha, that can touch it. Music is a metaphor for transformation, a holding action while humanity waits out its appointed term, but this *is* the transformation, the release of spirit into the universe."

"But what of the danger, Your Holiness? If I understand the project, and I don't think I do, you are running enormous risks, you could . . ."

"Of course it's dangerous," the High Priest said as he impatiently brushed Viracocha's caution aside. "Everything of value is either dangerous or delicate. We prize things exactly to the degree that they are delicate. I can smash a harp, a vase, a baby's skull, or a civilization for that matter, in an infinitely shorter time than it took to create any of them. Does that mean we should create things that are not so delicate and susceptible to damage? No, we treasure them because of their fragility, because that fragility speaks of our condition as men. Danger is no different. We value it because it speaks of our condition and makes us more conscious, more aware of our fragility."

"And if the earth cracks under the Tower, what then Your Holiness?"

"It depends on *when* it cracks," the High Priest said with a smile. "If it cracks *before* we have made it out, then that is tragic and some future poet should write our tragedy, but if it cracks *as* we are leaving, then it's no matter, for the thirteen of us will reabsorb humanity in the Great Death. And if we fail, it's better that the civilization be destroyed at its peak than for it to degenerate as the ancient Lemeurians did. We're condemned to a world where everything dies. Very well, then; so we take this given death and use it as a vehicle of expression, just as you take sound and use it to create music. You know, I think His Excellency the Archon was right, you're wasted in the College. It just encourages your tendency to self-indulgence. It's time you got acquainted with the work in the Institute and lent your quick genius to the real work of the spirit. How long will it take you to transcribe your notes onto plates?"

"If Your Holiness means the designs for the Five Hyperborean Solids, no more than an hour. It's all complete in my mind, I just have to copy it all out."

"Good. I'll send a page over with you to wait while you transcribe your designs. The page can take them over today, and then later this afternoon, we'll arrange for you to be given a tour of the work. In your condition now, you just may be able to effect a lifetime's growth in a day. This is going to be a very important day for you, Viracocha. You now are being given a chance to learn from me, and, who knows, perhaps someday even succeed me. But be careful with your volatile emotions, for if they get the better of you now, they will destroy you. Your stay with Brigita and your studying with Abaris have opened you up to the psychic realms, and that will be dangerous unless you can shoot through them quickly to get above the psychic. Otherwise, like a swimmer who doesn't return to the air because of the beauty of the mermaids' songs, you'll drown in that medium of illusions."

"How does Your Holiness know about Abaris?" Viracocha asked, beginning to feel a sense of fear that he did not know or understand anything or anyone, not Abaris, Brigita, or the High Priest.

"How would I *not* know?" The High Priest laughed at Viracocha's naïveté. "Of course I know all about everyone who comes and goes in and out of the City of Knowledge. Abaris especially, since he was traveling far too much to be up to much good."

"How did Abaris die?" Viracocha asked, almost not wanting to know.

"To understand his death, you have to understand his life," the High Priest said as he turned, and grasping the edge of the railing, looked out over the City and the bay. "Abaris was part of a secret police force. They claimed to be the custodians of human evolution, but actually they were the jailers sent to keep us locked into earth. Supposedly humanity was to wait for a certain cosmic moment when one of Abaris' group would come to release us. Our project here was challenging their scheme of things, for we were advancing the time of our escape by one entire Great Year. He came here, demanding that the project be stopped, a guard misinterpreted one of his so-called secret *mudras* as a threatening gesture, and shot him with a dart. Thus ended the career of Abaris the Great, though I suppose his ghost flies at night to cohabit with his consort, our Abbess of Eiru."

The High Priest turned round and leaned against the corner of the Tower. His face was in the shadow, but the sunlight gleamed on the large emerald in the medallion on his chest. Viracocha said nothing but gazed into the medallion as if in its light he could find an end to all the darkness and confusion inside himself.

"You see," the High Priest said softly, "it's a quarrel about time, or timing. Revolts in Anahuac or attempted coups by the military, these are the pieces of the game, but not the hand that moves the pieces."

"But Abaris' teachings," Viracocha blurted out in bewilderment, "they work, they're powerful, you can feel the effects inside yourself."

"Of course they work," the High Priest said in quiet confidence, "that is, they work on their level. But all his out-of-the-body techniques disassociate the student from the physical realm in order to energize the volatile and shifting psychic body. Then all these awakened emotions are focused on the teacher. Surely, you must have noticed during your stay with our witch of Eiru that she idolizes Abaris. He is, or was, everything to her: father, lover, teacher, god. And what was Abaris doing with all this devotion from his disciples? He was traveling around the world, setting up a shadow-structure to the Empire. He was clever, for he never used the same strategy. In Anahuac, he stirred up the indigenous people. With the Military leaders, he appealed to their ambition to rule. With the powerless, he appealed to their desire to escape to some new colony in a remote corner of the world. And with you? He simply gave you some meditational techniques to fascinate your overly abstract mind. So you block up your eyes and ears, you listen to inner sounds, you raise a stream of light up and down the inside of your spinal column, or you project out of your body to visit phantasm-schools with mysterious teachers. But all this trafficking with the dead doesn't *use* death to advance life. The disciples of Abaris keep spinning around from life to death and new life in the psychic dream world. Humanity could keep that up for millions of years, and still go nowhere. It's not escape, it's the trick of the jailer."

"I don't understand," Viracocha said quietly. "I truly don't understand. Where have I been all these years?"

"With humanity in its prison of illusions. But now you're waking up. It's time for you, just as it's time for humanity. I want to see you at the end of this day, Viracocha. You are fast, Your Grace, but today you are going to have to test the limits of that speed of growth. I look forward to seeing you tonight, for then I will know if I can take you up to the next level of initiation. So, let us say that we shall have a small dinner with the Archon and the Master of the College. But now it's time to go down to the Palace. I'll send the page back with you to wait for the Plates."

The High Priest walked from the corner of the Tower into the platform and Viracocha followed him. He touched his ring to the receptor and the platform silently began its descent. Viracocha did not speak, but kept going over all his memories and impressions of Abaris. Nothing in the way Abaris felt to him made any sense. The only thing that at all made him doubt Abaris was Brigita. She was clearly a witch, a woman who hated men and yet was insanely drawn to them in a lust for destruction.

The platform reached the level of the Palace and once again the High Priest touched his ring to the crystal receptor embedded in the stone and the trapezoidal megalith slid quietly to the side. The High Priest did not turn back until he came to the door of his private quarters, and then with a gesture to Viracocha to remain, he waited while the page opened the door.

"Go with His Grace. Wait for the metal Plates he shall give you to take to the Archon and inform His Excellency that His Grace will inspect the entire project at the hour of none. Until dinner, Your Grace. Full ceremonial dress will not be required."

The High Priest gave a last investigating glance at Viracocha, as if to say, "I wonder if you can survive the test," and then turned to disappear into his chambers. Viracocha bowed, and as he turned to leave he could hear the bells of noon begin to sound across the city; but he could not see the shadows from the sun shift quietly to the other side of the Tower.

It was all a cunningly designed trap. He could see that clearly now. Five Hypoborean Solids, five etherically-resonant metals, five planetary intervals, and five archetypal frequency-signatures: the systems of correspondence were certainly elegant. The ultimate correspondence was, of course, to the five human bodies: the physical, etheric, psychic, mental, and archetypal. If you took one Hyperborean Solid and resolved it from a geometrical to an algebraic expression, it gave the formula for the next Solid in the ascending sequence. The inseparability of the five human bodies came from the interlocking and overlapping patterns of vibration. The Hyperboreans had clearly known this and their Five Solids were not the teaching models for solid geometry that the Atlanteans took them to be; they were the architecture of incarnation.

Yet from another point of view, they were teaching models, and what they taught was that our incarnation was not simply *on* earth, but *in* a complete field of energy that was the solar system. Without the appropriate scale of the planetary intervals, the field of resonance in the five metals would not interact with the five bodies. The metals in the earth, like the blood in the physical body, were collectors that changed tonality under the strain induced by the changing geometry of the moving planets: and not just metals, but gems and crystals as well.

If a person were to fall asleep or go into a trance inside the geometrical lattice of the properly aligned Five Solids, the interlocking system that held all his own five bodies together would become unlocked. But what then? The being would ascend to the archetypal realm, there to cry out in joy of vision or torment of imprisonment. But he would not be able to move out of that archetypal realm, out of that meta-pattern of chains of causation that held the manifest world together. No, Viracocha thought to himself, there was no doubt about it; you could not unlock the system from inside the system itself. They were locked in.

And in more ways than one. The distance from the solar crystal to the center of the Five Solids in the foundation vault was the intended opening in space and time, but his hunch had been correct, for the real opening would be the distance from the center of the solar crystal to the center of the earth. Then the rip would not be simply in the subtle body but in the subtle body of the earth itself. The attempt to break into heaven would only raise hell in the form of a volcano. Any attempt to escape automatically activated a system of recontainment. Was the earth some kind of galactic prison or leper's colony from which escape was impossible? Or was there a missing key, a missing crystal to open the wall? The High Priest spoke of being abandoned by the gods, but it looked much more as if humanity had been intentionally locked in. Why? What crime was humanity guilty of?

And yet there was such beauty and elegance to the pattern of containment that was our incarnation. Whoever our jailers were, whether gods or Abaris' secret police, they certainly had an appreciation of geometry and music. Why had it taken him so long to see it? The High Priest had recognized it at once when he heard "The Canticle to the Sun" and appointed him to the Sacred College. It was all there, for the "Canticle" was theme and variation to the frequency-signature for the Fifth Hyperborean Solid. Its beauty and uncanny yearning were the cry of the soul that had ascended, without any Tower at all, to the archetypal realm, there to sing out alone against the lattice of the celestial geometry that still contained it. That piece of music expressed the affinity that linked him with the High Priest, and was the reason why the High Priest had first offered to supervise his indoctrination, and now dropped suggestions that, with work, he could become the successor.

As Viracocha compared the structure of his own music with the drawings of the Solids that he had etched on the thin metal sheets, he saw something he would not have believed before.

Always before he had prided himself on his differences, his genius and individuality, which had set him apart from everyone else. Now he could see what a fiction that had been. The more he had moved into the essence of his own individuality, the more he had moved closer to the essence of his own culture. The Tower and his music were isomorphs of one another, each expressing the yearning for transcendence. What one tried to effect through science, the other tried to effect through art. The Tower was a piece of literalism, a clumsy attempt to break out that was clearly doomed to fail. But what of his own music? All human civilization, every science and art in it, now seemed so much motion on the surface of a sphere in a futile search for the center. No amount of traveling could turn one in or lift one off. They were locked in. To be ignorant meant to ignore this fact; to be intelligent only brought one to an awareness of the geometrizing demiurge that had locked them in.

It hurt to think that there was no difference between his music and their Tower. Always before he had nurtured this feeling of difference between himself and his colleagues, between the College and the Institute. The intellectual style of the faculty of the Institute had always repelled him as aesthetically distasteful. It had been so simple before: they were ugly, they with their poisonous darts, but his music was beautiful. Now he had to admit that the patterns of beauty and ugliness in a civilization were related. The feeling of difference that he so treasured was simply an emotional illusion, a membrane that enabled the cell to work more effectively within the organism.

And yet somehow that did not feel right. There had to be another crystal to unlock the system, but, clearly not within the system itself? But where then? The system of correspondences worked on the principle of homology. Could the key be in the mirror-opposite, in difference? What was the difference that made a difference?

Viracocha stood up from his desk, placed the metal sheets within a portfolio, and tied the string. As he walked across his room to the door to give the portfolio to the page waiting outside, he realized just how tired he was. The month with Brigita, the still confusing and unresolved ambiguity of his flight from her, the revelations about Abaris and his planetary secret police, and now this collapse of the emotional foundation of his music: too much was happening too fast, even for him. He opened the door, handed the portfolio to the page in silence, and then closed it again to avoid contact with anyone.

It felt as if knowledge had hit him like one of the paralyzing darts of the Institute. He had no energy to move, to care. He was too tired to care about anything: Brigita was a witch, the High Priest was a great man, Abaris was evil; Brigita was good, Abaris was a prophet, and the High Priest was evil. He didn't know anything anymore. All he knew was that knowing didn't seem to make much of a difference. All he could feel was that he was tired, and that if he went to bed he would not wake for days. He knew that he couldn't afford deep sleep now, for he still wanted to know what was going on inside the Institute. If he could not know anything else, he wanted to know that much.

Not daring to sink down into the deep oblivion of his bed, he moved away from the door, grabbed a cushion from the chair, and collapsed on the rug on the floor. As he stuffed the pillow behind his head he told himself to listen for the bells of none, and then he let his mind drift out of control on a stream of images.

After a while the images collected into a dream. He was standing on top a high sea cliff with Brigita. He kept trying to stare up into the sun, but the light was blinding and he had to turn away. They were both naked and Brigita began to laugh and tickle him, saying, "It's not up there, silly!" And then she began to tickle him harder, pushing him closer to the edge. He tried to get her to stop, but she only laughed the harder at his elaborate and awkward movements at the edge. Then he lost his footing and began to fall, but all the while Brigita kept laughing at him. As he fell down through the air, she looked at him and laughed, and then she cupped her hands to her mouth and yelled: "Turn around, silly!" He turned over as he continued to fall and then he saw the water coming up to meet him. He stretched out his arms and tried to protect his head and neck, and then he hit the water and was surprised to find how good it felt all over his body. He wanted to see if he could make it all the way to the bottom, for somehow he sensed that there was something down there on the bottom that he wanted. He would take hold of it, crouch down on his knees, and then spring up to the surface to hold it up in the air so that Brigita could see it, wet and glistening in the sunlight. But it was dark at the bottom and the shadows from the large rocks made it harder to see. After a moment of searching, he saw it flash and he reached out to grab it, still not knowing what it was that he had taken hold of; then, pulling his legs under him, he crouched down to spring up from the bottom. He hurled himself toward the surface, and as his head came above the water he held it aloft to Brigita as the bells began ringing and awakened him.

It took Viracocha a minute to remember where he was and why the ringing of the bells was important to him. His first impulse, when he did recall, was to run out the door to be on time, but then he decided the Archon could wait and go over the plates once more while he walked over.

Viracocha crossed the room to a small cupboard that he kept filled with food for the times he was working and did not want to leave his desk for the society of the dining hall. He reached into the jars and filled his hands with raisins and almonds, and as he stuffed his mouth he thought again of the High Priest's allusion to his becoming the successor. The absurdity of the idea was immediately apparent to Viracocha, and he wondered why it was not to the High Priest.

With a mouthful of raisins and almonds, Viracocha filled his hands again, gulped down some cider from the ceramic jug on the shelf, closed the cupboard, and turned to leave. The more he thought about the High Priest's idea, the more bizarre it seemed. As he walked out of his rooms into the quadrangle, he began to take an imaginative inventory of the place. He tried to see himself presiding over meetings, making appointments, performing secret acts of ancient mysteries in the Solemn Assemblies, and fighting back assassination attempts with his own squad of secret assassins. It was a useful exercise, for the inventory of the City of Knowledge, as he walked through the College's cloistered gardens out to the Broad Street, made him quite aware that not only did he not want to be High Priest, he did not want to live in the City anymore. But where could he go?

Viracocha stopped for a moment inside the College Gate and looked up at the Tower. What was the difference that made a difference between his music and that instrument of cosmic vibration. If he left this City, there was no other place in the world where either his music or the hieroglyphic notation for it could be understood. The memory of listening to music in the island within the lake came back to him, but he pushed it aside at once because he knew it would be impossible for him to live his whole life in so primitive a place.

There was no place to go, except . . . But the idea was too frightening, and Viracocha knocked it aside; nevertheless, it came back. What had the High Priest meant when he spoke of the thirteen and said that "We may be able to take this great voyage together"? What would it be like to be inside the Solids within the foundation vault when the solar crystal was activated? He could see the High Priest put him into trance, as he had done before in the Solemn Assembly, he could see the volcano lift from beneath the ground to hurl their physical bodies into the air while their subtle bodies ascended to the archetypal lattice of imprisonment. He could hear the cries of millions as all the Islands began to explode and drop in fragments to the sea, but he could see no way to pass through the lattice of causation to the free world behind the stars; all that he could see was the entwined bodies of himself and the High Priest dropping into the sea where once the City of Knowledge had stood.

It was not in thought, but in the fullness of that atavistic faculty of vision that Viracocha realized why the High Priest could look upon him as a possible successor, why he could gaze at his spinal centers with a fascination equal to Brigita's. It was so clear that he wondered how he could not have seen it reflected in the ceremony in which the High Priest elevated him to the Sacred College. He should have noticed that the institution of the temple concubines was a test, an institution that expressed a contempt for women and the lesser men who were ruled by the mere biological urges of reproduction. Both the

High Priest and Brigita were obsessed with a mystery of the spiritual phallus with its magical potion that turned the flesh itself into some ritual of escape from incarnation. Both had taken the innocence of sex and twisted it into another direction in the hope that by reversing sexuality they could escape it altogether in a realm beyond male and female, generation and death.

Viracocha was walking very slowly down the Broad Street as the visions of the end flashed through his mind, but all the time he never took his eyes off the copper doors of the Institute. Behind those doors lay the Laboratory of Incarnation, but even before he had passed through he began to understand just how cursed incarnation was in everyone's imagining. Perhaps, he thought, humanity will never escape as long as it is trying to. Perhaps it is the very effort to escape that locks us in.

The guards at the copper doors saluted Viracocha and allowed him to pass unquestioned. The page at the desk of the guard inside immediately sprang to life, bowed, and motioned to Viracocha to follow him down the long corridor. At the end of the corridor, Viracocha could see another set of large double doors, but the page stopped at a door to the left, knocked twice, and then opened it to allow him to pass.

The Archon was seated in front of a table in which five Mercury Tablets were set up. The Emerald Stylus was still in his hand, and as Viracocha approached he could see the Five Hyperborean Solids shimmering in the liquid metallic gray of the Tablets. The Archon did not bother to stand or turn to greet Viracocha, but simply gestured with the stylus that he was to take the seat next to him in front of the table. Only when Viracocha was seated did the Archon turn from his study of the Solids to consider him.

"I was beginning to wonder if 'the fast Viracocha' was as slow in walking as he was fast in thinking," the Archon said as he turned with some difficulty to face him. "And then you appeared. I have, as Your Grace can see, induced your Plates into the displays."

"Good Afternoon, Your Excellency," Viracocha replied. "Yes, I can see that you have not wasted any time."

The Archon sat in silence for a few moments as he considered Viracocha. The only sound in the room was the gentle thud of the Emerald Stylus as he struck it against the cushioned arm of the chair. The silence deepened, and Viracocha decided that he would not be the one to break it. Instead, he began to study the Archon's face and noticed just how much his condition had deteriorated in the month he had been away.

Finally the Archon took in a deep breath and spoke:

"I knew Your Grace had a love for ancient knowledge and mysteries, a love that pulled him away from the Institute to the College, but I never thought that what would finally bring us together were these children's toys of the Solids."

So, the hostility is out in the open, Viracocha thought to himself, but what he said was simply:

"And does His Excellency consider the Five Hyperborean Solids to be merely toys?"

"No, not the Solids themselves," the Archon said with a stiff smile, "although I do confess to some residual anti-Hyperborean prejudice. No, it is not the Solids themselves, but your almost absurdly simple little gadget of thin metal rods with which you construct them. I mean, after all, we've been working on this project for years. The stones in the foundation vault weigh hundreds of tons, and now you come along and in a few hours suggest that pieces of induction wires and thin metal rods are all we need. Surely, even you must see the ironic nature of the proposal?"

"I think Your Excellency gives too much weight to matter and volume," Viracocha answered without animus. "As you will recall, there is more empty space in the universe than there is material, and what matter there is, if one truly understands it, is made up out of music and geometry. You know as well as I do, or else you would not have been able to move those megaliths into place so easily, that it is not size that is important, but the scale, the alignment, and the frequency-signatures you induce. You have the Mercury Tablets here to check my calculations, so what are we arguing about?"

"We are not arguing, Your Grace. We are discussing the ironies of your proposal, but it seems the irony of my remarks escaped you. When I used the word 'toy,' I was merely saying that it was ironic that these old toys, these children's blocks with which we were taught solid geometry, should have a role to play in the successful completion of our project. Am I clear now?"

"Yes," Viracocha said, "but Your Excellency is not exactly famous for his lighthearted and joking manner, so I was not prepared for irony and wit."

"To return to the subject at hand," the Archon said, annoyed but determined to ignore Viracocha's jibe, "which of the three possible frequency-signatures do you think will be the most effective?"

"The highest one, but it will also be the most dangerous. I hope His Excellency is fully aware of the risks of this project."

"Yes, of course, we are aware that there could be an earth-quake as the planet adjusts to the new galactic position, but that is a risk we shall just have to take."

"For what purpose, may I ask?" Viracocha said.

"For what purpose!? Yes, I had forgotten, you are not really aware of just what we have accomplished here. I had forgotten that this is actually your first visit to the Temple Institute. Well, that is a failure on our part that we must remedy immediately. As for the risks, His Holiness has said that the society that does not take risks degenerates. So, as you can see, we have given the matter some thought, but we are going ahead with His Holiness's encouragement."

"It's not my responsibility to make decisions," Viracocha conceded, "but it is my responsibility to pass on *all* that I know."

"Quite. And you have done that. I must say, Your Grace, that your knowledge is particularly significant for me because of all the time we shall save. I had not thought of the connection between the Hyperborean Solids and the planetary intervals, not to mention the quantum-steps of the subtle-bodies. We have ample stores of the five metals in question, and since the whole model is only a mere thirty-six feet in diameter, we can have the whole thing in place for you, oh, even by as early as tomorrow afternoon. As you can see from my worsening condition, this saving of time is critical."

Viracocha tilted his head forward in a not very deep bow of acknowledgment and then thought to ask in a very serious tone: "Who goes into the center of the lattice inside the foundation vault?"

"I'm sorry. Yes, of course, you don't know yet about the biology of the project. Come, it's time we showed you around. I think what will be of particularly interest to Your Grace is our study of the physiological effects of music."

The Archon rose, leaning heavily on his cane. When he was standing securely balanced on his two feet, he extended his cane over a receptor-crystal on the table to summon the page. "I think that with your knowledge of architecture and music that the Laboratory of Incarnation will be especially fascinating to you, for it is precisely with sound that we have come to understand the architecture of the body."

The Archon passed by Viracocha as the page entered and bowed before them; he walked slowly, taking a step with his left foot and then dragging his right side forward with the help of his cane.

The page held the door open for them and the Archon and Viracocha passed out of the study into the corridor. The double doors of the laboratory were to their left at the very end of the hall. Viracocha slowed his own pace to walk alongside the Archon; he listened to the sandal striking the stones, the long dragging sound of the Archon's right foot, and then the click as his cane came forward to bear his weight before he extended his left foot again. The Archon did not bother to speak but put all his thoughts to making the effort to walk. Finally, they came to the double doors; the page moved quickly inside and then held the door open as the Archon passed through.

As Viracocha entered the room he saw a semicircle of about twelve examining tables. The huge stomachs of the naked women struck him first, and then he noticed that all of the women were in the last month of pregnancy. Two wires were connected to each of their heads, one at the forehead and another behind at the base of the skull. Viracocha felt uncomfortable at the sight of all this vulnerable raw flesh, and did not know where to put the focus of his attention, since from where he was standing he seemed to be looking straight into the vulva of the woman in the center.

The temperature in the room was unusually warm but the atmosphere and tone of the place was even more immediately thick and oppressive. The page removed His Excellency's outer cape and then stood by waiting for Viracocha to release the gold chain at his neck so that he could hang the garments up with the others by the door. Viracocha released the clasp and then moved quickly over to the woman in the center to examine the wires fastened to her head. His memories of staring down the thighs of the concubines returned to mock him, and he felt embarrassed and confused.

The Archon seemed pleased with Viracocha's immediate attention to the details of the technology and began to speak to him in a friendlier tone:

"Very good, Your Grace. I see the fast Viracocha goes right to the heart of the matter. You see, we have found a way to reproduce music through the pulsed oscillation of emanating crystals. We can't, of course, repeat the exact sound and timbre of musical instruments, but we can take the pattern of the music and duplicate it. We induce this abstract pattern directly into the lattice of the skeleton, so that the bones themselves become the crystalline-receptors. We eliminate the orchestra, as it were, and make the subject both the performer and the audience."

"What on earth for?" Viracocha asked, as he tried to imagine what the sensation would feel like to have an abstraction of music vibrating in his bones.

"It eliminates the deleterious effects of prolonged coma, Your Grace. Observe the healthy skin tone and the firmness of the muscles. Although these women have been in a deep coma for several months, their organs . . ."

"Months!" Viracocha exclaimed, "but the fetus . . ."

"No, the fetus doesn't die, but it is born mentally retarded. We haven't solved that problem yet, but we have succeeded in being able to slow down the metabolism enormously. But you're ignoring the most important point, Your Grace. You see, the music we have induced into the lattice of their bones is your own 'Canticle to the Sun.' It has absolutely amazing mathemati-

cal properties, and these translate rather nicely into the ab-
stracted patterns. We don't quite understand all of it yet, and,
no doubt, you could be of help to us here, but the resonance
does seem to arrest the decay of the cells and alters the timing
of the rate of growth and decay."

It wasn't rage, though it felt like that, it was knowledge, pure,
immediate, and utterly without thought: Viracocha knew that
he could kill the Archon. He saw in the purity of image himself
twisting the neck around to see just how much twisting the
neck could take until it snapped. The murder would be poetry.
Nothing else would matter beyond the appropriate perfection
of the act itself. Viracocha began to take a deep and slow breath,
preparing to spring, but the breath, like a receding wave that
exposed the ocean floor before it hurled itself beyond the limits
of the shore, exposed something inside him. It took the form of a
voice, but he knew it wasn't a person. "If you kill him now he
kills your soul by succeeding in turning you into a twisting
killer." The withdrawing tidal wave of his breath stopped, and
with its force spent, everything inside Viracocha stopped. With
action canceled out, a paralysis of soul took hold of him.

The Archon looked at Viracocha to see what effect his words
were having on him, and then continued his lecture in that
artificially friendly and avuncular tone:

"We choose to use pregnant women in this study because, you
see, the etheric body is much stronger. And with the growth of
the fetus we have a marvelous opportunity to observe the formation of the etheric body itself. Even if the mother or the fetus
does die, we have the opportunity of slowing the rate of death
down so that we can study the various stages of the process of
disengagement in which the etheric body slips out of resonance
with the physical organism. For example," the Archon patted
the medallion on his chest, "we have developed a new lens that
permits us to observe the form and radiance of the etheric body
directly."

The Archon raised the lens, which before had seemed merely
to be a jewel inside the medallion, and looked at Viracocha:

"I must say Your Grace is in exceptionally good health. Why, I
have never seen . . . hmmm, interesting."

The Archon dropped the medallion to his chest and looked at Viracocha with a puzzled expression, but Viracocha simply stared down at the wires attached to the woman's head. Everything seemed to be so far away, as if he were looking down at her from a great height.

The Archon waited a moment to see if Viracocha had any questions, and then resumed his lecture as Viracocha stared down at the woman's face.

"The two etheric bodies of mother and fetus provide us with an enormous level of vitality, but eventually we had to move beyond this stage of research, for we were not able to detach the etheric body of either mother or fetus. The instinct for self-preservation is too strong, and so both etheric bodies stay locked into the physical. What you see here is actually the phasing out of this aspect of our work. Now we are simply monitoring the metabolic conditions of the deep coma."

"Then why not revive them and send them back before it is too late?" Viracocha asked, and it began to dawn on him that whatever horrible sight he was confronting, he was only at the beginning of his tour of the Institute.

"Oh, at first we did try to return them, but the mother and infant were always mentally retarded. We found out that by returning them we stirred up a bit of trouble in the villages of Anahuac. It was better to let them simply be taken away in the garudas, that way they could think that they were being carried off by the gods to heaven."

Viracocha remembered the Captain of the garuda that he had talked with that morning. Now he understood the tightness around his eyes as they had both watched the children pass through the gate.

"And what will become of these women?" Viracocha asked in a flat and steady voice.

"We will slowly deepen the coma by infinitesimal degrees to study, with meticulous attention, the moment of death and the behavior of the two etheric bodies. But, come, to appreciate the significance of what you are seeing here, you must see the results of our work in the next room."

As the Archon walked to the door that led to the adjacent

laboratory, Viracocha turned his back on him and pretended to survey the entire scene. He was stalling to try to gain some idea of what to do. He wanted to be anywhere but where he was, and was disgusted to think that all of this had been going on while he had wandered around the peninsula in long walks of contemplative solitude. Small wonder that Brigita had been disgusted with his artistic powers of concentration. But the thought of Brigita only contributed to his confusion and disorientation. If Brigita was right, could that mean that she was right in all the rest?

"Your Grace?" the Archon said to interrupt Viracocha's reflections. "There will be time to return if you wish to study the effects of your music more closely, but I would like to give you a higher perspective of the entire project."

Viracocha took one more look at the women, and their great rounded stomachs reminded him of the clay ovens the Anahuacan women used to bake their bread. As he turned round to follow the Archon into the next room, he saw that the Archon was once again looking at him through the lens in his medallion. He dropped the medallion to his chest, smiled as much as his stricken face would allow, and then waited by the door as Viracocha passed slowly by him into the room.

Once again Viracocha encountered the semicircle of a dozen tables, but this time the women were all quite old. Their withered breasts sagged off their chests and the flesh on their thighs listed to the side of their bones. And then he discovered in horror that they were all pregnant. He could see the corpse of the fetus inside their collapsed stomachs: a withered raisin inside a withered prune. As soon as he realized what he was seeing, the sense of disorientation came back with renewed intensity and altered the dimensions of the room. Everything was small and far away, not truly in his space, not touching his personal sense of presence.

"Although each of these women is only around eighteen," the Archon commented, "the drug without the musical analogue seems to trigger the aging process. But we have been able to remedy the situation somewhat, for now we are able to slow down the flow of time in their bodies. You see, what we have to do is to find a way to keep a person exquisitely poised between life and death, neither alive nor dead. It has been quite a challenge, for all too often they move past the desired point and simply die. Then we lose the etheric body, and we can't have that. You can see how important your music is, for it arrests the aging process. The glandular system is not confused in its sense of timing. But there was a negative side to your music, and that was that it seemed to increase the inseparability of the physical and etheric bodies. Beauty, it would seem, is too harmonizing, if you will excuse the pun."

Viracocha knew the Archon was watching him closely, so he turned slightly to the side to pretend to be interested in something the Archon had not mentioned. He looked at a leg of one of the tables, for there was one spot where he could focus and not be able to see either the wrinkled faces of the young women or the Archon's half-stricken, rigid face. He needed that neutral place to orient himself, for he was becoming confused and dizzy. Three different commands kept rising inside his being, but they were locked and tangled in a knot of conflict, with no one emerging as victor. One was a command of rage to kill the Archon, to stop that irritating, lecturing voice by twisting his neck, not just once after the first snapping sound, but again until the head would wobble on its empty neck like a puppet from which the supporting hand had been removed. The other command was to flee from his own delight in murder, to go deep inside himself where they could never get him, no matter what they did with his body. There he would be safe and silent and would never have to talk to anyone ever again. The third command seemed coming from some place on the other side of himself, above the other two commands locked in a wrestler's embrace. It was a mind without a body, a voice without a mouth, and it said simply: "Do nothing now. You will be able to end all this later." But the counsel of doing nothing seemed only to enrage the violence inside him, and thus strengthen his desire to escape the intolerable situation by fleeing from consciousness completely. Viracocha reached out to find some human support and took the wrinkled, withered hand of one of the ravaged young women, and held it. And that helped, for he thought he could feel the spirit of the woman respond, to accept his hand in gratitude.

"I am impressed, Your Grace," the Archon commented. "Most people who have had no training in biology are a little squeamish and are afraid to touch them. It is good to see that you are basically a man of science. As you will observe, the flesh is quite cool, but not yet deadly cold. Now, as I was saying, music was effective, but too harmonizing. But when I considered the power of sound, it occurred to me that if beauty could be so effective, then perhaps an equally intense, and sometimes even related, experience might serve as well. In other words, terror. We know from our research in sound that there are some screeches that are so horrible, so irritating, that the organism cannot tolerate them. As it turned out, that was an inspired intuition, if I may be permitted to say so, for the screech of terror immediately separates the etheric body from the physical. Come, let me show you the results of this work in the next room."

Viracocha knew at once who would be in the next room. The children would be there. The image of the twelve children passing by him in the morning fog returned. He did not want to go into that room. He did not want to see or even imagine in what condition they were. The struggle inside himself increased in intensity. His rage now knew no bounds, for he no longer wanted simply to kill the Archon, he wanted to kill the entire civilization: all of it, every temple, every garuda, every poem, even every piece of his own music that had found its way inside the Institute. It was all guilty. While he had been writing music, supported in luxury, less than a mile away, all of this had been going on. His music was like an exotic, beautiful flower that they grew because it produced a poison for their darts. The flower thought it was admired for its beauty, but did not know for what reason they could reach down into its center to come out with the perfection of death. But how could he destroy the whole civilization? Snapping the Archon's neck could not accomplish that.

As his imagination began to race through scenarios of destruction, his raging self quieted down, appeased for the moment with the fascinations of revenge; as the rage quieted, so did the balancing pull into absolute immobility. The strong buzzing sensation in his abdomen returned and he began to feel that he had the power to break the neck of the Tower itself. But the power was not there where he stood, but in the next room; he needed to go in there, deeper into the spine of the Tower where he had only to reach out to crack it and sink the whole civilization into the sea.

Viracocha walked with new vigor and speed into the third room. They were there all right, they, the children, just as he had expected. Once again there was that semicircle of a dozen tables. Once again there was that exposure of the complete vulnerability of the bodies that contrasted with the cleanliness of all the instruments. The children were stretched out in all the naked awkwardness of early puberty: the beginnings of pubic hair and the puffiness within the nipples of the girls. But unlike the pregnant women, their eyes were all open. They all seemed to be staring at the ceiling in a state of shock.

"I think you will appreciate the delicacy and precision of this operation," the Archon said as he moved over to one of the boys closest to him. "The drug is introduced into their bloodstreams through the tubes here in the right arm, but once they are all deeply comatose, we then remove all their blood, collect it in the large quartz vessel in the center of the room, and then sensitize it by vibrating it ultrasonically. We use a stabilizing fluid to maintain the bloodstreams for the few moments that their own blood is outside the body, then we return the transformed blood back into them, and slowly bring them up to the level of dreaming consciousness. It is at that point that we induce the screech of terror into the lattice of their bones and skull. The shock causes their eyes to open, and if the eyes do not open we know immediately that we have not been successful. We then maintain the screech, but lower their metabolic processes, and then, when we have them stabilized in terror, the etheric body flies off. But because we have confused their bloodstreams we are able to collect the twelve etheric bodies, if we simply drain half of the bloodstreams into the quartz vessel, there in the center of the room. If you were clairvoyant, Your

Grace, you could see the twelve etheric bodies now within the vessel. Unfortunately, we have found that if the screech of terror is stopped even momentarily, they die, and we lose the dozen etheric bodies, which, of course, we can't have. But everything is fine as long as they remain suspended, neither alive nor dead, in this state of terror."

The Archon turned away from Viracocha for a moment to survey his work. With both hands on his cane, he leaned forward like a commander surveying the battlefield that had just put victory into his hands. Then with a backward glance, he turned to see how Viracocha was taking his initiation into a knowledge beyond life and death. Viracocha stood motionless and simply stared ahead at the vessel of blood in the center of the semicircle.

"You see, Your Grace," the Archon said, resuming his lecture, "the difficulty with the pregnant women was that the protective instinct of the mother was too strong. We could not detach the etheric body of either mother or fetus. But children at the early stages of puberty were a totally different case . . ."

The Archon signaled to the page to bring him a chair. He leaned over with his hands cupped on the top of his cane and surveyed his work with a nod of satisfaction. Then slowly he lowered himself into the chair, and continued his lecture, as if the audience were not Viracocha alone, but a posterity looking in over his shoulder:

"You, no doubt, know, Your Grace, that sometimes pubescent children—girls more often than boys—will cause peculiar disturbances around them. Things will go flying around their homes without anyone touching them. This comes from the transformation of the etheric body at the onset of puberty. As soon as the girls menstruate, or the boys have their first ejaculation, the phenomenon disappears. Puberty also generates a psychic form of detachment. It is as if the soul resents what is happening to it. I suppose it is some form of racial memory of the entrapment into the animal body, so that the development of the genitals seems to suggest a further descent into animality, a loss of spiritual innocence, and so some souls resent it and pull away from the body. Girls are often moody and daydreaming in their detachment. Boys are simply clumsy, not truly into their bodies. Well, this detachment, this pulling away from the body was just what we needed, for it enabled us to detach the etheric body without terminating the physical body. By maintaining the screech of terror inside the physical body, we ensure that the etheric body will not return but will maintain its new association in the cluster. As long as we can prevent the child from dying, we can ensure that the etheric body will not disintegrate. The key to it all was in collecting and mixing the blood. Strange, isn't it? Savages often emphasize blood in their disgusting rituals, but they were on to something after all. Blood is the critical element, the true amorphous liquid crystal. Would Your Grace prefer to sit?"

"No, I prefer to stand." Viracocha blurted out the words and did not bother to look at the Archon. "I feel strangely energized after my month away. Please continue, I'm simply concentrating on all the possibilities."

"Ah, yes, they are so many, are they not?" the Archon said, as he took in a deep breath before resuming his narration.

The image of twisting the Archon's neck was still a pleasant thought, and Viracocha had not entirely put it out of his mind, but the thought of doing more cosmic damage was far more appealing. He went over all the possibilities, and as all the images of destruction flashed through his mind, he felt a strange sense of exhilaration that seemed somehow to be localized within his body. The peculiar buzzing had returned to his lower abdomen, except now it had become so loud that he felt as if he could hear it, but in his right ear only. He leaned his head slightly to the side to pay more attention, but the buzzing did not seem to become melodic as much as it grew louder and more powerful in an unsettling way.

"Your attention that is so sharply focused on the quartz vessel that contains one half of the united bloodstreams is well placed, Your Grace, for this is the receptacle for the dozen etheric bodies. The difficulties we now face come from the fact that the psychic dream bodies are still individuated, but, fortunately, terror is most effective on the psychic level, so we are continuing along these lines. Here we found that we had need of someone who could project the psychic body from its association with the physical to create a thought-form that could begin to unite the etheric bodies to a common dream body. We found a shaman from the Eastern Continent who was quite skillful at this. Strange isn't it, this relevance of the primitive to advanced science, but there it is. When the Tower is working again, we should be able to create an opening in the etheric range so that one of the Old Ones will be able to get through."

The buzzing was growing intolerable within Viracocha, for it seemed to have shifted from his abdomen to his spine, but still he could not ignore this reference to the Old Ones, for it meant that they were not simply trying to ascend, but were trying to bring something down.

"And who or what are the Old Ones?"

"We're not exactly certain yet," the Archon said. "They may be something precipitated from the collective unconscious of the children, something precipitated by the protracted state of terror in them. It is the shaman who sees and takes messages from these Old Ones, for they seem only to operate in the psychic dimensions and are not able to penetrate through the etheric into the physical. The voices themselves say that when the solar crystal is activated that they will be able to project with the power of the etheric-cluster into human sperm. We will certainly look into this, for conception is the next phase of the work here, at least a slightly more immaculate form of conception than the one we've been habituated to in our animal bodies."

Viracocha began to feel as if his own body were being taken from him, and he stared wildly ahead. His gaze was so distracted that the Archon shifted round to see what was disturbing Viracocha.

One of the naked young boys on the table just to the left of center caught the Archon's attention as the child's penis began to lift in an erection.

"Oh, is that all that is disturbing you?" the Archon asked with a bemused tone. "That sometimes happens. It means that he is too far advanced into puberty to be of any use to us. He'll ejaculate in a minute, which will actually indicate that he's dying. It is interesting, is it not, this continual association of sexuality and death. The ejaculation of the dying man whose spinal cord is snapped. It's much the same here when the screech carries the sexually developed over into death. They get this erection and then this last ejaculation, this last pathetic little spurt of life in the face of death. Ah, you see, here it comes."

The little penis waved back and forth in the futility of its search for a womb, and then it coughed up a small jet of semen, strained for a moment, and then collapsed. As it fell over with the last stream of life oozing out of it, Viracocha felt as if his own spinal column had been snapped and he doubled over and fell to his knees in sharp pain.

It felt as if something had kicked him in the stomach and then ripped him open with an electric knife that went up from his abdomen to his heart. The pain in his chest was so unbearable that he felt as if his heart were being ripped out. Uncontrollable spasms of vomiting took hold of him and he felt as if he were vomiting his own entrails onto the floor. Even when his stomach was empty, he could not stop but continued heaving. He was on all fours, like an animal, staring down into the brown pool of his own vomit. Finally the spasms subsided and he was left gasping for breath. As he gazed down into his own reflection in the liquid mass, he felt a peculiar sense of peace.

The Archon was utterly astonished and yet somehow seemed pleased with this unexpected display of weakness on Viracocha's part. With a new sense of dominance in his voice, he took on a more openly patronizing tone:

"Please help His *Grace* up," the Archon said to his page. "I had no idea Your Grace would be so affected by the sight of a boy ejaculating. Perhaps it means that you have some attraction to young boys that you have been ignoring. There's no need to be so ashamed that you have to expose your insides in this symbolic manner. The temple concubines are really not appropriate for a man in your high position, and when you have had a chance to take a new assessment of yourself, I suggest you come round. We have more young boys here than we need for the work. But, perhaps, I am being overly analytical. Perhaps, you have simply picked up some infirmity in the primitive huts of Eiru."

The page lifted Viracocha up and held onto his arm for a moment, but Viracocha did not take his eyes off the pool of vomit on the floor. Somehow in his mind the pool of vomit and the sea in his dream had become one. He had found something, but he still could not say just what it was. All that he knew was that the pain in his abdomen and chest had gone.

"I hope Your Grace will be feeling better by this evening," the Archon said. "It would be a pity to miss the great honor of a private dinner with His Holiness. Perhaps, if you lie down for an hour or two, you will feel better. Please escort His Grace back to his quarters, and send in one of the servants to take care of this."

Viracocha did not bother to speak or to look up, for the Archon's petty jibes seemed far removed from the important things going on inside himself. He could hear the sandal strike the floor, hear the long drag of his right foot, and then the click of his cane on the stones. He waited for several moments until all the sounds of the Archon's movements had disappeared; then he stood up straight, removed his arm from the page's grasp, and took command of the situation:

"I can walk back by myself. You need only go for the servant. I will return to my quarters by myself."

He turned quickly away from the page and left him to his bewilderment as to whom he should obey. Viracocha kept his eyes straight ahead as he passed through the three laboratories into the main corridor, and he kept his eyes fixed straight ahead as he passed the guards at the control point and at the copper doors. He was not interested in them, for his anger had become pure and more refined. Revenge against individuals or the entire civilization now seemed petty and irrelevant. He knew the Plates he had given them for the Tower would destroy the City, perhaps even the three Great Islands. He was not interested in them anymore; they were mere tools. It was God who was the real enemy; it was God that he needed to kill.

He did not want to look up at the Tower. He did not want to look down at the sea. He did not want to be in the College, the City, the Great Island. He did not even know if he wanted to be, but the only thing that still held him in the grip of life was his rage at God.

He kept his eyes to the ground so that he would not have to look at anything, but there was little chance that he would see anyone. They would all be inside chanting the evening prayers to the setting sun. But he could see the pale blue hem of his priestly robes that they still had on him and that sickened him. He wished he could vomit out everything they had ever put in him or on him. He was sick of priestcraft, sick of this religious analysis of misery that only seemed to produce more misery. The religious study of suffering only gave them a license to prolong it. Their sophisticated doctrines of reincarnation gave them the illusion of power over life and death with a transcendent dispensation to kill. What did one life matter in the great cycles of reincarnation, in that vulgar profligacy of verminous, abundant life after life?

But what did a hundred lives matter, if one did not? A hundred zeros still added up to zero. Nothing could add up unless there was a value to *one*. But he no longer wanted to be one. He no longer wanted to share existence with Evil, to say this side of the bed is mine, but you stay over there.

He had looked down into the ground of being and found that there was this filthy secret to existence. Evil was not simply a disease of being, it was Being. The Institute was not some kind of infection in an otherwise good civilization; it was the very essence of the whole civilization. Beauty and goodness were simply allowed a little season to flourish to make the ultimate desecration more delicious: like someone tenderly nurturing a pregnant cow, waiting patiently to slaughter her calf for the delicacy of veal. Nothing could stand in the face of Evil because it was the face of everything. Evil would always win in the battle of good and bad, for in fighting the bad one had to use the methods of Evil. He knew that if he had exploded in rage and killed the Archon and his dumb submissive attendant, he would simply have added one more murderer to history's lengthening list. One could not be alive to fight Evil, for life itself was Evil. Men were not locked into some prison by a geometrizing god, they were penned in like animals. No, worse than that. There was a malevolence of consciousness at work here, not simply slaughter. There was a Mind seeking to grow Evil like some dark flower in a pot. When "good" armies went off to fight "bad" armies, that malevolence steamed above the battlefields and enjoyed much more the hot pleasure of the "good" man killing the bad than the obvious, cold, dry, and prosaic evil of some dumb brute lopping off a hundred heads. And how that malevolent consciousness loved being prayed to as God, loved the pretense of kindness that only made the final revelation of cruelty more perfectly Evil.

Viracocha lifted up his head as he passed through the gate into the College. The City of Knowledge, he thought, was well named, for behind all the arts and sciences of civilization was the hidden truth of the Institute, and the Institute was the universe in miniature. It was that malevolence made manifest. The children in the Institute were the open expression of what all suffered. Not even death could deliver them from suffering. There was no escape, unless somehow one could find a way to undo existence. It would not be enough simply to die; one had to find a way to eliminate death along with life, and the only way to do that was to reach up and pull down this maniacal geometrizing God, the cunning author of all these restraining traps of love and beauty.

Viracocha passed through the last doorway and came into the columnal arcade that surrounded the residential quadrangle. He noticed someone sitting on the low wall in front of his door. The figure had his back turned toward Viracocha and his head was hidden behind one of the columns. As Viracocha approached, the man turned round, stood to attention, and then gave a formal bow. As Viracocha recognized the Captain, he also remembered in anger the appointment he had made.

The last person Viracocha wanted to see at that moment was another member of the staff of the Institute. His rage at everything flashed out at the intruder and he decided that he was not going to bother with courtesy any longer.

"Good Evening, Your Grace."

"Considering that I have just returned from a tour of your Institute, Captain, ·I do not consider it to be a good evening at all, and I would thank you to leave me at once so that I may be alone with my thoughts."

The Captain looked shocked and nervously glanced around to see if they were being overheard:

"Then that is all the more reason why I have to talk with Your Grace. It is as important for you as it is for me, *especially now,*" Bran said, as his voice trailed off into a whisper.

Viracocha stared at the Captain in silent anger for a moment, but the more he did look at him, the more he realized that he was not angry at him:

"All right, Captain," Viracocha said with an assenting tone of defiance, "but don't expect it to be a pleasant social visit."

Viracocha opened the door to his quarters and left it open for Bran to follow behind. He did not turn back but moved across the room to his cabinet and took out a crystal decanter of brandy and two goblets.

"I can't offer you any of your native Eireanne dry mead," Viracocha said as he turned to glower at Bran, "though I wish I could, for its power to take your mind away would be most welcome now. Unfortunately, we'll have to make do with a coarse brandy."

Bran moved into the center of the room and looked around to see if there were servants present:

"Thank you, Your Grace, but I didn't come to get drunk. Are we alone?"

"You are alone, but unfortunately I'm not," Viracocha said as he took a drink. "No, there are no servants present. I prefer that they clean when I'm not around. I don't like to be disturbed when I'm working, so over the three years here, I've been able to frighten them all away."

Viracocha moved into the center of the room, set the decanter down on the table, filled the goblets, and then sat down without bothering to remove his cape. As he took another drink, he looked up at Bran over the rim of his goblet.

Bran looked down awkwardly for a moment, then he picked up the goblet and sat down on the chair on the other side of the table.

"Why are you so dressed up?" Viracocha asked. "There isn't going to be another Solemn Assembly. As a matter of fact, I don't think there will ever be another Solemn Assembly."

"I thought it would be easier to be inconspicuous if I were more conspicuous, as if I were on an errand of official importance."

"You sound positively conspiratorial," Viracocha said. "I hope you've come to tell me that you're going to destroy the Empire, for I'll drink to that."

"I have come to tell you that I have done as you commanded and that the vessel will be ready to take us at dawn the day after tomorrow."

"As I have commanded?" Viracocha remarked with a laugh. "I haven't commanded anything, Captain. I'm afraid you're not making much sense."

"When you gave me the official password this morning, I contacted the 144 to prepare for the escape flight to Tiahuanaco. Did you make any contact with Abaris through Brigita when you were on Eiru?"

"Wait just a moment, Captain," Viracocha said in annoyance as well as surprise. "First of all, I spent only one day with Abaris when he was alive. Second of all, I was with Brigita, but I don't see how or why you should know about that. And third, I did not contact the ghost of Abaris, for that's not exactly my style. Now, what 'password' are you talking about?"

" 'It had no arms to fight/But only wings for flight.' That is the password that Abaris said the leader of the colony would give me to identify himself and to let me know that I was to prepare the 144 for escape to Tiahuanaco just before the Great Islands were to sink in the sea."

Viracocha took another large drink of brandy and then folded his arms across his chest as he considered Bran in a new perspective:

"Tiahuanaco *is* a beautiful place. I lived there once for over a year. If I were a leader of a colony of refugees, it is certainly the place I would choose. I hate to end this little fantasy, Captain, but I made up the end to your poem on the spot. Abaris did not give me any password, and he never told me about any colony of 144 for Tiahuanaco. As for Brigita, she never said a word about it either. I went to Eiru for the pleasures of cohabitation. I'd never slept with an Abbess before, and it held out a certain sexual mystique that I found exciting . . ."

Bran stiffened in his chair, lowered his goblet to the table, and looked at Viracocha in disbelief.

"Ah, I see I've shocked you. Well, you see it just proves that I am not a leader, and certainly not a good disciple of Abaris, so where does that leave us, Captain?"

"I'm not sure. You certainly wouldn't be my choice of a leader, that's true. But the facts remain: Abaris put the password into your mind, Brigita singled you out for the initiation with the dagger and the chalice, and you are familiar with Tiahuanaco and its native peoples. I guess it means that you've been kept in ignorance so that you could more effectively penetrate into the hierarchy here, for Abaris' prophecy said that the new leader would sit by the side of the High Priest himself. I guess the test would be to ask if you had a vision of the winged serpent when you lived in Tiahuanaco?"

"Shit!" Viracocha exclaimed in a feeling that he was being conscripted into an army against his will.

"So, there you have it, Your Grace," Bran said with an air of one taking command of the situation. "I would hazard a guess that your ostentatiously sacrilegious manner is simply a convenient blind that your higher Self uses to keep you out of the way while it goes about its business. You may have thought you were going off for a sexual frolic with Brigita, but you can be certain that she knew just exactly who you really were and just exactly what she was doing in preparing you."

"Then what do you mean by 'the initiation of the dagger and the chalice'?" Viracocha asked, beginning to suspect that Brigita was indeed not a witch and that he just might have failed in some important way.

"The dagger and the chalice are very ancient symbols in our religion. They go back to the time before farming. Originally, I think the dagger was a spear. Anyway, they are symbols of the male and female forces in the universe. The chalice is the vulva and the cup of the crescent moon. It is also a sacred wound. As the vulva bleeds every month with the moon, it is seen as wound that heals itself, the crescent moon that fills up with light. In the dark of the moon, all the women bleed, then the moon grows full. The dagger is the shaft of light from the sun that opened up the earth to light. It is the phallus, and the dagger that creates a wound to open darkness to new life. In the vulva, the phallus causes the bleeding to stop, to flow into the womb for the child. The child is also the higher self born into the world. All of these meanings are seen at once in these images, but didn't Brigita explain any of this to you?"

"I suppose she was trying to in her own way," Viracocha said in a feeling of embarrassment that was beginning to make him feel very tired. "I guess because she's a dancer, she believes in showing more than talking. Anyway, we were . . . meditating. The moon came through the window. It made me open my eyes, then I saw the chalice and the dagger on the altar. I became taken over by this vision of Brigita as a witch and that in some primitive rite in your Eireanne religion, I was about to be sacrificed to fill her chalice."

"That's really interesting," Bran said with an air of serious and sober concern. "In your state of psychic sensitivity brought on by meditation what you picked up was part of the religion of the past on Eiru. Abaris was able to drive the witches out of Eiru, but they still exist on the Eastern Continent. In their dark rites they prefer boys in puberty to men like yourself. They drug them and then hypnotize them to make them see themselves as beautiful. They stimulate them for a long time, and then they castrate them to fill the chalice with the blood and semen, which they drink in the delusion that the concoction will grant them eternal youth and magic powers. It's all a mistaken literalism, taking something etheric and trying to make it simply physical. It is sort of a demonic parody for something much deeper, and that is why Abaris was so angry and drove them out of Eiru. It's also the reason why Abaris was so secretive and would not give out the teachings to very many."

"Well, the ritual you describe is exactly what I thought Brigita had in mind for me, and I ran from her house in terror, all the way to the port. There I intimidated the crew into flying me back here before the old witch could wake from her trance."

"And just in perfect timing for you to accidentally bump into me, and to just happen to give the passwords," Bran said as he laughed at Viracocha's bewilderment. "Were you running from, or running toward?"

Viracocha said nothing. After a good long minute of silence, he lifted his goblet and took another drink, and then folded his arms across his chest and looked at Bran:

"And I am still going to keep on running *from.* I'm not a leader, Captain. You seem like a nice fellow, you take the 144, and I'll stay here to sink into the brandy before we all sink into the sea. I'm not very good with people, as you should be able to see by now."

"What we're good at, Your Grace, is not always the source from which our inner strength springs. People have been destroyed as often by their strengths as by their weaknesses. Look at your High Priest."

"You're a veritable fountain of wisdom, Captain. You're wasted in the Institute. It's a pity you weren't one of my colleagues in our blessed Sacred College here. I could have used a good drinking partner these last three years."

"Someone was needed who could fly, and even more than that, someone was needed who could fly the largest garuda in the Empire. I can assure you that if it weren't with the hope of being the only one who could get the people out, I wouldn't have continued, but would have gone off to a remote island to work on my poetry. But this last year has been the worst. You saw the children this morning, so now you know what it has been like waiting for you to show up and give the damn password so that we could get the hell out of here."

"Hell is not an inappropriate word, Captain, for not only have I seen the children with you this morning, but I have followed their career all the way into the heart, if you will excuse the word, of our blessed Laboratory of Incarnation. Have you ever been inside to see our noble work in perfecting the evolution of the human race?"

Bran looked down at his feet and spoke without lifting his eyes to Viracocha:

"No. But I saw what the women and children were like when we used to take them back. Bran raised his eyes to look at Viracocha, imploringly, but also accusingly: "Why did all this have to take so long? Why didn't you show up sooner?"

"Don't you start accusing me!" Viracocha exclaimed in anger. "Brigita did that too. Listen, Captain of the great conspiracy: I am not one of your 144. I am not a leader. I don't give a damn about anything, not you, or Abaris, or Brigita, or this whole rotten civilization, or God. You've been had, Captain. God is simply the Archon, writ large. This whole fantasy of escape of yours is his little cat and mouse game. He uses me to set up the Tower so that it destroys this whole wretched city, maybe even all the Great Islands. Then he plays a joke on me and uses me to give you some magic password to carry the 144 to safety so that a few dumb followers of Abaris will think that Good has triumphed over Evil. Then slowly at first, but with increasing haste as the new civilization gets going down there, he will begin again to grow a lovely little garden of Evil. And if we're all too primitive down there and have forgotten how to build our great towers, why then we can improvise with stones and rip out people's hearts and stand on our tiptoes to lift them up in prayers to the sun."

Bran stared at Viracocha in disbelief and showed in his eyes a fear that the plan he had based his life on was about to be ruined. He looked at Viracocha in a state of shock that began to modulate into anger, as Viracocha gazed back at him in defiance.

"You see," Viracocha said, "you've got the wrong man. It's God's little perverted joke on you. You thought I was going to be some holy and devout disciple of Abaris, full of faith in the Great Plan, in the great battle of Good and Evil. But the illusion of battle is just a trick to keep you fighting, for Evil always wins. I don't want to escape, and I am not thrilled by visions of survival, because we would simply carry sweet Evil with us to Tiahuanaco, and the whole thing would start over again. I'm sick of Evil, Captain, sick of playing its game, so I'm kicking over the table and the pieces and saying to hell with you all."

"*You're sick of Evil!*" Bran shouted. "You act as if you've just discovered it. Where have you been your whole life? No, I know the answer to that. You've been here, a pampered favorite of His Holiness's private collection of artistic geniuses. You've been playing here in luxury a little more than a mile away from the Institute. And now you've discovered that there are bad men in your private universe, and so you sulk. You feel sorry for your poor self whose private party has been ruined. Then you come up with some great dramatic anger at God to avoid your own guilt. This God of yours sounds more like an inflated image of yourself, a being who tolerates Evil in order to compose without disturbance. Who divided up your life with Evil here and Good there? Your great anger at God is just more of your own theatrical vanity. But even in your grand self-righteous anger, you indulge yourself and carry on as if Evil were a personal insult and affront to you. God! You would have thought Abaris would have taught you more than that!"

"Abaris spent a little more than an hour with me. He told me a few things about the winged serpent, gave me a few meditation techniques, told me to wait six months before starting kriya, and then he left. I never saw him again."

"You saw him every night," Bran said. "Especially if you were given kriya. Though how you can do kriya and not be aware of your psychic life amazes me."

"My, how you do sound like Brigita. Even like the High Priest, for that matter."

"Well, perhaps there was a purpose even in your being so self-indulgent. You don't seem to be very patient, so I can't imagine that if you knew about the conspiracy, you would wait for the right minute to move. You probably would have been rash and impulsive and moved too soon; God knows it's been hard enough for me to wait for you to show up."

Viracocha was silent for a moment and slowly sipped his drink as he considered Bran:

"If you had escaped before the elevation of the Tower and my revision of the design of the foundation vault, the Great Island would not explode and the garudas of the Empire could follow you down to Tiahuanaco at their will."

"So, there you have it," Bran said, beginning to relax and feel less threatened about the safety of the plan. "Abaris said that 'A grain of sand is more effective as a weapon in the eye than on the foot.' He prophesied that the leader would come from the hierarchy itself. Every time I came to the City of Knowledge, I kept looking to see if I could find him. And every time I had to fly back to Anahuac, I would try to think things out. I kept telling myself that if things were twisted, then they needed something straight to twist. That if there were some depraved being looking for the perfect evil, then he needed some idea of perfection. That if I were the Archon and wanted to have an army of torturers obedient to my will, then I would need them to be obedient, loyal, and truthful with one another. That if they became evil in every instant of their lives, they would kill one another and cease to be an effective force for Evil. I began to see that in order to *do* Evil one had to *be* Good, that Goodness was more basic, more fundamental to the nature of existence, that even Evil had to invoke it to try to thwart it. The greater the Evil, the longer the time criminals must spend in Goodness to effect their crime. Eventually, I think humanity will see the inherent contradiction within Evil and transcend it."

"Or is it simply," Viracocha asked, "that Goodness exists to make Evil more enjoyable? After all, you have to have straight things around for the fun of twisting them."

"But the pleasure of twisting, as you say, comes from the prior existence of the straight thing and the freedom that exists. If God had created the universe as a machine in which nothing was allowed to deviate from His will, He would not have to bother to create it, because He would know how it would turn out. But in an open and free universe, you must have souls who are free to deviate from the will of God. They can only express love if they are free, but if they are free, you open up the possibility for Evil to deny existence. The question then becomes: Do you risk being for love, or do you play it safe in nonbeing?"

"And so for you," Viracocha said, "the fact that we're having a philosophical debate while the world goes to hell means that our 'Beloved Creator' chose to risk it?"

"In a word, Yes. God emanated the Conscious, but it was the Conscious who dreamed the universe and became caught in the projections of their own dreams. God didn't create the universe, we did. So if the universe appears to be Evil, it is a description of our own nature, that we like a story with Evil and danger in it. Evil is a projection, an expression of humanity's inability to express Being without Evil. Humanity is fascinated with Evil. It has discovered this dark and secret thing that comes out of itself. It is like a child playing with its feces, enjoying its expressive power in the patterns it can create by smearing it around. Eventually, the infant loses interest and discovers other forms of expression, and humanity will too, someday."

"But in the meantime the mother comes in and washes the infant and sets him down again in a clean bed. Who is going to mother this infantile humanity if God doesn't come in and clean up the mess?"

"And just how could God do that?" Bran asked, enjoying his new found status of authority. "Actually, you, both of us, are in a better position to *act*, since we are within this dream called the universe. God can whisper to us in our sleep and try gently to lead us out and away from our self-inflicted torment, but if he destroys the dream and the universe ends, we'd probably project another universe with the same problems. Actually, it could be much worse. We have Abaris who has one foot in the world and one foot out of it. The rest is up to us, and now that you have finally shown up, I am more than ever ready to get on with it."

"You know, when I listen to you," Viracocha said sardonically,

"I get the impression that you've memorized your lines at the feet of Abaris, and that now you're thrilled to play Teacher and to show that hidden in the uniform of a Captain lurks the soul of a poet and a prophet yet unborn."

"Don't patronize me, Your *Grace!*" Bran said in a flash of anger. "You claim not to respect your own Sacred College, but you still don't respect anybody outside your little world. You think I have to be stupid because I am in the Military. Well even if I don't succeed in becoming a poet in this life, I'll keep coming back to one culture or another until I do succeed. And long after your music is forgotten, my story about you will be remembered."

"Well, it's great to see a little vanity and passion in Captain Perfect," Viracocha said, lifting his goblet in a toast. "Here's to your fame and my oblivion. Now, since you have taken over my role as artist, I humbly suggest you take over my role as leader."

"I'm sorry," Bran said, trying to regain self-mastery. "I didn't want to lose my temper. Look, it's silly for us to argue. All right, I got angry because what you said is true. I have memorized my lines and little speeches from Abaris. I studied with him for twelve years. You still remember him after only a meeting of one day. Well, I had twelve years of instructions, and it's the only thing that got me through this last year. I'm a follower, not a leader. Abaris said that the leader would sit at the side of the High Priest, that he and Brigita would be able to work with the angels and elementals to free the children and sink the Islands. I can't do any of that. All I have been able to do is go over Abaris' talks, again and again. Last month when I had to fly the Governor back to Anahuac, I sat there watching him drool, watching the idiot spittle drip from his lips, and I kept telling him in my mind that you were coming, that soon his people would be free again.

Viracocha's face became deadly serious. He lowered his drink and looked questioningly into Bran's eyes.

Bran looked back at Viracocha and was surprised that he did not seem to know what he was talking about:

"I take it you don't know. The Archon has a contempt for death. He prefers to maintain control. He prefers to return leaders so that the people can see what happens to those who try to oppose them. I'm told that he says that the death of a leader inspires his people, but his method completely demoralizes them. He has invented or discovered some drug that when placed into the bloodstream turns the person into a slobbering idiot. And it has had its effect. Anahuac is numb. He has crippled their will."

Neither man spoke. Viracocha set the goblet down and stood up. He turned away from Bran and walked silently to his desk. He looked down at the thin metal sheets of the transcriptions for his music. It all seemed so irrelevant. It was too soon for that kind of thing, another age, another civilization, perhaps; but not now, not in this world. He picked up the sheets of his music, folded them neatly into a leather portfolio, and tied the ribbon around them. He picked it up, but let the portfolio hang down by his side as he walked back to the chair where Bran was seated.

"All right, Captain. I've packed my things. Here's a souvenir to take with you in the vessel. I'm not certain what we do next."

Bran stood up and took the portfolio into his hands:

"I guess you do whatever is next. You seem to have been on course even when you thought you weren't. What is next here for you?"

"I have been invited to a private dinner with His Holiness, the Archon, and the Master of the Sacred College."

"Well, there you have it," Bran said. "The prophecy said the leader would sit at the side of the High Priest, that he would come from the summit of the hierarchy. Since it has been prophesied, you might as well continue to walk in the footsteps of prophecy. Perhaps there is more leverage to effect a shift of the whole society at that exalted level. Perhaps that is what was meant when Abaris said that a grain of sand is more effective as a weapon in the eye than on the foot."

"It doesn't seem that there is anything else to do. I really don't have much interest in escape or survival, but, I suppose, if we do make it out of here alive, I would like you sometime to take me to Eiru to see Brigita. I didn't exactly leave in the best of spirits, and I would like to see her again."

"She's been placed under arrest," Bran said quietly. "Her Captain has been ordered to bring her to the City. She'll be here tomorrow morning. So, we will have to work fast, otherwise she is going to end up in the Archon's hands. And I promise you that I will not let that happen."

Neither man said anything. As Viracocha looked at Bran and realized how much Bran was in love with Brigita, he felt his cynicism dissolve in the complexity of his hate for the Archon, his own confused feelings about Brigita, and his own amazement at the self-mastery and control of Bran. All these years he had been a disciple of Abaris as a symbolic way of making love to the virgin disciple. All these months, he had been ferrying victims to their dismemberment, waiting to be faithful to a prophecy. And here all the time, Viracocha had cared about no one, had lived in complete ignorance and privilege, and even been privileged to make love to Brigita, and he had failed everybody, especially Brigita.

"All right," Viracocha exhaled in an agreement that was more of an exhaustion of his defenses than an affirmation. "I don't know who is leader or follower in any of this. And I certainly don't know what I'm doing. But go on, get the garuda ready, and I will go sit by the side of the High Priest. After that, I don't know what to do. I don't have your self-control. I just may indulge myself and kill the Archon so that, at least, he won't get his hands on Brigita."

"If you don't I will," Bran said with quiet finality. "I'll gladly go to hell if I can send him there." Bran walked to the door. As he opened it, he turned back, bowed, and said in a louder and more official voice:

"Thank you for the transcriptions of your music, Your Grace. Your music has been an important inspiration to my service in the Empire."

The door closed and as Viracocha stared ahead he thought it was time for the leader to follow. He would take Bran's example and dress to perfection for dinner. The High Priest had said full ceremonial dress would not be required, but for this occasion, he wanted the irony of imperial disguise.

Viracocha walked into the bedroom, removed his cape, and

fell onto the bed. The brandy and everything that Bran had told him about Brigita made him feel deeply tired. He knew that he did not have time to sleep, that it would not be long before the page came to escort him to the dinner, and yet he had no energy to move. He closed his eyes momentarily, telling himself that he would get up in a moment, but a thick heavy darkness seemed to crush down on him, rendering him completely paralyzed. He knew in the darkness that was his shame and guilt, he had somehow failed Brigita and now she was under arrest. He had failed the children and now they were caught, as he was caught, in this thick, impenetrable darkness. If he could only move, he knew that he might be able to save them all, but the darkness crushed every muscle and the pain in the back of his neck held him in some electric paralysis. He tried to scream, but he could only grunt like a moron without articulate voice. He could hear his own voice, but still he could not move. Then into the darkness from another world he felt Brigita's hands reach down to shake him, to move him, to break the grip of the paralysis.

"Your Grace? Your Grace!" The page shook Viracocha more vigorously by the shoulders. "Wake up. I have come to escort you to His Holiness's presence."

Viracocha's eyes snapped open as he stared at the page in a state of disorientation. He could feel a buzzing in the back of his neck, and he realized that he had stuffed the cushion behind his neck in such a way that he had cut off the circulation to his head. As soon as he gained command of his body, he jumped up.

"I'll need one minute while I change robes. Wait outside for me."

The page bowed obediently, and Viracocha ran to his wardrobe and slid back the panel. He quickly removed his daily robe and threw it onto the bed; then as he took out his formal robe and raised his arms to enter it, he felt as if the robe descending on his body had become one of the Old Ones coming down within the Tower to settle on the human form. Who were these Old Ones? he asked himself as he brushed out the snarls in his hair. Would the High Priest know? Thrusting his feet into his gold slippers, he reached up for his midnight blue silk cape, and decided that he would bring the matter up at dinner.

Viracocha turned from the mirror and moved hurriedly across the room and out into the colonnade where the page stood in attendance. The page bowed and then turned round to lead the way to the Palace. As Viracocha looked down at his gold slippers, and midnight blue cape with its magenta lining, he felt as if he were dressed in an aura and not a priestly costume. The High Priest's ceremonial robe at the Solemn Assembly, with its broad peacock-feathered headdress, certainly seemed to be a rendering of the human aura. Perhaps, he thought, there was some kind of historical progression here. We start out naked with extended auras and no priests; then we move into a society of priests with simple white smocks like Brigita's, but with light pastel auras; and then the priesthood decays, grows richly elaborate as the gorgeous robes begin to cover the darkening auras with midnight blue, purple, and magenta. Thus camouflaged, the priest was safe and no seer could discern the true colors of his aura to see in what a depraved condition he truly was.

Viracocha felt not only disguised but armored as he walked with his hands hidden behind his silk cape. He had the feeling that he was indeed going into battle, but he had absolutely no sense of what he was to do, or what he could do; and yet he realized that if everything was true that Bran had told him, then he had never *known* what he was doing.

What a strange form of knowledge it is, Viracocha thought as they came out of the College Gate onto the Broad Street, to know that you don't know what you're doing. It made him feel as if his whole personality, his whole identity as Viracocha, were a convenient fiction. Some other being was playing him the way he played his own harp; even his own fear had been used by this being that saw over the curvature of the earth to send him running in terror to be on time for an appointment with Bran. If that were true, then what was he doing now, he wondered, as he headed toward the Palace for an unknown encounter?

It was easy not to believe in the substantial reality of the great City of Knowledge as he moved down the street toward the hypostyle hall. The whole architecture was nothing but a few metaphors of power that were truly powerless in their shallow life on the surface of the volcanic earth. The city was already dead and all those in it were simply ghosts who had not yet realized that they were no longer among the living but were actually dreaming the world that surrounded them.

The unreality of it all gave Viracocha a new sense of freedom and fearlessness. He did not care to escape to Tiahuanaco. Bran could worry about that. He had no other purpose than to shatter the Tower and to release the hold the Archon had on every soul kept from death and life within the Institute. How a mere dinner party could serve that end he did not know, but since he did not know anything, he would take it one step at a time.

One step at a time, he went up the stairs from the Broad Street to the terrace above the hypostyle hall. One step at a time, he went up the stairs in the reception hall to the private dining room opposite the High Priest's study. But where were all the guards? The squadrons that had stood in the reception hall this morning were gone, and merely two guards stood at either side of the door to the small dining room as the page led him into the presence of the hierarchy. Had the crisis been resolved? Was the High Priest celebrating some victory with this dinner?

As Viracocha passed the two guards and entered the room, he saw the three of them standing by the portals to the south. He could sense at once that they had been talking about him and his behavior within the Institute that afternoon. As the High Priest turned round to greet him the last of the evening light touched only half of his face, and half of the white robe whose central band of color was dyed reddish purple from the cochineal of Anahuac.

"And here he is!" the High Priest said as he walked away from the Master and the Archon to greet him. "We were just talking about Your Grace and were hoping that you were not too sick to join us this evening for our small celebration."

"Thank you, Your Holiness," Viracocha said as he bowed first to the High Priest, and then to the Master and the Archon. "I think the sudden change from the northern climate of Eiru to

our warmer climate here made me feel ill. But I have rested,
and feel well, if still a little tired from the journey."

"Good. Come, take your drink and join us," the High Priest
said as he signaled to the servants to bring Viracocha a crystal
cup of wine. "We were enjoying the evening light and its beautiful reflection on the copper doors of the Institute. By the way,
Your Grace, you didn't have to go to the trouble of ceremonial
dress. This is to be an informal celebration."

"Since this is the first occasion of my dining with Your Holiness, and with Your Excellencies, I didn't feel quite right in my
ordinary robes."

"Well, no matter," the High Priest said with a smile. "Perhaps, it adds to our festive air. You see, this is a victory celebration. The revolt in Anahuac has been crushed, and the attempt
by the Commander of the Military to join with the insurgents
against the Theocracy has been dealt with appropriately. When
the Commander was escorted to the meeting of the conspira-
tors, they found him to be a smiling gentle fellow who wouldn't
want to hurt an ant. He sang a few little children's songs to
them, and the other officers decided that revolutions were silly,
so they all joined the party and decided to be good boys. Now
we all can get back to the real work."

"It would seem, Your Holiness, that much has happened in
the month of my absence." Viracocha took his cup from the
servant's tray and wondered what drug might be in it to make
him at one with the party.

The High Priest watched Viracocha as he took his first drink,
and then smiled, as if to set him at ease.

Viracocha was surprised to discover that the drink was dry
mead:

"Unless I am mistaken, this is the dry mead of Eiru. I am
surprised to find this in the Palace, Your Holiness."

"Yes, I confess that I prefer it to our brandy. The herbs com-
bined with the honey have a soothing effect on the subtle bodies. But come, join us in our little corner over here."

Viracocha was startled to feel the High Priest lead him over to
the Archon and the Master by placing his arm on his shoulder.
He felt as if the High Priest were signaling by this gesture that

he was to be the successor. The Master and the Archon both showed by the momentary change of expression in their eyes that the gesture was not lost on them.

"I was just telling His Holiness when you came in," the Master said, "that I think we have all been too busy in these last three years. Here you are a Member of the Sacred College, and yet I hardly know you. The ceremonial dinners at high table are all well and good, but they really don't provide the occasion like this one for developing a true friendship, so we are indebted to His Holiness for this evening. I certainly hope it won't be the last."

"Not at all," the High Priest said. "Now that the political matters have been taken care of, we can all get on with the true business of our society. After all, that is why I had this City of Knowledge built in the first place."

"Yes, I quite agree," the Archon said. "Now that His Grace has been made the College's representative to the Institute for the work of redesigning the Tower, I think we can make progress more quickly. This specious opposition between tradition and innovation has been obstructive in the past, but now that we have the most innovative Member of the Sacred College working within the Institute, I predict that our progress will become astounding."

"Why then I think you owe the College a favor, Your Excellency," the Master said. "You should send us the most traditional of your team to work on a project with us."

"And what kind of project might that be?" the Archon asked.

"Astronomy, of course!" the Master exclaimed in a slightly artificial tone of clubbiness.

Viracocha looked at the flushed red cheeks of the Master, and the tiny beads of sweat on his bald head, and found it hard to understand how the Master had ever come to be an astronomer. Of course, that was a long time ago; now the Master did little work except run the College and dine with his cronies. It was no surprise to Viracocha that the Master did not know him. There wasn't anybody under sixty in the circle in which he hid himself. The Master must have felt Viracocha's penetrating stare, for he turned to Viracocha and tried to include him in his imaginary little circle of clubby intimacy:

"I must say, Your Grace, that I was very impressed with the Plates you drew up today. The system of correspondences between the Hyperborean Solids and the subtle bodies was fascinating; but the correspondence to the planetary intervals was brilliant. I am ashamed that I never thought of it. By the way, Your Holiness, are we permitted to discuss the project, or should we avoid discussions of work this evening?"

"How could we avoid the subject?" the High Priest said. "A cycle of 25,920 years ends in a few days in the coming feast of Sauwyn, what other subject is so compelling? When I said this dinner was to be informal, I meant that we could avoid formal protocol and polite, inane chatter. So, feel free to indulge your obsessions."

"Excellent!" the Master exclaimed obsequiously. "Well then, Your Grace, as I understand it there are only, in terms of General Vibration Theory, three possible frequency-signatures that can be induced into the solar crystal. Which one do you think appropriate?"

Viracocha turned from the Master to consider the High Priest, and without taking his eyes off him, he spoke to the Master:

"Knowing His Holiness's sense of imagination and daring, I would say that there is no question about it. The third, the highest and most dangerous one, is the only one that will provide the geometrical power to strain the galactic alignment and pull apart the fabric of space and time."

"Oh, come now," the Master scoffed, "it can't be that dangerous. We're only talking about setting up a restricted singularity within the foundation vault of the Tower."

"The point is, Your Excellency," Viracocha said as he turned his gaze from the High Priest to the Master, "that it may not prove that simple to restrict the singularity *to* the foundation vault of the Tower."

"Viracocha is right, Your Excellency," the High Priest said in appreciation. "There are always risks commensurate with the scope of any project. But the civilization that stops taking risks dies long before its institutions collapse."

"But surely, Your Grace, you can't think the danger that great?" the Master said. "Just what do you think could happen?"

"An earthquake, if the singularity creates merely a corona of force around the vault, but if the singularity extends to the center of the earth, then the earth's crust will crack, and the islands will disappear."

"All three Great Islands!" the Master scoffed. "Really, I find that hard to swallow."

"Let's hope the ocean does too, Your Excellency."

The Master appreciated Viracocha's witticism and laughed more strongly than the remark deserved, as if to make certain that lighter spirits would rule the evening.

"Well, let's put off the end of the world until at least after dinner," the High Priest said as he stepped back from the circle to lead them to the table.

The emanating crystals were set to a low ambient light which was reflected in the quartz goblets. Viracocha waited for the others to take their places, but the seating arrangement would have been immediately obvious from the size of the chairs around the table. The throne of the High Priest was flanked on either side with large chairs that were handsomely carved but had no gemstones. Viracocha's chair had no gemstones, but was composed of inlaid woods. It was, however, directly opposite the throne of the High Priest. As the four servants pulled out the chairs from the round table, there was a polite murmuring between the Master and the High Priest. The Archon was to Viracocha's left, and when they all were seated, there was a moment of silent prayer before the first dish was set down before them.

"Since this is the first time Your Grace has been to this table, I should warn you that all the food will be vegetarian. When I moved into the new Palace and began sleeping directly under the Tower, I found meat to be too heavy. It caused unpleasant dreams."

"That does not surprise me, Your Holiness," Viracocha said. "I have had no meat for a month, so I'm almost growing used to the diet."

"So, our witch of Eiru is a vegetarian. At another time, Your Grace, I will have to learn more from you about this curious young woman."

The High Priest began the first course, and the others followed. It was the custom to eat in silence, to make a meal an exercise in contemplation. Conversation was accepted only between the courses, but because the intervals between each course were long, the social nature of the feast was still preserved. As the old wine was cleared with the dish and new wine was set on the table, it was the custom to sit back in the chairs, sip the wine slowly, and savor the conversation.

And so they ate their soup in silence, a silence made slightly more contemplative by the performance of a harpist whose music came out of the darkness at the end of the room. Out of this darkness the servants would appear, carrying their dishes and decanters of wine; out of this darkness, the music would come, and disappear appropriately during the intervals of conversation.

As they ate the soup in silence, Viracocha thought how severe the table seemed compared with Brigita's. In Eiru they ate from potter's vessels on wooden boards, but there were always flowers, different settings of flowers for breakfast and dinner. Here they ate off glass plates and bowls, crystal goblets, and anything that could take up the light from the emanating crystals and continue it, endlessly. The table itself was a glossy white marble that was so highly polished that one could see one's own reflection as in a mirror. Only the facets of light and the shadowy reflections seemed to move, for otherwise the table was set in a geometrical perfection that seemed to mock spontaneity.

And yet the play of light within the crystal and glass did have its fascination. Viracocha gazed down into the ocean of his soup and imagined that the sprinkling of three leaves on the top were the Great Islands, and as he pushed them down under the soup, he imagined that he was playing avenging god. But because the music was soft and sweet, he destroyed the islands without malice. It was then that he realized that the dry mead was indeed made from psychedelic herbs as well as honey. He studied his mind for a moment, but found no distortion, no hallucination; it was simply that whatever thought he had normally seemed more heightened, more emphasized in its purity of sensation. The mead certainly did seem to enhance his sense of taste, for the soup had not one taste, but half a dozen following in succession like ocean waves rolling across his tongue. He remembered how the mead had enhanced his sense of smell before and how he had loved the odor of Brigita's arms and thighs. But with the image of Brigita passing through his mind, there also passed the thought she had to be now in the garuda on her way here to the City. Suddenly his emotions took a wild turn into rage and he looked down at the knife by his right hand and was sorry that it was a dull, round vegetarian implement, for he saw in an instant how quickly he could kill the Archon before any of the servants could stop him.

Viracocha struggled to contain himself, to force his mind to think of some ruse through which he could talk to Brigita to work out a plan for her escape with the others. He held his mind close to the thought of her and could feel just how much he wanted to see her again, wanted to atone for whatever failings within himself that had made him turn away from her in projected terror. He held on to the image of Brigita's love of flowers at the table. Here there was nothing but the cold precision of clear glass and crystal on white marble. Better the flowers, the clay vessels on bare boards of Eiru than this costly sterility.

As his emotions tossed back and forth between love and rage, Viracocha suddenly realized why the mead was chosen and why the High Priest had given it to him. It was some kind of truth-elixir that made you more of what you were and forced your personality out into the open. The dinner was to be a ritual of truth, a rite of initiation.

Viracocha put all his mind to tasting his soup as a way of avoiding his rage at the Archon, or his fear of the High Priest. But once his mind was steadied on sensation, he began to take an inventory of his other senses. The drug was not overpowering; he could feel that his will was still intact. It was only that tendencies and moods were intensified and exaggerated. Provided that there were no Anahuacan mushrooms in the soup, he should be able to observe his emotions without acting on them.

The High Priest leaned back from the table to indicate that conversation could resume, and the music of the harp in the darkness instantly stopped. It was the Master who signaled his desire to speak first by turning toward Viracocha and wrinkling his bald head in an attitude of serious inquiry:

"The music of the harp has set me to thinking that since Your Grace is also a musician, you could perhaps answer a question that has been troubling me for some time."

"By all means, Your Excellency," Viracocha said as he sat back in his chair and decided to go very lightly on the wine.

"Well, I have heard that you recently returned from a stay in the Remnants of Hyperborea. While you were there did you hear of any legends concerning 'The Singers from the Pleiades'?"

"I have heard some legends, Your Excellency, but it was not during my stay on Eiru. There used to be an old teacher who lived on Eiru, but often traveled around the world. His name was Abaris. He taught that the planets had their resonances within the centers along the spinal column, and that if one plugged up one's eyes and ears to listen to these centers, he could then hear this other celestial music. But I confess, it was not a practice that I ever mastered."

"So much the better for you," the High Priest said, and then turned to the Master. "You'll notice, Your Excellency, that the practice requires blocking up the ears and the eyes with the fingers. The whole teaching is nothing but a rejection of the physical world. Every technique is aimed at disassociating the psychic body from the personality, so that rather than transforming the world, the person sits in primitive squalor, but goes off, out of his body, to imaginary palaces in shimmering dimensions. Well, this Palace here is not imaginary, and we have built our temples out of mammoth stones to declare to the world that the mysteries of the spirit are to be found in matter, not in the shifting, intermediate realms."

Viracocha looked at the High Priest in surprise. He himself had said nothing about using the fingers to block up the eyes and ears. And why was there such unusual intensity to his words? Could it be that the High Priest, that they all were drinking this dry mead together? Was this truth-telling some kind of social ritual for the hierarchy?

The Master was about to speak, but Viracocha interrupted: "Your Holiness, I said nothing about stopping up the eyes and ears with the fingers. It could have been with cloth. How is it that you know about the practice in such detail?"

"When you were still a child, thirty years ago, I was a student of Abaris. Yes, even I. Like you, I had been bored with life on the Great Islands. His wandering all over the world fascinated me, and so I followed him until I coaxed him into giving me some of his 'secret teachings.' Then, again like you, I went off by myself and practiced with furious intensity. Nightly, I would fly out of my body and struggle with demons and witches. I would draw secret sounds up and down the inside of my spine, enjoying the energy, the private, secret ecstasy. Each day I would lift up the sun, and at night I moved the stars about. I became the Ruler of all the universes. Then one morning I decided I did not want the sun to rise in the east, but in the west instead. When it did not, I became enraged, and I stood up to strike it. But clouds came up suddenly between me and the sun, and it began to rain. It was then that I realized that I was mad and that Abaris was an old fool, playing with phantoms. Like little boys who play with their penises, but have no understanding of sexuality, Abaris played with his psyche, but had no real understanding of spirituality. The secrets of the spirit are in matter, not in the psyche."

"That is most certainly true, Your Holiness," the Archon said, "and yet I must say that I am amazed at the capacity of the dream-body to change the etheric conductivity of the blood. The blood does seem to be a physical medium that interacts with the etheric and psychic dimensions in the most amazing ways."

"I am not denying the existence of the dream-body and its imagery," the High Priest answered. "I am simply denying the wisdom of constructing a whole religion, or a whole civilization, on so limited a foundation. Eiru is an example of what happens when you do that. It is a culture of poetry and thatched huts. But let me put it another way."

The High Priest set down his crystal cup and picked up his white linen napkin and held it taut between his two hands: "One end is the physical world, the other end is the archetypal world of causative patterning. All the middle is the intermediate world, the world of the psyche. It is a shifting gaseous atmosphere of clouds and wind, not the world of the stars beyond, or the solid earth underneath." Then he overlapped one end on the other, and holding it by the corners, let the middle sag down.

"Of course, I agree with Your Holiness," the Archon said, "for this has been the basis of my work. But I am finding new things out every day. To use your own metaphor, the shifting and unstable atmosphere is the means by which the solar radiation is rendered usable by living things on the solid earth. Perhaps this pyschic world takes the causal patterning and renders it into organic form through the power of psychic imagery. I must say that our shaman from the East seems to be having a profound effect on the psyches of the children. He's an amateur, of course, compared to Abaris, and I think it a pity that Abaris refused to work with us, for our progress would have been much faster."

"You asked Abaris to work in the Institute?" Viracocha asked quietly, forcing himself to stay calm, as he felt again his violent rage whenever he looked at the Archon.

"He didn't, but I did," the High Priest said. "I had been informed that Abaris' travels had been increasing, and that his spider web had become world-wide. I was curious about him and we had a discussion concerning him in the Supreme Council. Then one day he simply showed up. I am told that he just sailed into the bay, docked at the quai of the Sacred College, and walked up the processional ramp, wearing that old medallion of his as if it were some kind of protection. He appeared in the throne room unannounced and said directly that unless I dismissed the Archon and closed down the Temple Institute that we would create, what he with his love of ghosts, called a civil war among the elemental spirits of the earth. I found it amusing to look at this sorcerer standing in the middle of the City of Knowledge and making pronouncements about the future of civilization on the basis of his traffic with the dead."

"Yes, I remember that day very well," the Archon said, turning toward the High Priest and so making only his paralyzed right side visible to Viracocha. "You asked him to help us, that we had need of someone who was so skilled in projecting out of the physical body and manipulating psychic images, but he, unfortunately, refused."

"Yes," the High Priest laughed, "he made one of those dramatic gestures he was so fond of, and the Palace guard took it as a threatening gesture and shot him with a fatal dart. I will give the old man credit though, he did go out with style. He looked at me as he pulled out the dart, and said: 'You wish to take hold of this body? Here, take it, but the body of the earth will take you.' Then he rolled up his eyes and his soul went out through the top of his skull, and he became the ghost he always wanted to be. His way is not for us. No, Your Grace, your music interests me much more than his magic, for your music is the wedding of cosmic, archetypal structures and physical sounds. Abaris' soul is still out there floating in the psychic sea, but your music goes directly up from the ground of the flesh to the archetypal realm."

"I confess, Your Holiness," the Master said, looking down into his cup, "that when you first proposed His Grace here to me as a candidate for the Sacred College, I was shocked. He was so young, and, well, unknown, outside the inner circle, so to speak. But now I can see what you are driving at. Altering the body through sound and music, accelerating the whole rate of evolution, it is certainly more exciting than jabbering with the dead."

"I am glad that Your Excellency sees the pattern now, for you notice," the High Priest said, looking at Viracocha, "that it is a question of seeing the *whole* pattern. It is one thing to run a College of the traditional forms of knowledge, another thing to run an Institute devoted to the new sciences, and yet another to compose a great piece of music. But what a High Priest must do is create a civilizational form in which all of these are possible.

But now to honor the art of cooking, let us move on to the contemplation of the main dish."

The High Priest extended his hands to left and right and immediately four servants removed the wine vessels, and four more servants set down the new dish before them, and brought with it a decanter of a clear white wine.

Viracocha studied the lovely pattern and colors of the spiral terrine before him. Each layer was a different food that faded into the color of the next turn of the spiral. The pastry shell that held it together was almost translucent, but it was impossible to tell what each layer was composed of, nuts or marinated mushrooms, and yet each turn of the spiral was distinctly different in taste, progressing from mild to spicy. At the center was a fruit that he had never tasted before; it was peppery and sweet, and yet seemed as if it had been marinated in dry mead. The basic idea of the dish seemed to be one of opposites held in unresolved tension: hard and soft, sweet and sour, savory and bland, hot and cool. And there in the very core of it all was that exotic fruit, the burning sweetness of the truth the dry mead was sure to bring out.

They ate in silence throughout the main course as once again the harpist played softly, but this time he had altered the tuning to play in the Hyperborean semitones. As Viracocha listened, the five layers of the spiral in the terrine, the five Hyperborean Solids, and the five modes all began to dance in his imagination, and he found himself thinking about the five levels of being, the worlds associated with each of the subtle bodies. The worlds spiraled around one another in Viracocha's imagination, and he could see each world feeding off the world below, just as he fed off this world on his plate.

As he considered all the images in a grand fugue in his imagination: the dish, the subtle bodies, the Hyperborean Solids, the five modes, and the five levels of being, Viracocha realized just how saturated with mead the small fruit of truth really was. But he no longer cared. He wanted to know about these other levels of being. As he looked up from his empty glass plate when the servant took it away, he noticed that the High Priest was eyeing him intently. Very well, he thought to himself, let us find out:

"Who are the Old Ones, Your Holiness?" Viracocha asked as he sat back in his chair and returned the High Priest's penetrating gaze with one of his own.

The High Priest regarded Viracocha with a curiously serious stare. He was silent for a moment, and then he relaxed slightly and began to answer the question as if he had come to some sort of judgment:

"Without giving you a long lecture on the history of the earth, I'm afraid that I need to know just a little more about the context in which you heard about these Old Ones. Was it on Eiru?"

"Not at all," Viracocha answered. "Quite the contrary, it was in the Institute this afternoon. His Excellency told me this afternoon that the new configuration would enable one of the Old Ones to join a psychic, dream-body to the new etheric body cluster. Considering Your Holiness's dismissal of the intermediate realms, this providing of a body for a psychic wraith does not strike me as the joining of the physical and the archetypal worlds."

"So now I must turn to you, Your Excellency," the High Priest said, leaning into the corner of his chair as he turned toward the Archon, "to provide me with a little more of the context of your remarks about the Old Ones."

"Yes, by all means, Your Holiness. Actually, this seems like the perfect moment. I was going to ask Your Holiness about the Old Ones, but our attention was so taken up with these military matters the last month, that we haven't had the time to explore these more theoretical matters of research. Also, I'm not quite sure that we have enough information yet, but what we seem to be finding is that as we energize the blood with sound, we seem to create a heightened receptivity to the intermediate realms. In our evolutionary ascent, we seem to be effecting a recapitulation of history, and the Old Ones are irresistibly drawn to our work."

The High Priest became strangely silent and it seemed to Viracocha as if some fascinating division or fault line had just opened up between them. He hadn't a clue as to what it all meant, but he saw the opening and he knew that he wanted to explore it further:

"I must confess my ignorance of history or mythology, or whatever it is we are talking about here, but the subject seems to be becoming even more mysterious."

The High Priest continued to stare at the Archon but clearly addressed his remarks to Viracocha:

"Mythology is simply a garbled form of the prehistory of earth. When our ancestors came to this world, it was not uninhabited."

The High Priest relaxed his hold on the Archon and turned to face Viracocha:

"On the physical plane there were two different species of hominids, but the dominant presence was on the etheric plane. When the solar system took its present form, after the explosion of the binary star, these beings were constrained to this world. Not wishing to disrupt the terms of 'the war in heaven,' when our ancestors came they made an agreement with these Old Ones that no attempt would be made to disturb their dominance on the planet. At first, this agreement was kept, but then after a considerable length of time, one of the species of hominids began to reach an evolutionary threshold, and this caught the interest of one faction of our ancestors. This group could not resist the temptation to facilitate the hominids in crossing that threshold, so they violated the agreement. They called their project 'Teaching the Serpent How to Fly,' using as a metaphor for their work the fact that both the snake and the bird had evolved from a common genus . . ."

"And is that why Abaris wore a medallion of the winged serpent?" Viracocha asked, beginning also to wonder about the sources for his vision on the island in the lake at Tiahuanaco.

"Abaris would have liked to think that his Order of the Winged Serpent goes as far back as all that, but that is an act of vanity, religious fantasy, and mythically self-created history. We're talking about millions of years, Your Grace, and there are no human institutions that can span that length of time. But, as I was saying, these Old Ones were furious at this interference with life on earth, for when the hominids crossed over the evolutionary threshold, the balance of energy was upset, and a great deal of energy began to pass over into the physical world. To use a metaphor, the Old Ones fed off the subtle energies, both etheric and psychic, that emanated from the animals. When the hominids crossed over into consciousness, then that etheric and psychic energy was no longer available to them. Instead, the group-soul of the hominids began to be its own collector to take its subtle energies directly from the sun, so that . . ."

"In other words," Viracocha interjected, "they did what we are trying to do again on another turn of the spiral, and so the Old Ones are drawn back into the scheme."

"So it would seem, but there is more that I need to know from His Excellency before I can determine the nature of their involvement. But to finish the story, so that we can choose our own appropriate response, the Old Ones became the enemies of the new hominids and constantly tried to pull them back. Basically, they used religious forms of inspiration, establishing various rituals of blood-sacrifice that enabled them to feed again off the subtle energies, and as well to pull the hominids back into the ancient collective animal psyche.

"That was when one of our ancestors, in this case, a female, took the forbidden step of having actual sexual relations with one of the most advanced of the hominids. From this union our race came into being. But with this intrusion, hostility broke into outright war, and the Old Ones, exercising their control over the etheric forces of the earth, pulled the entire Lemeurian Continent down into the sea. Scarcely any of the two species survived. Our ancestors, these 'Singers from the Pleiades' that His Excellency the Master asked you about, came to our aid and came between ourselves and the furious Old Ones. The Old Ones, having lost their evolutionary lead, were beginning to degenerate. This, by the way, is what I fear for us, if we don't press on and escape our planetary confinement. The new race was removed to Hyperborea, which was a continent then, and a treaty was established whereby the humans were restricted to the physical plane, and the Old Ones were restricted to the intermediate realms. The direct solar access was not taken away from the humans, but the Old Ones had the mineral and plant domains for their fields of energy. One faction agreed to cooperate with the Singers from the Pleiades, and they lifted this continent out of the sea to become our future home. But the other faction refused. There was civil war among them. At the end of that war, a new arrangement was established whereby the Pleiadean side of the Old Ones had dominance over the etheric, and the losers withdrew completely into the subtler intermediate realms. With their powers reduced, they became homeless exiles, filled with jealousy and an impotent rage. The Singers from the Pleiades remained for a while, until life on this continent was well established, and then they withdrew. The Hyperboreans insist that there were continual sexual relations between the Pleiadeans and themselves; in fact, they made sexuality into some sort of ritual, much as the Old Ones had turned blood and death into an atavistic ritual. But this is all superstitious nonsense. The way to alter the genetic linkage is not through clumsy forms of sexual reproduction, but through music and sound. The immaculate conception of the future will be with music. Eventually, we will have bodies of pure musical geometry; then we will have purged these hominids out of us entirely. So, you see, Your Grace, now you know why your music is so important, and just how in you the Sacred College and the Temple Institute can become united. Or should we say, 'Your Excellency' rather than 'Your Grace'?"

Both the Archon and the Master were shocked and felt uncomfortable as they realized that the ritual of the Meal of Truth was moving rapidly in a direction they had not expected.

Viracocha said nothing for a moment, drank down his cup of wine in a single move, and then slowly returned it to the marble table.

"Not yet, Your Holiness, not yet. You move too fast even for me, for I still do not know if *His* Excellency our esteemed Archon is working for one faction of the Old Ones, or the other."

"I'm sure I have no idea," the Archon said with an aloofness that tried to float at a level above the atmosphere of political intrigue the High Priest had introduced into the discussion. "I shall need to ask the shaman tomorrow when he goes into trance and starts channeling these Old Ones. By tomorrow your metallic rendering of the Hyperborean Solids should be in place within the foundation vault, so tomorrow should be time enough to find out what this is all about. Biology, much more than history, is my field. I confess that most of this is rather new to me. In fact, some of this I am hearing for the first time."

"One aspect of the period of initiation," the High Priest said, "is that the old High Priest must take the new one into training. In that period, the successor is given the true and complete history of this planet. There is more than I have presented here, but only the successor himself is permitted to know. Human beings, it would seem, cannot stand too much reality. Now, Your Excellencies, the time has come for us all to share the cup."

Once again the High Priest extended his arms out, and once again the four servants cleared the table of all the dishes and goblets of wine. When the table had been cleared and wiped clean, one servant set a crystal goblet of the golden dry mead before the High Priest. His Holiness waited for the servant to disappear into the darkness, and then, taking the cup, he lifted it with both hands. Through the facets of the crystal, it seemed to Viracocha as if the High Priest had a dozen eyes. Then he lowered the cup and drank a fourth of it, and passed it to the Archon.

The Archon took it with his one good hand, drank the second fourth, and passed it on to Viracocha. Viracocha took the cup, rotated it so that the place the Archon had touched would be away from his own lips, and drank half of the remaining mead before he passed it to the Master. The Master held the cup aloft with both hands trembling, and then drained it. As he set the cup down, he closed his eyes and looked down. He seemed visibly shaken, and the High Priest did not wait for him to return the cup, but reached over to place it perfectly in the center of the table.

And there it sat, an empty vessel of invocation on a table that had become an altar in some ceremony unknown to Viracocha. The Archon closed his eyes, and the Master kept his head down, but he seemed to be clasping his hands tightly together under the table. Very slowly, the High Priest sat back and touched his fingertips together and looked at Viracocha, who did not try to avoid his stare or follow the example of the others to close his eyes.

Viracocha watched the eyes of the High Priest go out of focus, and he might have grown nervous at the thought of him examining his aura were it not for the fact that he began to see the High Priest's emanation. A deep dark and midnight blue seemed wedded to a powerful red creating an evening purple more vivid than any sky he had ever seen before. Then the High Priest's faces began to change, slowly at first, then with an increasing speed as face after face flickered and then disappeared. Were they all the faces of his previous incarnations, Viracocha wondered, or the images of all his possibilities?

Viracocha would have continued to study the High Priest's face, except that his attention was now drawn to the Master, for he had begun to sob silently, and tears were streaming down his face.

"I can't take it anymore. The stars, they're too frightening. I don't want to hear anymore about these spirits and these demonic wars. The stars, the stars frighten me. I don't want the Tower. I don't want the Tower. I don't want any of it. Leave the stars alone! Leave me alone! I don't want any of it."

Viracocha looked from the sobbing figure of the Master, slumped down in his chair, to the High Priest, whose eyes were still set in their unfocused gaze. He could feel the presence of the mead working inside himself, and yet he felt nothing except disgust at the sight of the Master and anger at the Archon, who had closed his eyes, seeming to be bored with the whole ritual.

And yet, Viracocha thought, the Archon may be right after all; the whole ritual was a farce, for nothing could be changed with this moment of mead-induced truth. They would all go on just as before: the Master would blubber, but return to hide from the stars with his studies of astronomy, the Archon would go on torturing children, and the High Priest would go on babbling about the secret thread that ties College to Institute, and City to Civilization. The whole thing was a stupid farce, for what difference would the Truth make to these people?

Viracocha reached out and seized the cup, turned it upside down, and smashed it down on the table. The High Priest's eyes snapped back into focus as he looked at Viracocha, and then at the cup, which had cracked but not yet broken apart.

"I have had enough of this stupid, meaningless ritual," Viracocha said as everyone stared at him in shock. "In fact, I have had just about enough of everything. Here we are building a Tower that is aimed at cracking open the heavens and stealing primacy from the sun, and the Chief Astronomer is afraid of the stars, and the Archon is sucking the blood out of children to draw down devils that have hated the human race since the foundation of the world. Good God! What on earth do you two demented fools *think* you are doing?"

A wry smile crossed the lips of the Archon, as if to say that he was glad that his suspicions about Viracocha had been confirmed, but the Master stared at Viracocha in disbelief and his tear-reddened eyes appeared as pink and bulbous as his bald head. The High Priest looked at Viracocha for a moment, and no trace of emotion or judgment escaped him. Then slowly he turned to the Archon:

"He has a point, Your Excellency. You do seem to have gotten in over your head. You should have come to me at once as soon as the shaman began to channel the Old Ones."

"Your Holiness!" the Archon exhaled in quiet but still expressed exasperation. "We have not exactly been idle these last months, and in spite of illness and an aborted revolution, we have still managed to keep this project on schedule for the feast of Sauwyn. I was fully intending to bring this matter to you, but I needed more information. And so I decided to complete the test with the shaman and the dozen subjects. Then His Grace's proposal for the use of the Five Hyperborean Solids was sent over, and so I decided to test it all together, and then report to you. If I reported to Your Holiness every day, I think neither one of us would get much work finished."

"The principle of what you say is true," the High Priest said, "but you need to develop greater sensitivity to the whole context in which you work. When you shifted your studies from captives and criminals to pregnant women from Anahuac, you did not give me sufficient notice, and we had an insurrection on our hands, a native insurrection that quickly promised to develop into a military coup. Then you went on with the studies of children, and now this working directly with the Old Ones."

"I wouldn't call it 'working with' the Old Ones, Your Holiness," the Archon said. "When the shaman in trance spoke about conception, and providing a body for the Old Ones, I was more interested in his words about conception than Old Ones, simply because we had not yet progressed from our studies of the children to conception itself. Since the shaman seemed to be anticipating our work and your instructions about 'immaculate conception,' I became interested. I would have informed Your Holiness sooner or later."

"And I am telling Your Excellency that it should have been sooner rather than later," the High Priest said with finality.

The Archon bowed his head in silent submission, but even before he could raise it, Viracocha blurted out:

"And I am telling both of you that it should have been *never* with the whole project. This rage for transcendence or escape, or whatever it is, is insane. To escape death we seem to be inflicting it all around us."

"Stop!" the Master screamed with his pink eyes bulging in a rage against disorder. "This is against all the rules of our society! You can't do this! I can hardly call you, 'Your Grace.' You're a disgrace! Your Holiness, are you going to permit this outrage in our presence!"

The High Priest kept his eyes on Viracocha in complete fascination with the move he had just taken, but with a casual and contemptuous wave of the hand at the Master, he dismissed him:

"You are excused, Your Excellency. Leave these matters to your superiors and go back to your cloister. You will find nothing outrageous there."

The Master stood up quickly, looked at Viracocha as if to say, "Now you are going to learn your lesson," and then he bowed quickly and turned to leave as he snapped his fingers impatiently at one of the pages to open the door and so honor his exit with ceremonial dignity.

The High Priest never took his eyes off Viracocha as he waited for the Master to leave and the door to close. The only sound was of the fingers of the Archon lightly tapping on the marble table. Once again the High Priest regarded Viracocha's aura in that diffuse, examining stare. After a moment, he took a deep breath, and returned his eyes to normal focus. Almost as if he had come to some final judgment, he looked without anger or malice and spoke sympathetically to Viracocha:

"I am sorry, truly sorry, Viracocha, that you have made your decision against us. I had hoped for more from you, but human beings are curious animals, and sometimes when they come near power or success, they run from it in a fear they like to think of as innocence. Since you choose to remain within the prison of your ignorance, you give me no choice but to place you under house arrest and confine you to the guest rooms within the Institute. If you are right about the danger of the project, then your term of arrest will be short, as catastrophe overtakes us all. But if, as I think, you are wrong, then perhaps you will come to your senses to realize that you are not omniscient.

"And since you are not omniscient, let me tell you a few things you do not understand, things you can think about when you are in your new quarters.

"Let us suppose we stop the project. What then: The kairos of our time is lost, and we fall down into another cycle of 25,920 years. I doubt very much whether our civilization, or even any priesthood with knowledge, will be intact when we come to the opportunity of the next opening. You seem to have a particular sensitivity to death in the illusion that the individual organism is some sort of solid foundation on which to build a civilization. Well then, consider the future. War has a way of stimulating more wars. Consider a time when the High Priest is weak, and the military class succeeds in displacing the Priesthood. Consider a cycle of 25,920 years in which dreary militaristic empire follows dreary militaristic empire. All music will be marching songs, all science simply the cunning craft of weapons. When the next opportunity comes along for humanity, what traditional body of knowledge will be intact to enable us to move beyond this dull eternal round? No, by then humanity will have sunk so deeply into warfare that there will be no spiritual knowledge surviving anywhere, and this planet will become the place where the human race is buried alive.

"You object to the people who have died in the Institute, though it can't be more than a hundred, perhaps two. Well, add up all the deaths from wars that are going to come in the next cycle. Whole cities burned to the ground. Pregnant women with their bellies ripped open and the fetus put to their breasts by laughing soldiers. And perhaps someday the military mind will learn how to destroy continents, or the whole planet. Then humanity will have to wait in suffering for another solar system to evolve and carry them to the point where we are now. For what great destiny are you saving humanity, you young, ignorant fool?"

"I don't see the difference," Viracocha said in defiance, "between the soldiers disemboweling pregnant women and what is now going on in the Institute. Except for the fact that the women and children of the future will at least be able to die. The soldiers won't be able to go after them to continue the torture in the space between life and death, but we will. And perhaps soon with the help of the Archon's colleagues, the Old Ones, we will know how to continue the torture long after death, so the wretch is prevented from escaping in death or life. Of course, that is all assuming that our Lord the Archon is an infallible genius. But let's assume he's not. Let's assume he and I are both wrong: no opening and no earthquake. Do you think he will release his addiction to human blood? Do you think he'll say, 'No more experiments for 25,920 years'? I doubt it! No, His Excellency has seen a more powerful reflection of himself in the eyes of the children glazed over with terror."

"All life is supported by terror," the Archon said with cold contempt for Viracocha's hot passions. "Your self-deluding sentimentality is disgusting, disgusting because under the pretense of knowledge you refuse to see. Had you the sensitivity of a savage, you would hear the tree scream as it is cut down to make wood for your harp. Personally, I would prefer it if beauty were the foundation of life, if all beings did not eat one another to live, that stars did not periodically explode, wiping out whole solar systems, or that galaxies in their epochal swing did not sometimes collide with other galaxies. But I was not consulted on the design of the universe, but the mocking archangel who built life on a foundation of terror seems somehow to manage to keep the universe in some kind of order. And so I accept that, even learn from that to use death and terror as merely the tools of Order that they truly are."

"You don't accept death," Viracocha answered with his anger fully released. "You hate it. You take it as a personal insult. The mocking archangel you describe is your own self-image thrown up in the sky. You inflict torture on others because you think that if you, great as you are, have to be subjected to this slow and rotting death that takes bits and pieces of your body and removes them from the control of your will, that lesser beings have no right to object if they become one with your half-dead body." Viracocha turned from the Archon to look at the High Priest:

"Here we sit eating the delicate vegetarian cuisine of adepts. Well, why don't we all be honest with ourselves and serve up the tender fetus? We sit here in elegance, but really we should be sitting around the roasting spit, waiting for the great belly to boil and burst to drop the fetus onto our plates."

"My, what an imagination Your Grace seems to possess!" the Archon exclaimed in a mockingly jovial tone. "But you don't seem to understand civilization. Everything in the Pyramid of Life feeds off the creatures underneath it, as savages feed off animals. When we moved up to become civilized, it did mean that we were entitled to feed off savages, but not literally in the way you suggest. Because we are now beings of knowledge, we feed off them through science, just as you as an artist feed off society to produce your music. And just as the artist sentimentalizes his perception of mental suffering to make his work sad or tragic, so we rationalize pain to put it to the higher use of knowledge."

As if the word "pain" were a signal, Viracocha brushed his thoughts of restraint aside, seized the fork at his side, and lunged toward the Archon, who moved quickly enough to avoid the stab touching his head or neck, but could not move fast enough out of the chair to avoid the thrust striking his shoulder. The High Priest touched his ruby ring to the receptive-crystal in the arm of his chair and Viracocha could hear the guards running from out of the darkness at the end of the hall. But the sound he paid much more attention to was the scream of the Archon.

"There! Rationalize that!" Viracocha said as he twisted the tines around to enlarge the wound.

The guards grabbed Viracocha by the arms, but the High Priest held up his hand to stop them. Viracocha did not take his eyes off the Archon but watched the blood soak through the silk of his robe.

"There," Viracocha said with satisfaction, "you see the pain is real, and its reality takes place *in* and only *in* the individual. So much for your theories of the abstract human race, or your Pyramid of Life."

The Archon leaned back for support into the corner of his chair, reached up with his single good arm, pulled the fork out, and set it down on the table. Slowly and with dignity, he rose, bowed to the High Priest, and then picking up the napkin to stanch his wound, he turned to face Viracocha:

"I see that when our passionate artist loses the argument, he also loses his mind and resorts to force. Interesting revelation, don't you think? I, for one, will gladly accept this pain and rationalize it, for in revealing yourself tonight you have saved me from the pain of having to work with you in the Institute, and, perhaps, you have even saved our society from the pain of having you in a position of power.

"Your Holiness, may I be excused?"

The High Priest said nothing, but with a wave of the hand, he dismissed the Archon. Then with a deep breath of acceptance he folded his fingertips together and looked over his hands to consider Viracocha:

"You didn't have to blurt out your feelings here," the High Priest said calmly. "You could have observed your feelings without acting on them, for that is the training for which the mead is used. But you are so self-important in your moral outrage that you think that if you have a feeling, why then the whole world should have it too. And that may be all well and good for an artist, but when you walked out of the ranks of the College, you showed me that you were interested in Power, in what holds a civilization together and not simply the voices of a choir. But you have failed, Viracocha. Think about that during the long days of your confinement. You, the brilliant and fast Viracocha could not get beyond your own emotions to understand the impersonal nature of Power. And as you think about your own emotional life, ask yourself just where your moral indignation is coming from, and why it can so easily flip over into cruelty. There is no cruelty in the Archon. He uses terror the way the sculptor uses a hammer and chisel, not to 'hurt' the rock, but to make Order out of chaos. But his cold and impersonal use of terror, like your hot and personal use of emotion, is unstable. Just as you flip over from dramatic moralism to cruelty, so he could flip into a self-dramatizing saintliness to become something like old Abaris. You see, the reason that I am the High Priest, and that neither you nor the Archon could be, is that I know another level. You are fond of beauty and self-expression, His Excellency is fond of terror and the illusion of impersonal control it gives him, but the universe is neither wholly beautiful nor terrible. His Excellency wishes to extend his range of control from life into death. You simply want to extend the theater of your personal expression from music into governance. Ironic, isn't it? You can't even govern your tongue. Ruled by your feelings, and deceived as you are with your own perception of yourself as a 'good' man, you would make a very dangerous High Priest indeed. The Theocracy was ruled by 'good' men before. They didn't do much good.

"Well, your training is over, Viracocha. You didn't even last a single day. You should have stayed a garden flower in the College, for now you're going to become a potted plant. Perhaps you can turn the sadness of your confinement into great music composed under tragic circumstances. If not, and if I see that you are degenerating, I will honor your gifts and mercifully order your execution."

"You're sending me to prison," Viracocha said in a struggle

against the wave of exhaustion he felt coming over him, "but I think you'll find that you've built only a slightly larger cell for yourself. Even you must see from this evening that neither the Archon nor the Master serves your vision. You're all locked into your cells of private fears and obsessions. You alone rule, and you rule alone, and no one will ever succeed you. You have nothing to pass on, small wonder that your obsession is of solitary escape."

The High Priest stared at Viracocha, but Viracocha did not try to avert his gaze with the customary bow. Instead, he kept his eyes locked onto the High Priest as he took the three steps back and turned to be taken away by the guards. But even as he passed into the corridor, Viracocha still continued to imagine the High Priest seated upon his throne and enclosed within a geometrical lattice of light.

The touch of failure or misfortune for Viracocha was always a physical sensation, as if someone had pulled out the stop that held his blood in place. He could feel precisely the point in his abdomen where the life-force would pour out of him. Within seconds exhaustion would overwhelm him and his mind would drop into sleep as if he had been drugged. Mercifully, some higher part of his being knew better than to let his consciousness continue its collapse into depression or to let his powerful imagination loose in unending morbidity, and so it simply took his mind away for safekeeping.

So habitually supported was his personality by the joys of confidence and creativity that when they were not there, he did not know how to make do with life. If he was not filled, he was empty. Life had no meaning by itself for him; it had to be given meaning in the act of creation. Failure, therefore, was all the more threatening, and deep and abject depression was the shadow to all his creativity. Fortunately for Viracocha, he had not failed very often, had not felt more than once or twice in his life that heavy crush of annihilation as that black shadow became the form and measure of himself.

But just as he did not know where his sudden intuitions came from, so he did not know where the rescuing oblivion of sleep sprang from. All that he knew was that it was his salvation, for whenever he awakened out of that sleep of defeat, he did so with renewed dedication and formidable strength that had been somehow smuggled into his body under the cover of night.

As the guards had led him out of the Palace, it was the irony of his situation that had first struck him. On the same day that the High Priest had suggested that he might become the successor to the throne, he was being led away to imprisonment in the Institute. But then as he began to reflect on all the other events of that single day, his sense of irony faded into exhaustion. The High Priest had been right: he did not need to speak out, to try to triumph over them all as if it were some collegial debate. He could have remained silent and cunning, waiting for the right moment to spring to attack. But he was habituated to exhibiting himself and the contents of his own mind, so he had accepted the pull of the mead and blurted out everything.

The guards must have thought that Viracocha had passed out in terror as they approached the copper doors of the Institute; perhaps they even grumbled about the weakling as they carried him through the doors, up the staircase to the left, and down the long corridor to the apartment built into the living rock of the cliffs above the sea. And perhaps it was with some degree of satisfaction as well as relief, that they had thrown the body onto the bed and pulled the curtains around his imprisonment.

When Viracocha awoke at dawn he thought the bed itself was his cell. It was not until his fingers touched the curtains that he realized he could part the walls and step out onto the balcony that overlooked the sea and the neighboring island.

His prison was really a guest apartment for dignitaries visiting the Institute. It had a large living room and a dining table, and a bedroom separated from the sitting room by a series of sliding panels of translucent wafers of thinly sliced and polished rocks. Both the bed and the bath faced out to the balcony that looked on to the sea. But it was the bath that seemed to proclaim the luxury of the space. With its hot-spring-fed waterfall that cascaded down the enclosing rocks to fill a pool large enough for a sybarite with more than one attendant concubine, it showed that it had been built to impress its guests with the fact that the Institute was a good deal more than a laboratory.

After Viracocha had explored his new surroundings, he began to explore his own feelings. He knew that he should be afraid and he could not understand why he was not. He could remember no dream to account for any change of mood, for he had not awakened slowly out of sleep into drifting thoughts. His eyes had snapped open and his mind was instantly and completely alert. Once he had determined the shape of his imprisonment, he began to set his mind to the feelings of new resolve concerning his future. But resolve to do what? he wondered, and the more he tried to think about this peculiar feeling of resolve, the more confused he became.

Viracocha paced back and forth on the balcony that ran along the entire length of the apartment, but as the day began to lighten, his thoughts began to darken. An oppressive feeling of shame began to creep over him in the brightening dawn as he realized that his impulsive trip to Eiru had endangered Brigita, and with Brigita in custody, Bran might not be so eager to fly off, but might try some foolish effort of rescue that could endanger the escape of the 144. As his mood began to shift he found himself even staring over the wall of the balcony in consideration of the certain death that lay far below on the surf striking the broken rocks. In moments like that he knew he was indulging himself in histrionics of shame and despair and his inner voice seemed to ridicule his need to think or to feel, when clearly neither thought nor moods were of any use at all in that particular moment. What was of use was patience, but the fast Viracocha simply was not a patient man.

And so he paced back and forth in useless exercises of useless thoughts and feelings until at last he began to grow bored with the endless circles and decided that he would meditate to get above the confusion of rational investigation and irrational moods. It was then, as he turned away from the balcony, that he heard the knock on the door and the shuffle of several feet and went into the bedroom to see what was going on.

He noticed first the soldier carrying the stretcher and saw the other soldier before he saw the long hair trailing over the side and almost touching the floor. When the soldier turned to move to the bed, he recognized Brigita at exactly the same moment that he caught sight of the Archon coming through the door:

"My God! What have you done to her?"

"On the contrary," the Archon said, smiling, "we have to ask you what *you* have done to her. Her servant told the pilot of her garuda that she has been like this ever since you left. I don't know what the two of you were up to on Eiru, but it would seem that she is in some kind of deep ecstatic trance."

As the soldiers lifted her onto the bed from the stretcher, Viracocha began to smell a strong odor of wild roses, and as soon as the soldiers had moved away, he leaned over the bed to determine whether it was really emanating from Brigita.

The Archon walked slowly over to the stairs but did not make an effort to come up into the bedroom. Instead, he lifted his medallion to his eye and began to examine Viracocha as he leaned over Brigita:

"Yes, it's curious, isn't it?" he said in his studiedly artificial manner. "She seems to be giving off a strong emanation of a floral scent, and if you observe her closely you will notice that she only takes a breath once a minute. Hmmmm. Fascinating. Yes, I can see that I was right in my intuition to bring her here."

Viracocha turned momentarily to see the lens-distorted eye of the Archon staring at him, but he quickly returned his glance to Brigita to consider the strangely beatific smile that rested on her full lips.

"No, there seems to be little doubt," the Archon said as he dropped his medallion to his chest. "Your etheric aura is twelve times stronger in intensity than what would be normal for a man your age, and hers practically fills the room. But the most curious thing is to observe what happens at the edges where your two auras meet. Very curious indeed."

"What are you talking about?" Viracocha said in annoyance as he turned away from Brigita to glower down on the Archon, who seemed to be smiling up at him like some doting parent.

"Yes, I think I shall have to do a few tests with the two of you later when I have finished the attunement of the crystal to the foundation vault. You two do seem to make such a lovely and interesting couple. Later, you must tell me all about your stay on Eiru."

"Will you please stop this little game and tell me what you are talking about?" Viracocha said as he noticed his anger and hatred of the Archon returning.

"Sometimes the slowness of the fast Viracocha amazes me," the Archon said in clear enjoyment of Viracocha's confusion. "It is obvious, isn't it? Our esteemed Abbess of Eiru was initiating you into some Pleiadean ritual, the results of which are that she is in a deep ecstasy in which she has slowed down the rate of time in her body, and you have increased the intensity of your etheric body enormously. As you will recall, both the metabolic rate and the etheric body are keen interests of mine. So, you can understand why I thought it was more appropriate, and perhaps even more productive of discovery, if we kept you here together. Besides, her servant says that the two of you were together for a month, so please make yourselves at home. Who knows, perhaps she will awaken from your magic kiss."

"You're disgusting!" Viracocha exclaimed quietly but intensely. "Just what do you plan to do with us?"

"Why, make you my guests, of course! Rest assured that I will not stick a fork into you. Perhaps a tube or two, but only for a few tests. In the meantime, enjoy your comfortable surroundings. Your Hyperborean Solids have given me a little work to do, but when I have finished with your helpful suggestions I will come back to bring you news of how your invention is coming along. By tonight the children should be all nicely arranged within the vault."

Viracocha moved from the bed toward the Archon in anger, but the guard lifted his catapult and aimed it straight at his chest.

"That would be useless, Your Grace," he said as he turned to walk away. He walked slowly toward the door as the two soldiers moved to come between Viracocha and the Archon.

"Oh yes, I forgot." The Archon turned back and rested both hands on his cane. "Feel free to slide the bolt to ensure your privacy. It is a little bolt, but it will ensure that the guards knock before they enter with your meals. So make this your home and feel free to resume your Eireanne way of life. Good day, Your Grace."

The Archon turned and walked out of the room, and it seemed to Viracocha that his step was lighter and less pained, as if he were indeed happy to have the two of them under his control.

Viracocha waited until the guards had left before he walked

down the stairs to bolt the door. For a moment, he leaned against the door and looked back into the bedroom, as if that little distance could give him the perspective that he needed, but from that angle he could not see her; he could only detect the odor of wild roses that was slowly filling the room. He took a deep breath and felt the odor itself entering his body. It brought knowledge, as if scent were the equal of light in bringing forms and ideas to his body, and it was his body and not his mind that responded as his penis began to lift in an erection.

With the awakening of the body came an awakening of soul, as if from opposite sides the mind was being taken in hand and lifted up to some other level. He could hear again the voice of secret instruction, less primal than the smell that excited him, it seemed to be from a world beyond smell or sight, a world of disincarnate knowing. "She is trapped in paradise," it seemed to be saying. "Only you can bring her back, but you must go back to the point at which you abandoned her." For a moment it seemed as if his mind would rise up to come between body and soul to offer its objections and interpretations, but the primal, worldly wisdom of that erection took hold of his body.

Viracocha moved away from the door and walked toward the bed. Yesterday there had been no moment in which the rush of events had allowed him to find his casual release in the embrace of a concubine. Now there was nothing in his awareness but that feeling of engorgement that the ritual of the month with her had created in him. And yet there was a difference that he could feel inside himself. The fullness was there, but the pressure was gone. There were no thoughts as to how that could be, but as if he were dreaming with his eyes open he saw the semen flowing up the spinal column while a stream of light came down from his brain. When they had touched it was as if a star was created in white light, and it was that feeling that he had misinterpreted as having his heart ripped out of his chest; it was the shock of that dismemberment and that agony of love for the children that had torn him apart and sent him puking to the floor to find his own reflection in his vomit.

But now he could feel that his body had changed. While his mind had been occupied with the politics of the Theocracy, his body had gone on about its own business, little caring whether he *knew* what was going on or not. Now he could feel with clear intensity that that pool of seminal light had been transformed by rage and pain into another essence of life. The love that he had not been able to find in the paradise of bliss where Brigita remained, he had found in hell. And now deep in the center of this hell, inside the Institute itself, he would have to return to that terror.

Viracocha came to the edge of the bed and looked down on the smile of bliss that still rested on Brigita's lips and remembered in astonishment just how he had read that beatific expression as an evil, ecstatic leer. The odor of wild roses was now very strong, but he noticed an emanation of pastel light that seemed to shift from pink to a soft amethyst whenever she would take the shallowest of breaths. He climbed up onto the bed and sat at her feet for a moment and could feel her emanation enveloping him, as if he had already entered her body.

The simple act of reaching up to pull the curtains closed around the bed not only dampened the light, but also increased his sensitivity to the slight pulsation of light that hovered a few feet above her body. Enclosed within the bed and within her aura, he felt as if he were no longer within the Institute but had entered a vessel every bit as powerful as a garuda. Secure in that space, he clasped his hands together and bowed to her, not merely to honor her but to ask permission; and then he lifted his robe over his shoulders and set it to the side.

As if it were an act of slow, walking meditation, he took hold of her ankles and very gently pulled her toward him, lifting her silk robe above her waist. Unhurriedly, reverently, like a priest folding an altar cloth, he removed her robe entirely, and then sat down cross-legged at her feet. He waited a moment until his breath had quieted, and as he gazed down at her vulva he understood why the savages of Anahuac chose to bless an object by inscribing a triangle with a line in the middle of it. The savages knew what the priests of the Theocracy did not, in their domestication of women into servants and concubines, that this softest of forms was both origin and altar, and not until he had made a vulva of his own heart and had felt it break open to give

birth to a love he had always felt to be the embarrassing, illegiti-
mate bastard of his secret life, did he dare approach this other
altar of the immediate, intimate God. With her permission, he
touched her legs to allow her thighs to encircle him. With her
permission, he lifted her back to allow her arms to encircle his
neck; and with her permission, he lifted her hips and entered
her entirely. With arms, thighs, and vulva all about him, he
closed his eyes in meditation and allowed the slowness of her
breath and the slightest pulse of her heart to draw him into the
time and rhythm of her own being. In less than an hour, their
pulse was one.

Whether she awakened or he joined her in trance, he could
not say, but slowly he felt her body open and take him up. Once
again he began to feel the strange vibration and the strong,
vortex-like sensation that felt as if it were trying to pull his
entire being into hers. He remembered the time before, remembered how his mind had interpreted this sensation first in
fear, then in panic, and finally in complete terror, but now he
knew that it had been his own self that had been the source of
that terror, the fearful author of that inadequate interpretation.
This time he would not interpret, not raise his defenses against
her. He would surrender and allow his thoughts to become
merely clouds passing through the sky. He was the sky and not
the clouds.

As he relaxed she widened enormously, unbelievably, taking
him all in: legs, hips, half of him had already disappeared into
her. He saw a vision of binary stars in space, alternately consuming one another in complete intercourse, but he felt no fear in
this vision of being utterly consumed. He felt her body move up
along his stomach and back, and then peacefully, gently, he was
completely taken in. The moistness of her vagina was soft on his
face and the taste of her moved past his lips into his mouth and
tranquilized him, as if he were sipping some richly sweet opiate.
The physical pleasure of a close and intimately embracing
peace allowed him to stretch out in relaxation to feel the caress
of her body everywhere at once all over his skin. He did not
linger there but slowly continued as he was eased up further
into the ultimate embrace of her womb. Space widened to

receive him and he began to float. The smell, the taste, the touch all over his body were so intensely enjoyable that he floated on a perfect concentration of effortless pleasure.

The sea grew enormous as he grew small, and then the sea became all space. Suspended in that infinite space, he felt no need to do anything and he knew that he could rest there forever in that absolute bliss. But no sooner had he felt the wish to rest in dark eternity that he felt the pull of motion drawing him through space as if he were moving in approach to some distant planet. And then he saw it. It must have been the earth of long ago, for it was red and molten and slowly turning. He saw it struck by a shower of meteors and he knew that these meteors and comets brought strange metals from outer space to startle this world with the possibilities of others. The red molten earth cracked open, and light met light, but not alone, not without sound. There was a music to it all that he had never heard before. There was a theme and then a complex variation on the theme as the earth underwent so many changes before his sight. He had entered down into the sky of this world and now overhead he could hear the vault of heaven respond with variations of its own. Like a primitive drumbeat moving toward some climax, the monotony of the double beat began to push him toward a shore he could not make out. He wanted more space. He wanted to float in the sea, but now there was nothing but the muffled dullness of distant sounds. Sound began to thicken but as it did, taste returned and he felt again the drugged tranquility it induced in him to allow him to relax to enjoy this moist kissing all over his body. As his head emerged into the light and he felt her lips glide down the back of his neck, he remembered the first time one of the temple concubines had taken his penis into her mouth to glide her moist lips up and down the entire length of it: this was like that but better because these erotic lips could glide down the entire length of his body at once. It felt so unimaginably good as his head emerged and her lips slid down his neck, and then down his back and legs. He hung there suspended in the light that announced that he had eyes and that she had a face, a face that drew him toward her as new lips began to kiss again. The taste of her lower lips was still lingering on his mouth as she began to kiss him as if the taste of her own life was an offering that he had brought up to her in gratitude. How lovely was this gentle tongue in his mouth, these warm living arms around his neck, and the soft words of surprise breathed into his ear:

"It's morning! We must have meditated all night!"

Viracocha opened his eyes and saw Brigita's green eyes smiling at him as she leaned back to look at him while she clasped her hands behind his neck.

"Where are we? Are we in the body, or have you magically transported me to the heaven of lovers?"

Brigita looked down in amazement as she began to notice the feeling of Viracocha completely inside of her. She shifted her hips from side to side, enjoying the new sensation of his presence within her.

"I guess we really are in the body. I've never experienced this feeling in the ethereal worlds."

She took her hands from around his neck and leaned back, pushing her hips tight against his. Her long reddish-brown hair fell like a waterfall and collected in a deep pool on the bed, and as she stretched her head back, her little breasts lifted high, and Viracocha admired again the full, soft, pink areolas whose color seemed to match the odor of wild roses that still hovered around her. As he looked at her he wondered how he could ever have seen her as plain, or how he could ever have seen her as ugly to run from her in terror. How could he not have seen the beauty that was so completely revealed to him then?

Brigita straightened her back and returned her hands to clasp them behind his neck as she looked into his eyes with a depth of feeling that needed no other expression:

"Thank you," Brigita whispered. "I'm glad that I've never experienced any of this before now. And I am glad we've both survived. I would never have come out of it without you diving down and lifting me up. I feel rather ashamed. I collapsed into myself completely and could have floated in that trap of paradise forever."

Brigita looked into Viracocha's eyes and began to comb his

hair away from his forehead with her fingers. They were silent for a moment, then Viracocha took in a breath and said:

"Well, since this is a time for naked confessions, you should know that paradise wasn't my trap. You may have collapsed in on yourself in bliss, but I exploded and ran from you in terror, completely possessed and completely out of my mind in fear. I had better tell you now where . . ."

"Not now," Brigita said as she placed her fingers across his lips. "Not now. I can feel the changes in both of our bodies. Now we need to put aside all of the restraints of the last month. Now it's time to let go."

Brigita fell back and pulled Viracocha on top of her. She smiled and kept brushing his hair back as he responded with surprise to her and struggled to unlock his legs and stretch them out against the length of hers. She quickly wrapped her legs around him and became a different woman: her thighs lifted high, her hand reaching under her legs to fondle him, her tongue fluttering in his ear. The more excited she became, the more lifted up he was. He could see and feel every center along his spine open and tremble with hers so that he could no longer tell who was male or female to the other.

Brigita's head rocked back and forth on the bed, and then her eyes opened wide in uncomprehending wonder as her body became the being she had never known in her eagerness to escape it. Like a woman completely taken over in the shock of sibylline possession, she stared at miracle and then reached up to take his head with her hands and cover his ear with her mouth. She began murmuring oracles, wild images, and then thrust these teachings of the god into his mind with her tongue. If Brigita had told him before, he might have questioned revelation, but she breathed her visions into him precisely at the moment of his own release, and so he followed her as word, image, and moving bodies became a dance.

They rolled over, as soon the continent would. And then she towered above him and as he looked up from underneath her high floating breasts, he understood that she was the only tower given to man for the return to the stars, that the "Singers from the Pleiades" had placed in both of them the true crystals that could be touched by light. With wild astonished eyes she looked down at his face between her thighs and blessed him, and then like a mother in graceful birth she reached down to lift him up to her. Face to face, kneeling in complete communion, they drank from the light-transfigured chalice of their bodies and became, not mystic vision or beatific scent, but the incarnate taste of each in the other: tasted, the way an anemone tastes the sea and opens.

Gently, with a slight downward pressure of her fingertips on his shoulders, she led him back into the seated posture of meditation, and then encircling him once more with her thighs, she sat with her arms around his neck. Lightly with her fingertips she closed his eyes, and then with one finger she touched the crown of his head. It felt as if she were opening a door, for immediately he could feel a shaft of light descending into it. She took his fingertip and placed it onto the crown of her own head for a moment only, and then she moved his hand to her waist. He could feel her heart beat against his chest and soon the beat of their hearts and the lifting tide of their breaths became one.

He could not tell whether time slowed down, or whether it took a long time for their heartbeats to disappear and their breath to stop, but he could feel that this time all was effortless and easy. As if they had removed the impediments that before had made the vibrations seem shattering, they now could simply accept and not resist the disappearance of their flesh. Viracocha saw with a colorful intensity beyond physical vision the bright centers along Brigita's spine, saw the blue light that shot out from the base of her spine into his. Back and forth, as if it were a shuttle weaving their two beings together, the light shot from center to center, from the base of the spine to the crown of the head. When the blue light reached the crown, he felt himself being pulled up out of his body completely into the light. As he emerged out of his body and hovered in the ethereal light, Brigita reached over, took his hand, and the feeling of ascent continued.

They seemed to pass into a world not built of the stark contrasts of light and shadow, but simply different qualities of light. It seemed as if the sun were shining in the sea rather than on it, and if Viracocha looked closely he could see that this ocean was composed of numberless crystalline beings, just as a field of snow is composed of numberless crystalline snowflakes. The light was never still or monotonous but was constantly changing in color and sound. How primitive and limited his lists of earthly colors now seemed to him, for he would need the names of over a hundred different kinds of white and gold. As he listened to the sounds the colors made he realized by some inner form of direct knowledge that this ocean of light was a membrane all around the earth that took in the energy of the sun, stepped it down to a safer level for animals and plants, and spread it throughout the world in all the innumerable variations of climate and weather.

The feeling of ascent continued and they passed above the ocean of light into an ambience of radiant indigo, and as he moved out of the earthly orbit he could feel a burden being lifted from him and he began to be able to think purely, no longer in words, but in the crystals he had seen when composing. As these forms moved, they rotated through more than three dimensions, and the friction of their passing through a higher dimension created a sound that was also a meaning, a glyph. The unpacking of all the information in a single crystal would take ages, for the language they generated from the crystal's unfoldment was what humans experienced as time. These crystals did not sit in space, anymore than they were located in time, but space seemed to be an emanation that came out of them. As the crystals sounded and rotated in and out of their several dimensions, Viracocha could see that in some baffling way the inside of one crystal became the outside of the other.

Still they moved higher, or deeper, for there was no longer an up or a down. The only frame of reference was the vestigial sense of holding Brigita's hand, but Viracocha knew that that was merely a habitual thought-form. Although he could "see" in a complete circle, and was no longer limited to what was ahead, still there was a horizon to his perception. And from the edge of that horizon he could see a being appear moving toward them.

He knew that something was before him, but he could not

make it out because it had absolutely no relationship to anything he had ever known. He could feel the being reach into his mind to find some frame of reference or image with which to establish a relationship, and he could sense its frustration at all the limitations his consciousness imposed. It seemed to settle for a collection of images, as if they were hints or metaphors, but not its own substantial nature. First, it became one of the multidimensional crystals of blue ice, then it shifted that image slightly so that every one of the thousand facets of the crystal had a pair of eyes staring at him in the most amazing, a-human way. He looked back at this creature of the thousand eyes in puzzlement, and then he understood the hint. His own being was polar; he had eyes at one end of his spine, organs of generation at the other, and he was more located in his head than in the other parts of his body. But this being was omnipresent in itself; it was not a polarized creature at all. Then all the crystalline facets with the thousand eyes were set into motion and it gave him the feeling of wings, of the speed of hummingbird wings. Accepting the limitations of images and perceptions, the creature moved and passed into Viracocha, and then drew Brigita inside as well. As soon as they were all "inside" one another, Viracocha lost all sense of his subtle body with its imprinted image taken from the physical body. What had been Viracocha became a geometrical lattice of light and enormous energy. What had been Brigita became the music vibrating and emanating from and around the lattice.

They became a single being. Before the foundation of the world, they were. They had only parted in an act of offering and sacrifice that made entry into the limited world of dense matter possible. Before the adventure of the world they had been with this creature of the thousand eyes in another universe entirely, and now that they had come out of the world, it had come to welcome them in the joy of return, of homecoming. In an act of recognition and communion, Brigita and Viracocha offered up to this being from another universe their own new consciousness of matter and flesh that they had brought with them out of the world. But there arose this felt difference and the communion was touched by their differences. The world of matter and flesh was inconceivable to it, and with a tone of peace and acceptance, the being moved out of them and the atmosphere began to lighten from vibrant indigo to a pearl-white iridescent with many colors.

Into this color-scape that seemed to hover at the edge of becoming a transfigured earthly landscape, the sun behind a beautiful cloud began to speak to them.

> *I am Melchizedek.*
> *I formed this earth as a vessel*
> *To receive the fall of light*
> *In which humanity descended.*
> *From Godhead humanity came,*
> *To Godhood humanity will come*
> *When time is finished.*
>
> *But you have come out of time*
> *As a twin-being only,*
> *While all the others*
> *Who went down with you*
> *Remain below in suffering*
> *And dark forgetfulness.*
> *The great being that is Humanity*
> *Has not gathered itself back*
> *Into its future form.*
> *Why do you abandon time*
> *Before it is time?*
>
> *I offered this earth as a cup,*
> *But can a cup be filled*
> *With a pulp of grapes*
> *That has not turned to wine?*
> *I offered this earth as bread*
> *For nourishment of Spirit,*
> *But a mass of dough*
> *Is neither grains nor bread.*
> *Why do you abandon time*
> *Before its time?*

You are now what you were
When you chose to descend,
But have you forgotten
Why you chose to fall?
Spirit had become a vacant sphere
Whose inner surface was
A vacant reflecting mirror.
The love you now hold
In your bright duality
You did not hold before
In your vacant solitude.
How much more will there be then,
When each is in All
And humanity reflects
Mind to Spirit, earth to sun,
And bright ecstatic carnal love
To the innocence of virgin stars?
Why then do you stand
Here two as one,
But not All as One?

But greater than the Plan
Is freedom, novelty, and creative joy.
Now if you should choose
The return to the Pleiades,
Then the Plan for earth
Must change of Necessity.
The vessel will be cracked
Where you came out of it.
The unremembering souls
Will spill and fall
Out of form to nothingness.
Not until another sun
Can shape another world
Will they be able to return.
Out of ignorance and fear
They will create hell-worlds
from their broken, aborted minds.

> *One who is beyond our sun,*
> *Even beyond our galaxy,*
> *Is preparing to descend,*
> *First in the form of*
> *Origin and Emergence,*
> *Mother and Child,*
> *Then into the life of death.*
> *Only at the end of time*
> *When Humanity was One*
> *And Earth another*
> *Would they become lovers,*
> *As you have become,*
> *To consume the world*
> *In the last copulation*
> *Of matter and of light.*
> *What you have invoked*
> *Is a future far off for humanity.*
> *But all this can change,*
> *For eternity is in love with time.*
> *You are gods*
> *And freedom is your divinity.*
> *You are free*
> *And now must choose.*

The archetypal pulse and tone of the words was in no earthly language, and both Brigita and Viracocha realized that what they were experiencing was being translated from a higher life into a familiar religious form, but just as the timbre and tone of this prehistoric language seemed to suggest a liturgy of sacred utterance, so did it seem to recall what they were before the world began. The power of this sacred language seemed to be capable of harmonizing dissonances and in its presence the creature of a thousand eyes was able to become completely one with Brigita and Viracocha. But once they were a Unity, they felt the formation of a higher pattern that Melchizedek himself could enter, and then as an unimaginably powerful quaternity they could feel the intimate emergence of a Being so cosmic that it could take form only in precisely that Unity of hitherto separate streams of universal existence. There was no thought whatsoever except the return that would make the emergence of this inconceivable level of consciousness possible in the nature of humanity. As soon as the emotion of willing their return cried out in affirmation, the cloud passed away from the sun, and Melchizedek stood before them as the Archetype of Humanity in its sublime and future form, a being in whom evil had been taken in and transformed in the erotic transfiguration of matter into incarnate light. Now in a new voice and in the natural language of Eiru, the being spoke with a voice of love and compassion that was at once everywhere in space and in the deepest recesses of themselves:

"Before there was Mind, Being was entranced with its own reflection. Love did not exist for there was nothing other to itself. When Being broke apart into beings, love became possible. The risks that you are now about to take will not be yours alone. In the opening you have made in space and time, the one you know as the creature of a thousand eyes will accompany you back to the edges of matter. And Abaris shall return to earth from the sun, and here I promise that the Fellowship of the Sun will never be absent from the earth. From here to the end of the world, it will remain on earth to guide it through its crises and seizures of hate and forgetfulness. Go now, you are a priest forever after the Order of Melchizedek."

The cloud returned to cover the sun, and then slowly, beautifully, the sun set, and they were again in the deep indigo of planetary night. A sensation of falling came over them, and as they fell they could feel their unity as a single being come apart. Now alone in a denser body, Viracocha could feel the wrenching sense of loss.

The descent continued and the spherical sense of global consciousness, in which the inside and the outside of a hypersphere were a single surface, collapsed into a merely circular field of consciousness. He felt as if he were at the edge of time and as he passed through the barrier, like someone falling into the sea, there was a splash that was more like an explosion. In that explosion, with its fragments or sparks flung out, he could see all his incarnations at once. It was not a line of life following life; rather, the fragments were the effects of the impact of his spirit with time. He knew that he was none of these incarnations truly and entirely, that they were not so much beings but relationships between his being and time. Only with the ending of time could he gather up these sparks, these fragments to make a being such as he recognized himself to be. Although each of the sparks was flung outward by the impact, yet each still had the possibility of tracing itself back to its origin, its original spirit.

But then as he fell more deeply into time, the fragments took on a more substantial reality; they seemed more solid, more like trees in a forest than sparks from a disintegrating meteor. The quality of each life seemed to be directly related to the quality of the culture in which it was embedded. In some cases, the lives were strong and flourishing; in others, weak and stunted. In some cultures, the Spirit was known and life could grow and reach up; in others, everything was forgotten or denied and the stunted beings gasped in a poisoned air.

As he looked down at the circle of his "lives," four seemed to stand out, like the points of orientation on a compass. There was the life of Viracocha, then another as a monk ten thousand years later in the Remnants of Hyperborea. There again Brigita appeared as a mate, but in that culture sexuality was forbidden as sinful and they chose not to meet in their personal lives, but simply spiritually join their different monasteries while their bodies were asleep. Then, in a later time, they were together again in Anahuac; there they struggled to remember in chastity the rituals they had experienced as Brigita and Viracocha. But they could not achieve, either in chastity or in the shame of their falling into carnal love, anything remotely close to their previous transfiguration, for the culture was hopelessly broken, and eventually the priesthood was overrun by warriors. Viracocha could see himself dying amid flames in the splendor of his priestly robes as the morning star rose over the sea. The last life was at the end of the world when they all were reunited in the consummation of time itself.

He fell, entering the circle which contracted to a point in which he became Viracocha only. There he could see Brigita once more, and he reached out in human space to take her hand. Together they continued their descent until they hovered over their physical bodies. With a renewed sense of loss, he released her hand, was drawn thickly down, and returned to a sense of the almost unbearably dense and heavy animal body.

Viracocha opened his eyes and stared into the crying eyes of Brigita. He reached over and kissed her tears, tasting the salt, and accepting it. Brigita took a deep breath, and then slowly unwound her thighs from around Viracocha's hips. She moved a little away from him and then sat back on her feet and looked down on her thighs. As Viracocha followed her eyes, he thought that her thighs looked like the iridescent coloring of an abalone shell, for the glazing of semen and blood had flown together to create a new quality of light.

"I haven't menstruated in three years," Brigita said quietly. "I really have returned to the body. Strange, isn't it, this unconscious sense of timing? That too was written on the pages I saw in my vision of the mind of the future. Along with the instructions for this ritual of love, there was a poem:

> *"Let the moon and sun*
> *become*
> *A single light.*
> *Let the red and the white*
> *Be taken in delight.*
> *When One became two,*
> *Heaven broke apart.*
> *When two become One*
> *Humanity will start*
> *Returning to the sun."*

"I wonder," Viracocha said, "if you saw the writings in a vision of the future, or, if in a life to come, you will look back on our lovemaking to write that poem?"

"Well, whatever this has been," Brigita said sadly, "it is over."

"In more ways than one," Viracocha added as he pulled back the curtains to reveal the balcony looking out to the sea. "We are back on earth in a prison all right. We were both arrested and brought back to the Institute."

Brigita looked up at Viracocha with a seriously determined look. For a moment she probed his mind to orient herself amid the danger, and then with a look of formidable resolution that revealed to Viracocha just how strong this passionate lover could be when called upon to play the role of warrior, she stepped up off the bed and extended her hand back to him:

"Come, let's bathe together before we go into battle; the fools don't know what they have made possible by bringing the two of us back together."

Perfectly at sunset, when the light behind the mountain let it take growth from its shadows, the volcano on the other island exploded. They heard the crack and then the deep percussive boom and ran from the table out to the balcony to see a sunset that was no sweet farewell to day, but a war between light and dark. Intense orange, raging scarlet, and demonic purple were more vividly present in the sky than in any sunset Viracocha had ever seen before. Light and dark fought openly as they had not since they argued over the inhabitants of the world, when the clouds were ripped apart to let in the stars and when a new celestial quiet was forced down upon the heaving earth. Now the old debate raged again, and the cloud rising up to darken the sky seemed the largest, most powerful being there could be. The claim of man to rule the earth seemed about to be hurled aside.

"It looks as if we are going to have some help," Brigita said as she gazed across the sea to the island.

"Do you think it can take care of this island to do any good soon enough?" Viracocha asked.

Brigita gave Viracocha a smile of exasperation: "I don't expect you to think like an Eireanne, but it might help you to see into the volcano if you didn't call her 'it.'"

"It's hard to break old habits," Viracocha answered. "But why a 'her' and not a 'him'?"

"We like to think of volcanoes as breasts of the Great Mother."

"I don't think that I would like to nurse on that," Viracocha said as he nodded toward the smoking cone.

"Infants don't nurse on hot blood; they nurse on the milk the blood helps to produce. It's the same for the volcano. The lava produces soil, the plants nurse on the soil, the air nurses on the plants."

There was another cracking rumble and a bright red stream of lava found the sea and sent up a great cloud of steam.

"She obviously agrees with you. What else is she telling you?"

"That your work on the Tower has helped them speed up the process of change. This explosion is a result of today's tests."

"If that explosion is coming from the Archon's tests in the foundation vault, then I have a lot to learn about how etheric waves are propagated through the earth. That explosion should have been on this island."

"It will be tomorrow, or whenever the sun strikes the solar crystal when the opening is made. This volcano is simply the beginning. All the three Great Islands will disappear. The elemental Spirit whose outer physical body is the volcano is telling me that there is war among themselves, among those you called the Old Ones. One group is using the Archon to break into the human body. He thinks he is advancing human evolution, but actually they are trying to take it over, the way a parasite takes over a host. But what this volcano is saying is that they are not going to let things go that far. They take their energy purely from the sun, and if the Tower were to succeed in displacing the primacy of the sun's position in the larger configuration, the whole solar system would be destroyed."

Viracocha imagined the new geometry; he could see the new galactic pattern disturb the inner core of the sun, could see it explode in a supernova that wiped out the entire solar system, could see the multitude of souls wandering in dreams of agony, bodiless and unevolving for the eons until another world could spin into form.

"I begin to understand what Melchizedek was talking about, if I can use the word 'talking' for that kind of communication."

"The side of the elemental Spirits that is aligned with the Hyperboreans will not allow things to go that far. They will work to destroy the Tower as soon as the sun touches the crystal. They will not allow enough time for the opening to establish itself in relationship with the distant sun."

"So, we need to get the children out of the vault tonight, and

Bran needs to leave before sunrise. It's going to be a busy night."

"Bran probably won't be able to make his move until the middle of the night," Brigita said. "And I don't think we should wait that long. The children must be in unimaginable agony. I think we should project down there now."

"Projecting down into the Tower vault in your psychic body won't help the children, Brigita. That screech of terror is oper-ating in the etheric range. I would have to get down there physically to dismantle the thing."

Brigita was silent for a moment. She closed her eyes and tried to feel her way into the vault. "But I can eliminate the thought-form the shaman is creating with the Old One."

"You've lost me there."

"The Old Ones feed off fear. The more frightened a person is, the more power they can suck away from him. The shaman is terrifying the children to create a thought-form that the Old Ones can use as a temporary vehicle, until they can enter the physical body itself."

"It sounds like a nightmare," Viracocha said.

"That is what nightmares are. But if I project down there, I can eliminate the shaman's thought-form and that will force the Old One to withdraw out of the etheric."

"But what if the Old One goes after you, Brigita?"

"They can't, unless of course, one is afraid. If one has no fear, one can walk right through them and they disperse like a mi-rage in hot air. I'll deal with the Old Ones, but I'm going to have to leave the screech of terror to you. Since I don't understand how it's being produced, I don't know how to annul it."

"It would be easy enough to annul it on the physical plane, but to annul it on the etheric, one would have to hear it even before you could get near it, and I certainly don't look forward to that. But what makes you think I can just pop out of my body and follow you down there? You know I'm no good at that sort of thing."

"You didn't seem to have any difficulty this morning, and that voyage was far more elevated than anything I have ever experi-enced before. We went far above the etheric and psychic realms. Perhaps if we come together again and align the spinal centers, we could become a single being with the angel and shatter the crystals that are generating the vibration."

"That might work," Viracocha said as he tried to imagine how to produce a counter sound to cancel out the frequency of the oscillating crystal. "And if we fail, there isn't a nicer way to die. But what if we fail, what then?"

"As we all die in the morning when the volcano explodes, I'll take the children to Abaris' school, but I guess you'll have to try to find a life in Tiahuanaco. It would certainly be better if that doesn't happen."

"Well, then, I guess that's the plan," Viracocha said with a smile as he reached out to take Brigita's hand. But before he could turn to lead her back to the bed, there was a loud knock on the door.

"It's the Archon," Brigita said quietly as Viracocha looked toward the door. "We'll have to work alone to start with."

The knock sounded again, but this time more loudly. Viracocha moved toward the door, but he did not hurry. There was a third knock by the time he came to the door and opened it.

It was the Archon, the Archon and four guards. Two of the guards entered before him and held their catapults aimed at Viracocha.

"Good evening, Your Grace. The servants who brought you your dinner passed on the good news that Her Reverence, our esteemed Abbess, was up and about. You do seem to have many talents. Ah, and there she is."

Brigita came in from the balcony and stood at the top of the stairs between the bedroom and the living room. She stood there silently looking at the Archon in that unfocused way that told Viracocha that she was trying to find out as much about her enemy as she could. The Archon returned the compliment by lifting his medallion to stare at Brigita through its crystal.

"Fascinating!" the Archon said. "The two of you do make such an interesting couple. Good evening, Your Reverence. It is an honor to have you here as our guest. It is not often that we have a guest with such amazing faculties, and so I hope you won't mind if we request your presence in the examining room. It's only a matter of some routine tests to measure the intensity of the etheric radiance."

Viracocha flinched and was ready to jump, but the guard immediately placed a restraining hand on him. As soon as one guard moved, the other grabbed him while the other two pointed their catapults at him.

"Don't be alarmed, Your Grace. I will return for you in an hour or so. You will, no doubt, be glad to know that your model works beautifully. We induced the frequencies into the metallic rods and tested the first two of the frequency-signatures. Tomorrow at dawn we shall be able to test the third. You might be interested to know that our shaman has been in touch with the Old Ones who interest you so much, and he tells us that this volcanic eruption was to relieve the strain and the pressure on the crust, as well as to provide a release passage for tomorrow's activities. So, you may put aside your anxieties about an earthquake. Right now, all is prepared. The children are sleeping comfortably in the foundation vault with all your lovely Hyperborean geometry around them. I find it hard to sleep with all this excitement, so I thought I would take an hour or two to have a closer look at the two of you."

The Archon signaled to the guards to lead Brigita out, but Brigita did not wait for them to set hands on her and walked quickly to the door and out into the corridor.

"Do stay up, won't you, Your Grace?" the Archon said as he turned from watching Brigita leave to look at Viracocha. "Since the two of you have lived together, it might be interesting to examine you together, for your auras interlock in the most extraordinary way. It should be only an hour or two before I send for you. Until then, Your Grace."

The Archon smiled in that absurd grimace of his that was more a twisting of half of his mouth than an expression of ease, and then turned his back and walked out the door. Two of the guards followed him, but two kept their catapults aimed at Viracocha until the Archon had passed out into the corridor. As the door closed after them, Viracocha felt his hatred of the

Archon begin to take over and he struggled to remain collected in his search for a new strategy.

The images of the Archon putting his stricken hands on Brigita to examine her sprang up in his mind, and he found his rage boiling up again. He struggled to gain distance, to rediscover that connection inside himself with that other presence, as he paced in circles in the bedroom; but the more he looked at the bed, the more disturbed he became. He went out to the balcony, but there the red streams flowing down the volcano in the black night called to his anger to come forth. He paced back and forth on the balcony and tried chanting the *Ome ulubi ra, se tata mak,* but the melodic call of that work now seemed to be a faint memory of a past life. The suffusing presence in him now was not a lifting up into the spaces of detachment and concentration, but an unknown and secret power that he could feel singing in his muscles. It wanted to have the time and place for its own recital. Viracocha closed his eyes to try to see into this undiscovered part of his own being.

The first thing that he felt was that there had been something false about his image of himself as a composer. It was not what he was, but what he wanted to be precisely because it covered up something he did not want to see in himself. He had never been self-indulgent; he had been self-escaping into his little dramatization of the artist. The surprising thing was just how good the music had been, or just how plastic any being was and how it could be molded into artist and lover, lunatic and warrior.

But it was the warrior he felt inside himself now. The solitary walker lost in artistic contemplation had allowed him to ignore this other being of muscular power and instantaneous violence. And yet the artist had taught this other being something in the process of disguising it. The force he could feel inside now was not inchoate rage, but an empowering presence that was as forceful and direct as his music had been. More than anything, it loathed the perverse cruelties of the Archon. The Archon hated the body and was waging war against it, but Viracocha could feel that he loved the feeling of this presence inside his marrow and muscles and that he was about to fight with the body and not against it.

He was ready. Viracocha knew just how he would do it: he would fall to the ground, and as the two guards struggled to lift him, he would move quickly to strike their heads against one another, take their catapults, and rush downstairs to the laboratory. With a clear resolve that the time for action had come, Viracocha moved from the balcony back into the bedroom, but before he was past the three stairs and into the sitting room there was a loud perfunctory knock on the door and four guards entered, two with their catapults already in hand.

The vision of his strategy flashed through his mind, and Viracocha could see that although it would work with two easily, and maybe with the right kind of kick, with three, it would not work with four. Why had the Archon sent so many guards for simply one man?

But he knew the answer to that question. The Archon's medallion had told him that if Viracocha's etheric aura was that intense, his phsyical strength would also be doubled as that swirling vortex in his abdomen sent its empowering light into all his muscles. The Archon knew Viracocha's secret even before he himself had known it.

The guard gestured with contempt for Viracocha to move out the door, and as Viracocha passed by him into the corridor he tried to think of a way to isolate two of the guards while he grabbed one of the catapults. But nothing seemed to work out in his imagination. Two guards walked beside him, and two guards walked behind. He would have to wait for a moment of opening, a moment when they did not expect him to strike.

Viracocha walked down the corridor in a hurry; he was glad that the waiting was over. As he came down the stairs and passed the sentry desk, he noticed for future escape that there were only two guards posted, with probably another two outside at the front of the copper doors. He would need to take a catapult away from one of the guards. They passed the sentry desk and moved into the main corridor; he could see that there were no guards posted in front of the Archon's study, or in front of the double doors to the laboratory itself, so that meant that he had only four guards to deal with immediately.

The guard to his right opened the door in front of him and as they went into the first laboratory, Viracocha saw that the pregnant women had been removed. Where were they now, he wondered, and an image of a long slide flashed into his mind, a long slide that carried round body after body down into the green sea.

They entered the second laboratory, and once again Viracocha observed that the withered bodies of the young women had been removed. But the Archon was there in the very center, with his cape thrown back over the edges of one of the tables. As Viracocha came closer he wondered why he had exposed the stricken arm that was frozen to his side. Always before he had kept that arm hidden within his robes.

"Ah, there you are," the Archon said in a state of obvious pleasure. "Sorry to keep you waiting. Again, I find that I must congratulate you. Very much like your own, Her Reverence has an etheric radiance twelve times what would be normal for a woman her age. It seems that we have been working with people at the wrong stage of life. Pregnant women and pubescent children, why they're nothing compared to the two of you. We will, of course, need to know more about these meditational practices that the two of you have been using. They must be rather original, I would say, considering that I found traces of semen in her vagina."

The Archon moved from the end of the table and his cape fell away to reveal Brigita lying naked on the slab. The tube inserted in her vagina was directly in front of him and he could see the menstrual blood being collected in a vessel. There was no thought or premeditation in his mind, but simply as if lightning had flashed, Viracocha moved with a speed that yet seemed slow and precise to him. With his right foot he kicked out to the side of the guard's knee at a point where he knew he could drive it out of its socket and immobilize him with pain, and at the same time he reached out to his left and seizing the guard by the neck, he snapped the cervical vertebrae and then pulled him off his feet to strike the third guard, whose catapult discharged into the swinging body that Viracocha released to send him hurtling against the other as he jumped onto the fourth. He could tell that he had the force to stop him from reaching for his catapult when he felt the sharp electric wasp sting in his back. He had both of the guard's hands pinned and a knee in position to give him the leverage to snap both of the wrists when he realized that he couldn't move.

The guard spun his own wrists out of Viracocha's loosening grasp, and seizing him by the upper arms, he spun him round to see the Archon smiling at him as he held up a slender white cylinder:

"Actually, these are medical darts. We haven't used this particular drug on the battlefield, but we soon will. You will notice, Your Grace, that it takes effect instantly, much more quickly than the old poisonous darts. They, of course, paralyzed for life, but these are more subtle and precise. In this dosage, the effects of paralysis are temporary. Please put His Grace on this table here.

"You will observe, Your Grace, that with this drug, you can see everything, hear everything, but you can't move any of those powerful muscles of yours. By the way, thank you for that demonstration. I had rather thought that the intensity of the etheric radiance would mean that you would also be much stronger physically than normal."

Viracocha tried to turn his head to keep his eyes on the Archon, but all he could do was stare helplessly ahead or up at the ceiling as the guard lifted him and stretched him out on the slab. He could hear the moaning of one guard and the shuffling of feet, but there was no way to move his head to the side to observe them.

After a moment the Archon intruded his head into his field of vision, and Viracocha felt that the face was even more disgusting when seen upside down. The Archon smiled down at him and patted him approvingly on the shoulder:

"Most heroic, Your Grace. You've actually managed to kill one of the guards and break the other's leg. You see, it's not all that difficult to kill. It is, however, much more difficult to keep the balance at the point between life and death."

196 / *William Irwin Thompson*

The Archon stood back so that Viracocha could only see the middle of his robes.

"Take him away. And you go into the infirmary. Post two guards at the door and then leave us."

Viracocha listened to the shuffle of feet and the noise of the departing guards. To his right he saw the blue cloth and the head of the Archon's assistant peering down at him.

"Remove his robe. I want to do the same blood tests," he commanded.

"This evening, Your Excellency?" the assistant asked in surprise.

"Yes, tonight. I feel intuitively that we are close to a great discovery. I don't think either one of us will sleep much tonight. But you, Your Grace," the Archon said, patting him on the shoulder, "you shall have a good rest. But before you do, since you are a man of knowledge, let me explain our process of examination here. First, we will introduce this tube into your right arm. This will strengthen the dosage of the dart and begin to take you down into a deep coma. Then we introduce this tube into your left arm so that we may remove some of your blood to subject it to glyphic analysis. By the way, should you find yourself hovering above your body here, I would recommend that you don't go into the Tower. The screech of terror is activated, and though I do find that an amusing touch for a musician, your sensitive soul might be disturbed. Now, have a pleasant rest. When you awaken tomorrow morning, we will share the results of our tests with you."

Viracocha felt as if he were falling backward, but falling slowly back through darkness into warm sunlit water, water that was pleasant on his skin. The water was rich, bright aquamarine, and lovely in the thick liquid softness of its silence. There was no need to breathe. There was no need to move; he had only to float there suspended in peace. Somewhere from above he began to hear a voice. It was distant and unclear, mere vowels mumbled in oil. Still, his body seemed to lift and float toward the sound. Now that he could hear it better, he could make out that the voice was calling his name. It had a familiar tone to it, this voice, and it kept telling him to wake up. But

BEAR & COMPANY
P.O. DRAWER 2860
SANTA FE, NM 87504-2860

If you wish to receive a copy of the latest BEAR & COMPANY catalogue and be placed on our mailing list, please send us this card.

Name _____ Date _____

           (please print)

Address _____

City _____ State _____ Zip _____

Please check the following area(s) of interest to you:

1. ☐ Creation Spirituality   4. ☐ Healing/New Age
2. ☐ Medieval Mysticism   5. ☐ Native American/Mayan
3. ☐ Ecology/Sacred Sites   6. ☐ Other _____

why? He wasn't asleep, simply comfortable. Then his face emerged above the surface, and he could hear the voice more distinctly. It was Brigita. But why did she just stand there in her white robe, why didn't she take off her clothes to drift naked in this bright, warm water?

"No, come up, Viracocha. Don't sink back. We've lost a few hours already. Viracocha! Wake up! Come up out of your body."

Brigita held out her hand and touched Viracocha's forehead, and instantly he came awake. He moved up out of his body and looked around in confusion through the grayish, indistinct light.

"Are you clear?" Brigita asked. "We shouldn't move if you're still disoriented."

"Yes, I'm not dreaming anymore, I'm just trying to figure out this light, and why you're wearing a white robe when your body is naked on the table."

"We're on the etheric plane. You won't be able to soar. You'll move in leaps and float back down like a sinking feather. We can pass through the walls though, so now we will be able to get into the Tower."

"But why the clothes?" Viracocha asked.

"All perceptions are habits of mind, interpretations. Dispensing with the interpretations is transcendence, but come on, we can discuss philosophy later. We need to move, I think it must be after midnight."

Brigita set off in the direction of the doors at the opposite end of the laboratory. The first thing that Viracocha noticed was the intensely physical sensation of flying. He could float, with the energy perfectly balanced like a garuda, if he stayed about three feet above the floor. If he jumped, or tried to fly higher, he would always settle down to that level. He stretched out, floating on that stream of energy and found that he could move forward simply by willing himself in that direction. Brigita led the way and he passed through closed doors and walls like a swimmer moving through colored water. Within a few moments they were out of the series of laboratories and into the underground tunnel that connected the laboratory with the foundation vault of the Tower.

They passed through the enormous megalithic stones of the

foundation and moved from the gray indistinct light into total darkness. Viracocha lost sight of Brigita as a force pulled him into the center of a viscous blackness that increased its compressive hold on him. He lost all sense of orientation, could see nothing, hear nothing, but could feel this mass crushing him with a black suffocating heat. He couldn't even move his fingers. The compression began to increase, and the pain became excruciating, as if each finger were being smashed in a vise, and then when the pain was unbearable, he heard it, and the pain became inconceivable.

Sound returned to his void in the form of a shrill, high-pitched screech that kept pulsing back and forth between two notes. One note produced a sensation of extreme irritability, as if all the nerves were being confused in their impulses and were reporting every painful sensation they knew: burning, freezing, tearing, breaking. He was being flayed alive and disemboweled at the same time. Then the note oscillated to its demonic twin and the extreme irritability concentrated itself into an unbearable itching under the skin. If he could have moved his hands he would have gladly torn his skin to pieces in a frenzy. The rage against his own body was so intense as he hung there suspended like a fly in black amber that after he had heard the screech only twice, some power took over and he found that he had flung himself out of his etheric body and was now flying in some kind of dirty black tornado.

He was not alone. Others had been sucked up by this psychic tornado and had been pulled from their sleep by the power of this nightmare that hung over their world. Some of the others tried to grab onto his ankles or hair as if he could save them from the force that was pulling them down to the center of the vortex. His speed increased as he drew nearer to the center, and then he saw it. And he knew at once that it was an Old One.

At the end of the vortex was a cauldron of blood in which the Old One stood as if it were bathing, but it wasn't bathing as much as it was kneading itself into shape. The creature was a conglomerate mass of the twelve children's bodies. It would seethe like a pool of lava in which bubbles would come to the surface and explode, but the bubbles were the children's faces.

From one moment to another, one of the children's faces would emerge and scream in agony the single syllable of "God!" and then the creature would hear and thrust its head back into the molten mass of its slowly congealing body. The closer he came to the Old One, the more horrible the smell became. Every foul odor he had ever encountered in his life seemed gathered into the thing. Then the Old One saw him and reached up to grasp his ankle to pull him in. As he stopped stuffing the children's heads into his body, all their faces came out at once and screamed "God!" over and over again in a dissonant chorus of despair. The touch of the Old One felt as if a leech had gelatinously stuck itself to his skin, but the odor that came up from his hands was the smell of black, oozingly wet and rotten potatoes.

Then a rational thought shot through the emotional stream of his panic like a salmon leaping up a waterfall: "Why rotten potatoes in hell?" And then he remembered the experience in Tiahuanaco and knew that the thing was into his mind, into his own memory, and was playing back at him every fear and revolting thing he could think of. And with a great liberating laugh at the gross banality of this aggregate monster's mind, he pulled his arms up and dived head-first into the misshapen, screaming mass.

It popped like a bubble. Then there was only an enormous cauldron of black obsidian and a bent little old man standing in the center. He looked totally ridiculous in his animal skin and horns on his head. His spindly legs were wrinkled and from hopping about in his little dance, his testicles had slipped out of the dirty skin that served for a loin cloth and they now sagged and bounced against his withered thighs in rhythm with the drum and stick he beat with his hands. All around him, tightened up in fetal knots, were the twelve children. One of them looked out at nothing with insane eyes.

The shaman stopped beating his drum and looked at Viracocha with a puzzled expression. He mumbled a few incoherent syllables, beat his drum in Viracocha's face, and then backed up a pace when the magic did not have its intended effect. Fear began to form in the old man's eyes, and as he lifted his glance to look beyond Viracocha's shoulder, the eyes widened in terror, then panic. With a scream, he threw down his drum and stick and flew out of the cauldron in the shape of a startled owl. Viracocha turned around to see Brigita floating above him.

"Anyone who rules by fear is always afraid of something," Brigita said as she came down to stand next to Viracocha. "I simply played his own magic back at him."

"And the Old One?" Viracocha asked.

"As soon as you broke the connection between it and the shaman, it lost its point of contact with our level. The souls in the whirlwind have been flung back to their sleeping bodies."

Brigita knelt down to look at the children. Each one of them still seemed locked into its individual nightmare.

"The terror has been sustained too long," Brigita said. "If we brought them back to their bodies now, they would be insane for the rest of their lives. The best that I can do for them now is to carry them safely over into death. They can rest with Abaris until they are ready to move back into life."

"How are you going to do that?" Viracocha asked.

"If you can get rid of that screech, then the dream body can join the etheric. Together they will have enough force of will to sever the connection with the physical body to experience death peacefully. But as long as that screech is sounding, they'll be paralyzed in terror."

"The sound is vibrating in the First Hyperborean Solid," Viracocha said, feeling once again the paralytic grip of his own fear. "To annul the oscillation, I would have to be able to function on the physical or the etheric level, both of which are impossible. So where does that leave us?"

"We'll have to go back into the sound," Brigita said as she reached out to grasp Viracocha's hands.

"No! That's impossible!" Viracocha shouted. "I can't do anything inside it. Why can't we just wait? We'll all be dead in a few hours anyway."

"If the children die in the state they are in now, they will attract the Old One back to them and he will be able to take them down into his level. Then I would have to go down there alone to try to get them out, and I just might not be able to do that. Look, I lost you last time because I didn't know what I was getting into. Even in my worst nightmares as a young girl, I've never experienced anything like it. But now that I know it, I think that I can stay with you. We have to do it. There's no other way."

Viracocha became silent for a moment, searching for the courage to will himself back, but he couldn't find it; all he could find was the feeling of panic at the thought of being buried alive in that blackness. There was no courage in him at all, but suddenly there was understanding. The calculations flashed into his mind in a complete and detailed analysis of the oscillatory pattern.

"That's it!" Viracocha exclaimed in excitement. "If we can produce the right overtones from *hoomi* singing, the screech will be annulled and will leak right out of the metal rods as the wave pattern is flattened out."

Brigita saw the vision in Viracocha's mind and felt a wave of joy and gratitude sweep through her:

"Abaris comes from the Eastern Continent where that singing originates. He taught me the woman's part when I was also learning how to dance. Now I know why."

"It will be stronger and the effect will take place sooner, if we can do it together. Here, follow me. Try to sound the occult reciprocal of the overtone. Don't overpower it. It's a question of geometry and not force."

Viracocha began the low twang that at first sounded absurd, like a ridiculous emphasis on sound in nasal passages and skull cavities, but then, like a sacrament of the mystery of incarnation, all the physical absurdities of the ridiculous body began to gather into form until high above, this clear, crystalline angel came down to hover in beauty above it. When Brigita heard the overtone, she closed her eyes and began to intone the occult reciprocal, and no sooner had the two sounds married, that the creature of the thousand eyes manifested in the resonant space between them. Brigita's eyes opened wide in the same expression of astonishment that took her over in her first experience of orgasm. The ecstatic resonance of the angelic being inside them was so erotic that for as long as they could produce the sound they remained a single being of three in one.

"I don't think I'm afraid anymore," Viracocha said as he steadied his breath. "But to be certain, hold my wrists tightly, and I will lock mine on yours. I don't want to loose you again. All right. Remember, sound the music in the interval, in the trough between the two waves of that screech. Let's go then."

With an act of resolution, they willed themselves back, but as soon as Viracocha heard the first note, he lost all resolve. He did not sing. He screamed. Brigita collapsed into herself in mute silence as the black compression became a suffocating coffin. Then the second note sounded and Viracocha became hysterical and if he could have moved a finger he would have ripped his face off his skull to get the underside of his skin away from his body. He could not observe his pain with spiritual detachment. He could not spiritually transcend that maddening itch of perversity, but he could gather his being together in anger, and in the concentration of his being in anger, he found a new strength. His whole being rose up in one united and enormous burst of anger at the Archon. The musician in him was in a state of rage that anyone could take sound and put it to so perverse a use. The rage lifted him up and the anger ennobled him as his spirit rose in revolt to the torture that was being inflicted on it. He sang out his note as the second note ended, and the sound released Brigita from the crush of annihilation and she joined him.

The overtone was even more beautifully present than before, gaining power as it approached closer to the world of matter in the turbulent shore of the etheric. As the overtone hovered in the ether above them, they felt again the creature of the thousand eyes take on a body from the sound, and as it took its body in the space between them, the hot liquid blackness froze into a dark crystal of obsidian and then shattered as light reentered hell.

Space returned with its familiar dimensions and they saw themselves standing within the complex alignment of the five interlocking Solids. Within the space of enclosure were the twelve tables with the bodies of the children, connected by tubes to the large basin of blood in the center. Slumped over, dead in the basin, was the body of the shaman.

Brigita and Viracocha moved to the center by the basin, and to ensure their reconstitution of that space, they held one another's hands, and sang out the overtones once again. With the emergence of the creature again, the Solids became a singularity of exquisite sensitivity and Viracocha knew that with the first touch of sunlight at dawn on the crystal far above, the crust of the earth would begin to resonate and part to allow volcanic fire to mate with sunlight.

Like the touch of a mother's hand on a child tossing in nightmare, the music completely transformed the atmosphere of the vault. For a few lingering moments, the three of them continued to sing, not in triumph, but for the love of the sound. Its beauty was so strong, so completely antithetical to everything in that world of torture, that the children heard it and awakened from their nightmares. They rushed to Brigita and shouted out in Anahuacan the name of their mother goddess and reached out to touch her skirts.

The mother of none became the mother of all, and as Viracocha stepped back to look at Brigita with each of the twelve children kneeling and touching the hem of her skirt, it seemed as if Brigita had become the sun and each of the children the sign through which the coming age would pass. The aeon of Atlantis was indeed over, and a new cycle of 25,920 years was about to begin at dawn with the sound that would soon come from the solar crystal high overhead.

"Thank you," Brigita said as she looked at Viracocha, wanting to say more, but not knowing how to say it. "There is something more I want to say, but after being melted down, body and soul into one another, I don't know why I'm still reaching after words. You'd better go back now. I'll take the children to Abaris and then come back to be with you. I can't see how Bran can rescue us now. It must be getting close to dawn. Anyway, I'll come back to be with you at the moment of death."

Viracocha turned away and began to flow on that stream of energy that was a membrane between the physical and etheric planes. He passed through the tunnel that connected the Institute to the vault, but found no one at work in any of the inner laboratories. When he came back into the main laboratory, he found the Archon and his assistant seated in front of a table of a dozen Mercury Tablets. He moved behind them to try to understand what they were doing, when behind him he heard a shout in a strangely distorted voice. As he turned round to question the source of the strange call, he saw the High Priest enter with two guards on either side, one of whom he recognized as the man who held him when the Archon had shot him with the dart.

"Your Excellency!" Again the command rang out, but this time Viracocha realized the distortion was coming from the interference between the physical and etheric. Evidently, the Archon was in the process of slowly bringing him up out of his coma and his consciousness was being pulled through a buzzing thickness back into the waking world. But Viracocha did not want to return to his body; he wanted to hold onto that spectral freedom long enough to find out why the High Priest had suddenly appeared. Had he discovered Bran's conspiracy to escape?

The Archon and his assistant rose immediately and bowed as the High Priest approached. He stopped momentarily at the tables where Brigita and Viracocha lay stretched out amid a tangle of wires and tubes, and then he looked up at the Archon with anger in his eyes:

"Who gave you permission for this? I placed them under house arrest for good reason. I did not give you permission to make them subjects of midnight research."

"One moment, Your Holiness. It is much better than it would appear. Tonight has been a time of unimaginable discovery."

"I gave you permission to examine their etheric auras," the High Priest said, and reached up to fling the Archon's medallion into his face. "I said nothing about subjecting them to this kind of mutilation until I had determined what Pleiadean rituals of transformation they had uncovered."

"But, Your Holiness, that is precisely what I have determined. What we have learned tonight equals almost everything we have learned in the whole project. I have not injured either one of them."

"One guard is dead, two are wounded. That is injury. You have acted without permission once again, and that is injury. You have taken a Member of the Sacred College, as well as the hereditary custodian of the Treaty with Hyperborea, and subjected them to research as if they were common criminals. You have done all this flagrantly in the presence of the Palace Guards, and then act as if this were not the most serious affront to my authority."

"With what I have learned tonight, Your Holiness, I may have given you authority over death."

"*You* have no authority to give *me!*" the High Priest said with a deadliness that unsettled the Archon. "I begin to see now. In a way, Viracocha was right. I had thought that you men of knowledge would be different, but you are just the military in different uniforms."

"Please, Your Holiness, when you hear me out, you will see that what I have discovered is of the most use to you. After this morning's tests, I was going to come with the full report, not just of the new attunement of the solar crystal, but of the discoveries with His Grace and Her Reverence. Hear me out now, and if afterward you wish to order my execution, so be it. But at least let me show you what is in the Mercury Tablets. They are right here for you to see. Nothing that we have discovered here in the Institute equals what we have discovered tonight."

At that proclamation, Viracocha's interest shifted from the High Priest to the series of Mercury Tablets and he moved over to the table to study the glyphs shimmering in the liquid crystals.

The High Priest signaled to the guards to remain by the doors and then he turned and walked to the table where the assistant quickly pulled out one of the chairs for him to sit on. The Archon picked up the Emerald Stylus and pointed to the first Tablet:

"We analyze the blood by inducing a sound into it when it is inside the quartz vessel. This then produces a three-tone melodic sequence, which is in turn transposed into its mathematical isomorph. Then, through the normal procedures of glyphic resolution, we generate the associated hieroglyph, and as these all come in pairs, we take the melodic sequence associated with the twin, and reintroduce it into vibration of the blood within the vessel. This produces a four-tone melodic sequence, which can be resolved into its associated glyph. So far, this is what we have tried on the women and children, but always with uninteresting results. But tonight I noticed that Her Reverence was menstruating, and when I did an analysis of the menstrual blood, it produced a new and completely different melodic sequence, and this glyphic resolution."

The Archon pointed to the first of the Mercury Tablets with his Emerald Stylus. As he activated the Tablet, a four-note melodic sequence sounded and a spiraling mandala appeared in the liquid metal. The Archon watched the High Priest closely and then smiled as he noticed his attention quicken.

"Precisely. His Holiness immediately recognizes the chant still used in the Remnants of Hyperborea. Now, the curious fact is that there were traces of semen in the blood, which, of course, leads me to suspect that their practices were not at all what we know of as meditation, but some form of intensification of incarnation through sexual practice, or, perhaps, concentrations in trance upon the blood and semen. It would seem that in our work on pregnant women and pubescent children, we were working on the wrong stage of life. They evidently chose to concentrate on the essence of the sexual act itself. You see, I think that I now know that what is being expressed in this glyph is the effect of the female blood and the male semen, not in conception, of course, but in self-conception, as it were. Later we shall need to study the blood and semen separately, but this initial analysis led me to think that it might be worthwhile to do a tonal analysis of their bloodstreams together. And it certainly was."

"You mean to tell me," the High Priest said with returning anger, "that you removed their entire bloodstreams without even asking for permission for this kind of extreme activity?"

"Your Holiness, there is a momentum and an excitement to scientific discovery. If I stopped in the middle of it, I would lose touch with my own intuition, and it is that intuition tonight that has produced these, if I may say so, inspired results. Besides, there is no danger to them. As long as they are in deep coma and I keep the blood flowing through the vessel and back into them, they cannot be harmed. I was in the process of finishing the return of their blood when Your Holiness arrived. They will revive shortly and should have no effects more than a mere headache."

"*Should* have no effect," the High Priest corrected, "but the point is, you don't really know. And the more that you argue how unusual they are, the more you indicate that you cannot possibly know what you are doing."

"I believe Your Holiness said that we must take risks or risk becoming a decadent civilization. Well, men of knowledge must take risks as well if they are to make new discoveries."

"The point, Your Excellency, is that *I* am to decide which risks to take by looking at the whole situation, something you are incapable of doing."

"Your Holiness, you must choose your leaders and then trust them. If you are going to lead on the battlefield, do research in the laboratory, and write poetry and music in the College, then you will have to be a civilization by yourself."

"I observe that Your Excellency is now trying to tell me what I 'must' do and what I can be. You really are like the military. In your ignorance you try to make the eyes into the brain. The military wants a society of warriors. You want a society of scientists. You're all the same, the same blindness, the same ignorance."

"In my ignorance, Your Holiness, I discovered that the glyphic resolution for the mixture of their bloodstreams together was the Pleiades."

The Archon struck the second Mercury Tablet with his stylus and a four-note melody sounded and a new geometrical figure shimmered in the crystal. The High Priest looked at the figure with intense interest as he heard the melodic sequence.

"This glyph is extremely ancient," the Archon said. "I had to go through the Temple Archives to identify it, but I see that Your Holiness recognizes it. We see this glyph as the one for the

Morning Star, but the most ancient records show that before the last reversal of the poles, this was the glyph of the Pleiades. What I think this means, this signature of the stars that they carry in their blood . . ."

Viracocha moved from the edge of the group to come closer to the Tablet as soon as he saw the glyph. He wished he could activate the other three Tablets and turned impatiently to the Archon, as if to command him, when he noticed Brigita's subtle body descend and hover over her physical form before she turned to look where he was standing. She moved within an instant to his side, and Viracocha pointed to the Tablet. Brigita nodded, removed a ring from her finger, and showed him the same glyph ingraved on the inside. Viracocha did not need to ask who gave her the ring, but realized at once that Abaris must have given it to her at some level in her initiation.

". . . is that when the Hyperborean Custodians defeated the Old Ones, they must have introduced the lattice of the subtle bodies and spinal centers into the upwardly evolving animal body of the mixed race. Perhaps they saw this as some sort of rescue mission to make up for the bungling of the earlier forbidden experiments. Into the geometry of these spinal centers, they constructed various mathematical and musical patterns. In effect, they signed their work with the musical traditions of the Pleiades."

It flashed into Viracocha's mind all at once. The Tower, like the black magic of the witches' brew of blood and semen, was a crude literalism, and that was why the solar crystal would always rebound in dense matter to create a volcano. They had not been locked in by some demonic geometrizing demiurge; they were misunderstanding the message of the geometry. The centers along the spine were the solar crystals that resounded behind space to tell the Pleiadeans when humans had reached the next level. As soon as he and Brigita had ascended through the inner Tower of their own spines, it was not a volcano that appeared, but Melchizedek. It was the dense, literal, cruel materialism of human misunderstanding that was dooming their civilization and not the traps of some demented god.

"What Viracocha and Brigita seem to have been able to do,"

the Archon continued, "is to carry this mathematical-musical structure from the psychic, through the etheric, and directly into the physical bloodstream. They have turned the bloodstream into a liquid crystal of enormous, and I truly mean, enormous power and renewed etheric radiation. The most obvious and immediate ramification of this is that their blood could have tremendous healing powers. And, as His Holiness can appreciate, for someone like myself, dying of a blood-clotting disease that is daily taking bits and pieces of my body from the control of my will, such healing properties are of truly *vital* interest."

The High Priest did not say anything for a moment, but simply stared blankly at the glyph. Finally, he took a deep breath and looked up at the Archon:

"Once again, I see that you are not looking at the whole situation, though I suppose with your sickness you could not be expected to do so. Can't you see that if what you say is true, then the Priesthood is ruined? It means that women are not simply the old animal bodies of our entrapment, but that they carry a transformative power of the spirit. Can't you see, this would make a sacrament out of the grossest form of sexual intercourse, make a joke out of the ceremony of transference of power from the old High Priest to the new one, and tear apart all our institutions, from the Tower down to the temple concubines themselves."

"With all due respect, Your Holiness," the Archon said with the slightest of smiles touching the left corner of his mouth, "that is only true if the emphasis of our institutions is on escape *from* incarnation, rather than manipulation of it. Perhaps, it is time to set aside these archaic institutions of the Priesthood to have a new priesthood of science. If we placed Brigita in the Tower and controlled her conception, one of the Old Ones would be able to descend into her and we could begin to create a new generation, not for the stars, but here for earth."

"You still don't understand, do you?" the High Priest said in a tone of weariness. "The reason I came here myself in the middle of the night is because I could trust no one else either to ask or to know if what I feared was true. You fool! Brigita is the hereditary custodian of the Treaty with Hyperborea! In manipulating her like this, you may just have sounded an alarm that will bring the Custodians back to reestablish Hyperborea. That was what Abaris was all about. Do you begin to understand now? The Empire is finished. And it is all because you did not come to me immediately when you contacted the Old Ones. They are not the future of the human race, you idiot, they are a race of psychic parasites who would like nothing better than to attach themselves to the human race. You see, you don't know everything in this science of yours, and that is why the Priesthood can never be replaced with the likes of you. Now revive these two immediately. Tomorrow, after the morning's test, you are to report for a meeting with the Supreme Council. Now that the military is well in hand, it is time to take care of all of you. Guards!"

The Palace Guards came running from their station to the side of the High Priest.

"Now, revive them. I wish to know exactly how much damage you have done tonight."

The Archon gestured in silence to his assistant to remove the wires and tubes.

"Their bloodstreams were returning to normal while we were speaking. My assistant will revive them now with the antidote. I hope that when Your Holiness sees the beneficial results of tomorrow's test, that you will have renewed confidence in my ability to provide you with all that you need for the opening of the new cosmic cycle. I can assure you that I am not interested in challenging your authority, or in any kind of political power. Power over life and death, yes. Power to take the ovum of Brigita and project myself at the moment of death into her womb, yes. And power to create a new etheric body so that one does not have to go through the inanity of childhood all over again, yes. Power to flush out my blood to replace it with Viracocha's, yes; but power to rule, no, not at all."

Brigita shivered in disgust as the Archon spoke of projecting himself into her womb, but Viracocha reached out to take her hand as a plan of escape began to form in his mind. He looked at Brigita to question her willingness to try it, and she nodded her assent just as they began to feel the strong pull back to their bodies.

Viracocha stretched out above his body and began to sense the realignment of the two energy fields pull him down into sleep. He did not want to go to sleep. He did not want to move through that swamp of confused dreams that would, in its garbled jumble of images, produce a confused memory and interpretation of what he had experienced in the clarity of this other state of mind. But, for all his resistance, he sank into unconsciousness.

He saw himself standing in front of a mirror. It was confusing, because he could see clearly that he now had Brigita's breasts. He still had a penis, but he could sense that behind the scrotum there was this secret, hidden vagina. He began to reason with himself, telling himself that he remembered the single body of crystalline light that he shared with Brigita when they were with Melchizedek, but he should not have come down from there with her body confused with his. He opened his eyes to question the ceiling about his descent, and then he woke up, then he remembered his plan.

"My breasts! My breasts come from the sky!" Viracocha shouted in a childish voice.

The High Priest, the Archon, and the two guards came closer to the table.

"My breasts! My breasts come from the sky!" Viracocha shouted once again.

"Is this what you call normal?" the High Priest asked in disgust.

"He is merely dreaming, Your Holiness," the Archon answered. "He is simply creating dream images out of his perception of the presence of her blood in his. His mind will clear in a moment."

Viracocha turned his head to look at the High Priest:

"Please, Daddy, don't let that bad man hurt me again. Please take me home with you. I've come back from the stars to be with you. Please take me away from here."

"Marvelous piece of work!" the High Priest said. "You've found yet another way to turn a genius into a babbling idiot. But notice, that even in his babbling, he's talking about the stars. They have made contact."

Brigita began to shout in a little girl's voice:

"I have to pee. I have to pee bad!"

Viracocha picked up on Brigita's suggestion and the High Priest's fear and began to chant:

> *"Peepee, peepee,*
> *Please, please.*
> *Peepee on the Pleiades."*

"I have had enough of this. Guards, take them back with me to the Palace and keep them under guard in the guest rooms."

"But Your Holiness, I *need* them here! Even a small amount of their blood might be able to cure my disease."

"The only thing you need right now is to learn how to obey. You will return to your quarters, and you will remain there under guard, until I summon you to a meeting of the Supreme Council. Now, pick these two up, and let us all go to the Captain of the guard together."

The guards moved quickly to slip their arms under the neck and thighs of Brigita and Viracocha, but as the two of them were lifted from the table, Brigita began to urinate on the hands and arms of the guard, who dropped her feet to the floor and stared at the High Priest in confusion as the stream of urine spilled to the floor. And all the time, Viracocha clapped his hands and kept up his little chant:

> *"Peepee, peepee,*
> *Please, please,*
> *Peepee from the Pleiades."*

As the second guard struggled to hold the giggling Viracocha in his arms, Viracocha shouted "Now!" in his mind to Brigita and both sprang into action at the same instant.

With a single maneuver they lifted the dart-catapults out of their sleeves and shot each of the guards in the thigh. The assistant saw what was happening first and ran to the table to seize one of the white cylinders that contained the medical darts, but Brigita shot him in the back before he reached them. Viracocha kept his catapult aimed at the High Priest and the Archon, but ran over to the table to pick up one of the cylinders.

"Now, Your Holiness," Brigita said as she moved closer to him, "I feel uncomfortable walking about in the nude, so if you will please slowly release the chain at your neck and drop your cloak to the floor and step back, I will put on the robes, but not the office. No, I wouldn't try that. If you swing the robe into my face, I'll shoot you now."

"So, our esteemed Abbess reads minds," the High Priest said as he released the thin chain at his neck to let his purple cloak fall to the floor. "I suppose that is all part of the training with Abaris."

Viracocha approached the High Priest and the Archon as Brigita fastened the cloak about her neck.

"Surely, Viracocha, you don't think you can get very far with this escape. How long do you think it will be before the garudas of the Empire will follow you?"

"This is much more than an escape, Your Holiness," Viracocha said. "Can't you see? Your Empire is a fantasy in your own mind. The Military has its agenda, the scientists have theirs, the Old Ones have another, and the Society of 144 waiting now with the largest garuda in the Empire to take us away have more than an agenda in mind. They have a whole new era. This is over, Your Holiness. The Empire has broken into pieces even before these islands break apart and disappear into the sea."

"Not quite, Your Grace," the Archon said with an air of superiority. "If the two of you leave now, before you receive the antidote which only I know, now that you have killed my assistant . . ."

"What?" Brigita exclaimed. "I thought these darts were only to paralyze temporarily."

"The medical darts stun," the Archon said, "but the Palace Guards are not part of the medical force, Your Reverence."

Brigita picked up one of the white cylinders from the table, but Viracocha still kept the catapult aimed at the High Priest and the Archon.

"Your ruse won't work. I stood by you as you gave His Holiness a lecture on the magical properties of our bloodstreams."

"Be reasonable, Viracocha," the Archon continued. "You have discovered some new practices, but we had the knowledge to join your bloodstreams. What you are now, you owe to us."

Viracocha shot the Archon with the medical dart and spoke to him as he slumped to the floor:

"What we are, we certainly do not owe to you. You will excuse me if I have difficulty hearing you out, for ever since I heard your screech in the Tower, I find your voice harder to take."

Viracocha looked up from the Archon, collapsed on the floor, to the High Priest, as if in his eyes he could find an answer to it all:

"I wonder if *you* had experienced it, whether you still could inflict it on anyone. Do you even begin to realize what you have created in your 'City of Knowledge'? Why did you let him do all this? It's all so completely unnecessary. Had you meditated inside the aligned Solids, you could have ascended out of the physical world all the way to the archetypal realm."

"You know as well as I do, Viracocha, that the archetypal realm is simply the bars of our cage, the grid of cause and effect that lock us in. You've rescued a dozen children for what? For a thousand more lives of torture and unending misery. I'm not interested in mystical experiences anymore. I'm interested in ending this whole wheel of torture called existence."

"And you think by torture you're going to end torture? You admit that the Old Ones are parasites. Well, what kind of torture would there be if they had attached themselves to humanity, the way a lamprey eel attaches itself to a fish? In a little while at sunrise, you are going to have a few moments to gain understanding. I am going to put both you and the Archon in the center of the vault, staring up through the hollow spine into the solar crystal. If I am wrong, you can come to get me and we can have civil war. If I am right, you will have a few seconds when all the human dimensions, etheric, psychic, mental, and archetypal, implode into you. But it will be only a few seconds before the whole city explodes and drops in pieces into the sea."

"I observe, Viracocha, that you have become my successor after all. In struggling to defeat me you have changed enormously. Think about it. You are much closer to me than you were before. Now that you have taken power from me, rather than accepting it, you have killed three or four people. You weighed their deaths against the whole and made a decision to execute them in order to execute your own plan of escape. And I have done no differently. And so, Your Holiness, I pass on the succession to you and offer you my medallion of office."

Before the High Priest could lift his hands to his chest, Brigita shot him with the paralyzing dart from the white cylinder she had exchanged for the more deadly catapult. As he slumped down to the floor, she spoke to Viracocha without taking her eyes off the High Priest.

"He was going to shoot you. There's a dart-catapult hidden to the side of the large emerald."

Viracocha stared down at the High Priest on the floor and then bent down to pick him up to place him on the table. Very gently and with great respect he removed his white sleeveless robe and medallion and chain. He set them to the side, folded the High Priest's hands over his chest, and then put rolls of cloth to support his head so that it would not turn to the side and away from the point of the Tower.

Very slowly, Viracocha lifted the High Priest's robe over his own naked body and let it fall down over his arms and shoulders. He stood for a moment, looking down at the robe, and then spoke quietly to Brigita:

"He's right, you know. I'll take this robe with me, and when I forget, I'll take it out."

Viracocha turned to look questioningly at Brigita, took a breath, looked around at the four bodies sprawled on the floor, and took command of the situation:

"We had better put them all in the vault, so that everything goes on as usual in the morning when the work begins."

"But if the Archon is not here, won't they become suspicious?" Brigita asked.

"I'll leave new instructions in the Mercury Tablets and warn them all to stay out of the foundation vault. I can sign the order with the imprint of his ring. We'd better put them on the tables now and try to straighten up in here."

Brigita and Viracocha worked together picking up the dead and setting them on the tables on which their victims had lain before. As they set the last guard down and folded his hands over his chest, Viracocha recognized him to be the one who had reported to the High Priest.

"We owe our lives to this one," Viracocha said. "If he hadn't reported to the High Priest, we might still be stretched out on these tables. Not exactly a fitting reward, is it?"

Brigita said nothing for a moment, then she looked up at Viracocha as she still held on to the ankles of the dead man:

"He is the one I shot."

"Would it make you feel any better," Viracocha asked, "if I told you that he was the one who shot Abaris with that same catapult?"

"Yes, but that only makes me feel worse. I asked Abaris once about this problem of becoming evil to fight evil. He said: 'Those who swim in dirty water will get wet, but those who drink it will die.' We're not innocent, and we will have to accept our purification, however it comes."

Brigita moved away from the body to pick up a cloth to clean the puddle of urine she had made on the floor. As she bent down, she could see her own reflection, hesitated for a moment, and then spoke to it:

"The virgin has become a lover, the Abbess has become a warrior. Love and Death."

"And if they had carried catapults that only stunned, they would not be dead, but would be in a few hours. We won't be able to sort this out for a long time. Come on, let's take them into the Tower."

Brigita stood up, placed the cloth under the table, and then looked with confusion at the wheelless slabs:

"How do these move?"

"They're like tiny garudas. Touch the amethyst there, and then they will hover weightlessly above the floor. Then you simply push or pull them wherever you want. We'd better take one at a time to leave a hand free for the catapult, just in case we run into anybody else. But at least this time we can use the paralyzing darts."

As Viracocha set the white catapult down between the feet of the High Priest, he heard the sound of running feet, and picked up the cylinder as he pulled Brigita down behind the table. They listened intently for a moment.

"It's all right," Brigita said. "I can feel that it is Bran."

"I know," Viracocha answered. "They're running in bare feet: invaders, not defenders."

The doors burst open and Bran and six men rushed into the room, with catapults in hand. Viracocha did not take any chances with a nervously discharged dart and shouted before he stood up:

"It's all right, Bran. We're over here."

"Thank God both of you are not drugged," Bran exclaimed. "We've got to hurry." Bran ran over to them, noticed the High Priest and the Archon, and then the dead assistant and guards:

"Good God! How did you do all this?"

"Since you were a little tardy in rescuing us, we had to rescue ourselves. Great bladdered Brigita pissed on the Empire, and it went under. By the way, Brigita, that was a brilliant tactic."

"It wasn't all that clever," Brigita said with an embarrassed smile, "I really had to pee."

"Well, it was a godsend, however it came out," Viracocha said. "Bran, we have to hide them all in the Tower. The High Priest and the Archon are alive and only temporarily paralyzed. I want them both to see what they have done when the sun strikes the crystal in the morning."

Bran looked down at the Archon:

"I will move him in. After all the people I have had to bring to this wretched place, it will be a great satisfaction to make him my last."

"Let me take his ring off first to put the instructions into the Mercury Tablets for the staff in the morning," Viracocha said as he took off the ring from the tightly clenched fist of the Archon.

"Now, he's all yours, but I suppose, according to protocol, the High Priest should go first."

They moved down the aisle to the end of the laboratory where Viracocha erased the Tablets, set in the new instructions, and then impressed the ring into the template of the living metal. Meticulously, he placed the ring back on the withered finger of the Archon and then took up his position at the table bearing the High Priest.

Viracocha led the way down the underground tunnel to the vault, and clothed as he was in the robe of the High Priest, it seemed as if he were leading a funeral procession down into the great megalithic chamber. No one made a sound. There was no wailing or chanting, but only the slight serpentine hiss of the irradiating crystals that lit the way.

When they came into the vault, Brigita went over immediately to the bodies of the children, crossed their arms over their chests, and began to chant a prayer in Eireanne. Viracocha placed the High Priest and the Archon side by side, staring up the hollow central axis to the golden pyramid that held the solar crystal at the very peak of the Tower. Then Bran placed the two guards and the assistant between them and the children, and when all were in place, he waited nervously while Brigita completed her circuit around the twelve children.

When she had finished, she bowed to the children, turned to Bran, and said:

"We can go now."

"And we had better go quickly, on the run," Bran said as he signaled the others to go ahead.

They started to run with a nervous energy at first, but when they had come out of the vault into the underground tunnel, the power of the deep quiet that had descended onto the city settled on them, and their run became a more rhythmic and steadily beating trot. As he listened to the repetitive beat, it seemed to Viracocha that he was hearing the heartbeat of the whole civilization moving out from the Tower to pulse its last in the arteries of the streets and passageways.

The fog was thick and conspiring with them as they came out of the entrance to the Institute onto the Broad Street. It was first light, but no bird sang. No person stirred, waking in his bed. The only sound that could be heard was that of their bare feet striking the stones and scattering the few grains of sand and dirt that the winds had brought into the city from the wild.

No guard stirred in his post, and no resistance sprang up in surprise to threaten their escape. As they passed the last of the guard posts, they came out onto the quai of the Institute where the two garudas lay covered by the thick fog.

Brigita stopped for a moment to catch her breath, and Viracocha turned round in a flash of anxiety to look back at her:

"Are you all right?" he asked. "We're almost there, it's just a few more yards to the vessel."

Brigita placed her palms on her knees, bent over to take a deep breath, and shook her head to say yes before she stood up straight to look at Viracocha.

Bran signaled the others to go on ahead into the ship, and then walked back to Brigita:

"I've changed your crew, Brigita. I thought you would want to go back," Bran said as he struggled to catch his breath and quiet his own beating heart.

"Thank you," Brigita said, and then she looked at Viracocha in surprise. "I'm sorry. I thought it would be obvious to you. It has to be this way. You have your work. I have mine. And now more than ever we're going to be needed on opposite sides of the world. I'm no man's wife, and you certainly would make a poor wife for me on Eiru."

Viracocha was stunned into silence. He had never really thought of what they would do, or could do in the future. He had only some vague romantic notion of their flying off in the dawn together.

"Good-bye, Bran. Although I know I'll see you again. You're not likely to stay in one place very long."

Brigita embraced Bran in gratitude, and Viracocha could see that part of her wanted to be a normal woman, free of the burden of her own psychic gifts, and if there were any part of her that could be a wife, that normal woman in her would be wife to Bran.

Brigita took a step back into the fog and looked from Bran to Viracocha:

"More time. We all need more time. Maybe only after we've loved everybody once, can we love everybody all at once."

Brigita backed into the fog and disappeared. Viracocha heard the creak of the footbridge to her vessel, heard the rustle of material and then its passage through the air. As he looked down at the cloak of the High Priest, which lay crumpled at his feet, he thought of Brigita standing naked at the doorway to her ship, and he remembered when she stood naked in defiance of his lust, and when she had stood naked in front of her meditation chamber to approach him and carry him out of time and space. What more did he want from her? And why did he stand there feeling so sorry for himself? With a gesture of sadness and self-disgust, he kicked the High Priest's cloak over the edge and down into the water, and then turned to follow Bran to the mooring of the larger vessel.

They passed in silence up the ramp and through the main chamber into the control room. Viracocha hardly looked up to examine all the faces of those with whom he would spend the rest of his life. Instead he stared out the window and watched as Bran slowly followed Brigita's vessel out into the center of the bay. They held their position for a few moments, waiting as the small garuda lifted into the air; then they began their own slow ascent. As soon as they were up a few hundred feet, they came above the clouds. The entire city was hidden by the fog, and only the Tower stood out alone in the sky.

In the distance Viracocha could see Brigita's vessel moving off into the lightening horizon.

"Do you wish to stay here?" Bran asked. "I mean, we can hover here if you wish to see the first beams of the sun touch the crystal."

Viracocha did not look up at Bran. Instead, he stared out the portal at the Tower and he began to speak quietly as if he were seeing a vision or reading from a history book:

"When the first beam of light touches the crystal, nothing very unusual will seem to have happened. One will only wonder why the birds have stopped singing. And then the animals will begin to howl, but that will quickly pass. Then the greatest silence on earth will come over the whole island. Those who are asleep will bolt upright in bed, fully awake, fully alert as they listen to nothing that they can hear. It will seem to them for a moment that a sound was coming to them without direction. No man will recognize sounds that no man has ever heard before. Here and there will be a trickle of sand, a gentle dripping of gravel, as a seam appears in the Tower. When the sides pull apart, the crystal will seem to hang there for a moment, supported on a shaft of light. And then it will drop, not very far, for by then the cone will have been drawn up to meet it. The buildings will not so much fall as slip to the side in their irrelevance to the cone's attraction to the crystal. Perhaps a few farmers far up on the peninsula will notice a peculiar smell soaking up through the grass. They will have a moment to wonder about the little jets of steam in the earth, but only a moment, for with the not very heavy touch of the crystal on the cone, the volcano will explode and the entire city will pass in fragments through the air where we are now. And that will simply be the beginning. By the end of the day, all the islands will have sunk into the sea."

Bran turned back to the controls and began to move the vessel round to face toward the south and the island where the others waited for their appointed rendezvous. Viracocha did not take his eyes from the portal, but simply accepted in silence the part of the sky that was being given to him as they turned, the part of the sky in which the Morning Star appeared leading the sun into the last Atlantean dawn.

Afterword

Where catastrophe still haunts the brittle edges of our land, there the mind dwells; no, not mind as we know it exactly, but that atavistic faculty of dream, vision, and spontaneous images sprung out of time. The skeptical mind is its own proud tower that resists the pull of the darkening sea. Not forgotten, nor yet accepted, is that other morning when the usual return to the body slipped and glanced off into dimensions of future time: there upon the palisades above the Hudson were seen the crowd of towers in midtown, but everywhere the water covered the streets, although not entirely the buildings, which seemed to sway like reeds in a tidal marsh. New York was at peace with nature in death as it had never been in life. Like an ancient and romantic ruin, the Empire State Building rose gloriously above the water which covered only six of its numberless stories. More beneficent than its ancestor had been, it did not need to be obliterated from the face of the earth. Its fall would stand for ages.